I0691507

Libidinous

Variations

Volume One:
Ladies in the Stairwell

Libidinous Variations

Volume One:
Ladies in the Stairwell

by
J. Laux Perren

Duclerc Press
Wichita, Kansas & Santa Barbara, California

Duclerc Press

An imprint of
Saint Gaudens Press
Post Office Box 405
Solvang, CA 93464-0405

Saint Gaudens, Saint Gaudens Press
Duclerc Press, Imprimerie Duclerc
and the Winged Liberty colophon
are trademarks of Saint Gaudens Press

Print edition ISBN: 978-0-943039-25-1

Library of Congress Catalog Number - 2015946622

Printed in the United States of America

This is a work of fiction. Any reference to real people, objects, events, organizations, or locales is intended only to give the fiction a sense of reality and authenticity. Other names, characters and incidents are the products of the author's imagination and bear no relationship to past events, or persons living or deceased.

—

Preface

—

This is the first volume of a compilation of short stories written over many years. A few of these stories are fictionalized autobiographical in nature; some are just fantasies; and most are just stories I found interesting and worth writing about.

A word of caution or forewarning might seem appropriate with respect to works of erotica. I tried to create a spread of sexual experiences. Thus, some will undoubtedly not be to your liking. Rather than cast this modest compendium aside in disgust, I urge you to skip the offending story and read on. Let your imagination wonder about what might have been, or what could be. The human experience remains a vast spectrum of colors, shades and nuance.

If you find these stories entertaining and engaging, please let the publisher know, so they will demand more stories from me. I will write as long as you wish to read.

Enjoy!

J. Laux Perren

—

Jenna

—

"Jenna, our man just left."

"Thanks, Margo. I'll meet you on the stairs in about ten minutes."

"OK," she responded.

God, this is more like we are on a military mission or something. I need this. I really need this.

Wandering aimlessly about the apartment, I picked up an occasional errant piece of clothing or misplaced knickknack. Stopping in each successive room to take a look around and assess the condition of the room, I moved like a vagabond throughout the apartment. This is incredible.

"What am I doing? I am acting like a schoolgirl. This is just a guy. Why am I doing this?" I kept muttering aloud to myself as I moved from room to room.

The baby, I'd better check on the baby. There he is, sleeping peacefully. The transfer to his carrier shouldn't disturb him. I'll take him with me out on the stairs. He's probably got another 45 minutes of sound sleep. That should be enough time for what I need.

With James safely installed in the carrier and still sleeping peacefully, I lifted him and looked around the apartment one last time. Everything seems to be in order. Oh God, nothing's ever right. This is crazy. Maybe I shouldn't do this. It's been so long. Well, let's just go a little further, I can turn around anytime.

Walking through the door, I instinctively closed and locked the door behind me. My heart rate is quickening, it must be the anticipation. The conversations with Margo over the last few weeks increased in tempo and focus. My best friend is the one who's brought me to this level of deprivation.

This meeting was planned. Some would say premeditated. Fantasizing about what this meeting might be like has stirred us both up too much. However, it was just something we needed to do, I guess, that I needed to do.

It had been a little over six weeks since little James was born. I was finally beginning to feel normal again. My body was healed, recovered and otherwise back to its unstretched version. It made me feel suspiciously better to see Margo close to four weeks from her date. The distended abdomen, the enlarged breasts and the darkened skin tone each added to the image of what I had been over two months ago.

"Hiya, Margo."

"I'm so excited, Jenna. What do you think he's going to do?" There was a strange reservation in her voice.

"I know what you mean. My heart rate has been a bit pumped up since your call. I kinda feel like a schoolgirl, Margo. I haven't felt like this since high school." I can't stand still. I have to calm down or I'm going to wet my pants, that is if I were wearing any. Motioning toward the landing, I asked, "Why don't we wait over there?"

Margo nodded her head in agreement. We walked the short distance to the stairs. I instinctively looked over to my closest friend on every fourth step or so, maybe just to make sure she was still there. Margo bowed her head, but the smile on her face was irrepressible. We slowly descended the several steps to the landing at the head of the long flight of stairs.

Upon arrival on the landing, both of us froze much as though we had just stepped into another dimension. After a few moments, I lowered the carrier to the floor with James still peacefully asleep. After moving the carrier over to the wall out of the way, I sat down on the second step above the landing.

Margo watched me sit and then walked over to the facing wall. Stopping with her back to me, she waited for what seemed like a long time.

Turning to face me with a more serious expression, Margo asked, "Are you scared, Jenna?"

"I wouldn't say I'm scared. I suppose I'm just excited and apprehensive. I've only talked to Joshua a few times. I don't know how he is going to react."

"Remember, they say that you should never act out a fantasy. Reality is never as good as the fantasy," Margo said, reiterating the thought they had talked about so many times.

Why isn't she looking at me, I asked myself? Something is bothering her.

"Nothing has to happen, Margo. We're just going to talk to him. We'll just see what happens after that. OK?"

"Sure. I guess so," she responded.

Nobody is going to get hurt. Where is our young Adonis? He ought to be here any time. We need to get on with this, before Margo chickens out. With her head bowed, it was almost as though she was sulking. Why won't she look at me?

The unique creak on the entrance door two floors below broke the melancholy of the moment. Margo's face brightened and became more animated. The stairway banister provided the supportive barrier as she looked down the central cavity of the building. With an expression mixing fright and anticipation, Margo said, "It's him. He's coming up."

"OK. Settle down. He's just a guy."

Footsteps ascending the stairs were becoming more distinct. This ought to be interesting. My heart is still reflecting the anticipation. What's going to happen? What's he going to think or do? Is Margo going to change her mind? The footsteps were becoming louder. His steps were rhythmic, but heavy probably from his run. He was out for a little more than 30 minutes by my reckoning.

Margo's head turned to watch the ascending stairs. Her eyes told the story. Joshua was on the last flight of stairs prior to his fate. The excitement in her eyes was intriguing. This is unbelievable. This was her idea and she is more scared than I am.

"Hi, Josh. Did you have a good run?" Margo asked the approaching young man. His head crowned past the edge of the stairs below.

"Hiya, Margo. Yes, great. Thank you. How are you this glorious afternoon?" he responded.

"Oh, I'm pretty good. Kinda enjoying the clouds passin' the skylight and talkin' to Jenna," Margo answered.

"Isn't this a pleasant surprise," Joshua said as he made eye contact with me. "It's great to see both of you." He looked over to the baby. "How is little James?"

"He's doing very well, thank you. He's been sleeping peacefully in his afternoon nap."

"Great. He's a beautiful baby. Of course, what would you expect from such a beautiful mother," Joshua said with a broad smile on his face.

"Thanks, Josh. You're such a charmer."

The shimmering moistness of his sweaty body was physical evidence of his recent exertion. What a body this guy has. He sure does take good care of himself. Damn, sweat is so erotic. Joshua wiped his face with a small towel he carried in his waste band.

"I'd better go get cleaned up. I don't need to be grossing out you two attractive ladies with my sweat," he said as he started to work his way past us.

"It certainly doesn't gross me out, Josh. Actually, I think it's kinda sexy. You certainly don't need to go on our account."

"OK," he responded with some hesitation. He probably doesn't know what to think. He looked over to Margo as if to confirm my statement. Margo nodded her agreement with a coy grin and averted eyes.

"We don't get a chance to talk to you very often, even though you live just a few doors down from us," Margo said looking at him and then me. There was a sparkle back in her eyes now. She's over the hard part and he's liking it.

Oh, God, there it goes. I'm letting down and there's no sense trying to stop it. I wonder if he's going to notice or if it will gross him out. I guess we'll find out.

"You're leaking, Jenna," Margo was looking at my breasts then at Joshua.

He looked for himself, and then caught my eyes with a slight flush of embarrassment.

"Maybe I'd better take care of this. I'm sorry, Josh. Can I borrow your towel?"

"Sure," he answered with a curious tone indicating his inquisitiveness. He's wondering what I'm going to do. Well, here goes.

The bewilderment on his face was both fascinating and precious. The wink from Margo confirmed her readiness and willingness.

This may not be a good idea, but what the hell. Let's give it a try. I took Joshua's small towel, which was unexpectedly soft and dry. I unbuttoned my blouse opening it to expose both breasts. The milk was flowing in small rivulets down my breasts and chest. Damn, these things are full. The texture of the towel was verging on sandpaper to my hypersensitive skin. I'm so full, they're going to leak for awhile until James has his after-nap feeding.

"I think I'm going to need some help. My breasts are so full." I've definitely got his attention now. He's trying not to watch, but I've got him. This kid doesn't know what to do.

"Ah . . . what can I do to help?" Joshua said with considerable timidity.

"Well, James is still sleeping. However, there is something you can do to help."

There was near shock drawn across his face as I reached up to draw his head toward my left breast. His resistance disintegrated with his realization.

Joshua took my breast. Naturally and immediately, he began to suckle. Wow, does he have a mouth. That feels soooo good, I can feel it in my groin.

My right breast is in need of some help also. I motioned to Margo. She knew what I was asking. There was no resistance from her. Margo's soft lips felt sensual as they took to the task. I may not be able to stand this. This feels far too good, but it's worth it.

The tension within me was increasing. I was approaching the point where I was going to have to do something about it. Margo looked up to me like a nursing baby. She winked. The woman was up to something. She must know what is racing through my body. What a friend!

Time became dimensionless. I have no idea what time has past. Margo rose from my breast. Joshua was thoroughly enthralled and consumed. I kept my hand on his head stroking his hair. He was enjoying this and that was a good sign.

Margo moved behind Joshua. She had a broad smile on her beautiful face. After several moments of undefinable time, Margo nodded as she reached down. Joshua released my breast as his head rose from me. The question on his face needed to be answered.

His response was not predictable. What is he going to think of me? What will he do? I've taken it this far, I might as well give it a try. It's worth a try. I turned my back toward him. He did not move. It was as if he was frozen solid by some unseen force. I bent over placing both hands on the stairs in front of me and waited.

Moments passed. Looking at him was not an option. I closed my eyes. Oh God, I've made a fool out of myself. Then, I felt my skirt being lifted over my hips. I've got him. It's working. Does he know what I want? God, this is going to feel good, so good. What kind of lover is he going to be?

Joshua's strong hands touched my hips, as if to hold them steady for his entry.

His penetration was slow and smooth. I had not seen him, but he was big. The fullness within me was more than I expected. His motion continued to be slow and rhythmic. His fingertips tensed against my pelvis although his rhythm did not change.

Pushing against him, I wanted more of him. I needed more of him. The groan from within me was uncontrollable, surprising me as my ears heard the sounds my body spoke. The friction, the rubbing was heightening the tension within me. The rope was twisting tighter. The rhythm of life was beginning to quicken. The unison of our motion was fascinating and intoxicating, as the union of our bodies became more complete. My breasts still heavy from the incomplete relief swayed with his thrusts.

Joshua was everything my fantasies had wanted him to be. He was strong and yet gentle far beyond his younger age. Patient and purposeful, his hands stroked the roundness of my flesh spreading incredible electricity throughout my body. He reached forward to caress the curves of my swollen breasts without missing a stroke. The touch of his hands was light, allowing the motion to move my skin across his. I could feel the release within me. Opening my eyes for a brief moment, I flushed at the sight of the puddles on the stairs below me, and his hands moving across my breasts. He gathered the wetness from my hard nipples and spread it to enhance the smoothness and curvature of my breasts.

The tension was building too fast. Oh God, let me hold on long enough to make it over the edge. The sounds of his enjoyment blended with mine. It served to amplify the tightness that was spreading so quickly from our coupling to the furthest extremes of my anatomy. My skin, my hair, my whole body was electrified and hypersensitive. Every touch of his fingers and the expanse of him within me were sending shockwaves reverberating throughout me.

He's going to send me over the top. I don't believe this. I am going to climax right here on the stairs. This is too fast. I've never cum this quickly. I don't want this to stop. He must feel the tension within me. He is swelling. His pace is increasing to a staccato frequency. He's going to split me apart, I can feel it.

"Oh, God. Oh, God. No. No. Oh, God." The words gushed from me as my climax raced through my body like a lightning bolt. My legs were shaking, losing their strength. Don't let me collapse. I've got to continue. I pushed hard against him as I felt his convulsions of ecstasy begin.

The sounds of his short, quickened breathing became louder and mixed with the primordial groans from deep within him. His groans became an animalistic howl as his body shook violently, and he thrust hard against me. His climax extended for an extraordinary time.

I felt him leave me as I heard his body hit the wooden boards of the stairs that supported us. He just lay there with his eyes closed. His muffled groans commingling with the panting of his body as it instinctively struggled to recover its strength.

Standing up, my skirt fell back to its normal position concealing the still burning site of our passion. My legs were weak and shaky. I had to sit down on the stairs above us. It was at that instant I saw Margo for the first time in what seemed like an eternity. She had a broad grin with her snow-white teeth cast against her full, rosy red lips. Her whole face was smiling at me. The wink of her eye was the confirmation of her contribution. Margo must have had a good time, too. Her expression was in sharp contrast to her mood before this glorious event. It could not have been as good as mine.

She nodded to me, motioning for us to ascend the stairs and leave the groaning, heaving mass that was young Joshua. I acknowledged her recommendation, wobbling as I stood up. Margo passed me as she led the way up the stairs.

Little James was still asleep. The tranquility of my baby was a definite contradiction to the electricity of this fleeting moment. My God is he a sound sleeper. All that energy and passion so close to him and he does not look like he even stirred.

Lifting James accentuated the weakness of my arms. The sweetness of our recent exertion brought a pleasant smile to my face.

"See'ya later, Josh. Thanks."

This had to be the exception to the adage. This reality was better than my best fantasy.

———

Joshua

—

The coolness of the air enveloped me as I left the building. It was a great day for a run. Not too warm, not too cool. On top of the perfect weather, the holiday provided very few people and even fewer vehicles. Each was an obstacle to avoid and a distraction to the serenity of a good run.

The first quick steps were always a shock to my body. Like a cold engine starting on a chilly morning, it took a few moments for the lubricant to reach all the parts and warm up to full efficiency.

The air is distinctively clean with the absence of automobile exhaust. Yes, this is going to be a super run.

——

My watch said 31 minutes, 24 seconds – not too bad for five kilometers. Several deep breaths ought to reduce my respiratory rate. Let's see, what's my heart rate. The pulse was distinct and strong – 27 times 6 – 162. Decent. Good heart rate. The beads of sweat rolled down my chest to be eventually captured by the material of my shirt. The first edge of coolness from the evaporating dampness was beginning to show. Lord, I love the sensations of a good run. The air passing through my lungs, the blood pumping through my veins and the heat within my muscles brought a comfortable ache and release, both physical and mental. The only thing better is sex, I muttered to myself like it was a secret password into another world.

Heart, lungs and sweat are all under control. I suppose I'd better go in before I cool off too far.

The entryway door creaked with an irritating scraping noise that annoyed everyone. Someone has just got to oil this door before it gets destroyed or hit hard. I'd better shut the door behind me. I suppose security and comfort are more significant than my annoyance over this damn door.

Each step ascending the stairs brought a dull pain to remind me of the temporary fatigue in my legs. It felt good. An affirmation of the success of my run. As I transitioned from the first to the second set of stairs, I caught the wisps of soft female voices above me. The ladies must be talking again today. I wonder if it's Margo and Jenna? Why do they always seem to do their talking on the stairs? What are they talking about?

Halfway up the long portion of the second flight, the bushy blond hair that was distinctively Margo confirmed the answer. Are they going to talk to me or leave me alone? They were no longer talking or they're whispering. What am I going to say to them? I never know what to say. I always feel like a fool around them, but they are good looking.

"Hi, Josh. Did you have a good run?" Margo asked looking straight toward me. It was another couple of steps before I saw Jenna's lush, auburn hair.

"Hiya, Margo. Yes, great. Thank you. How are you this glorious afternoon?"

"Oh, I'm pretty good. Kinda enjoying the clouds passin' the skylight and talkin' to Jenna." she answered.

There was Jenna sitting on the steps opposite Margo. My, my, is she looking good, or what. Her recovery from birthing her baby boy was exceptionally quick judging from the few experiences of which I was aware.

"Isn't this a pleasant surprise? It's great to see both of you." Jenna's bright green eyes were sparkling full of life. The carrier with the boy safely installed and asleep was tucked away in the corner out of harms way. "How is little James?"

"He's doing very well, thank you. He's been sleeping peacefully in his afternoon nap," Jenna said with her characteristic soft, coarse voice touched with a twinge of British accent. She was delightful to listen to.

"Great. He's a beautiful baby. Of course, what would you expect from such a beautiful mother." I looked quickly from Jenna to Margo. I hope I didn't offend her. Her broad smile remained.

"Thanks, Josh. You're such a charmer," Jenna responded.

Pregnancy definitely agrees with both of these women. Margo's got to be close to her delivery date. She's getting big. What is it about pregnant women that make them so sensual? Maybe it's just me, but I don't really care. Lord, her breasts are full and that blouse doesn't help me maintain control. And, she's not even wearing a bra. There ought to be a law. That's too much of a distraction. I've got to keep from looking. I don't need to embarrass myself with these two. I'd better get myself out of here before I make a fool of myself.

All of a sudden my temperature seemed to rise. I could feel the sweat beginning to flow again. I instinctively reached for my running towel to mop up the moisture beading up on my face and arms.

"I'd better go get cleaned up. I don't need to be grossing out you two attractive ladies with my sweat."

I started to move between them when Margo said, "It certainly doesn't gross me out, Josh. Actually, I think it's kinda sexy. You certainly don't need to go on our account."

"OK," I said not knowing what to say. Jenna's eyes and smile were almost predatory. What was she thinking of? I looked over to Margo who nodded confirmation of their collective opinion. Margo face was toward me although lowered slightly with her eyes off on some other object. The smile on her face was verging on deceitful. What are these women up to? Why do I feel like a rabbit in a trap?

"We don't get a chance to talk to you very often even though you live just a few doors down from us," Margo finally said as her crystal blue eyes swung toward mine. Wow, is this heaven or what? I've wanted to talk to these two beauties for so long, and it looks like today is the day.

Jenna's expression changed mysteriously. Out of the corner of my eye I noticed the growing dark spots over Jenna's breasts. She was leaking. It must be past feeding time for baby James. I can't look. Please Lord, don't let me look.

"You're leaking, Jenna," Margo said. It was like a slap in the face. Had she seen me steal a quick glance? Her blouse was becoming transparent. The darkness of the two spots was the distinct shape and color of her nipples. The cloth was transparent as though she had cut that section from her blouse. Damn it, I'm staring. As soon as I looked up, I saw the recognition in her eyes. She was not offended.

"Maybe I'd better take care of this. I'm sorry, Josh. Can I borrow your towel?" Jenna said in total innocence. There was nothing unusual or out of the ordinary for her.

"Sure," I said without thinking. My hand with the towel rose toward her.

Jenna nonchalantly unbuttoned her blouse as she faced me exposing her large, round breasts. The milk was definitely flowing uncontrollably. She began to dry up the milk running down her chest working her way toward her breasts. Cupping her hand with the towel over each breast. I could see her squeeze gently trying to relieve herself. It must have been quite some time since little James sucked on those beauties.

"I think I'm going to need some help. My breasts are so full," Jenna said looking directly at me. What the hell does she want me to do?

"Ah . . . what can I do to help?"

"Well, James is still sleeping. However, there is something you can do to help," she said as her left arm rose to my head.

She gently placed her hand on the back of my head and drew me toward her. What is she doing? What does she want me to do? She was pulling me down to her breast. Jesus Christ, she wants me to suck on her tit.

I took her in my mouth and began to suck like a baby. It seemed so natural. Her nipple was full and hard and yet so soft. The milk came out easily. It was warm, almost hot, and surprisingly sweet. I never knew that human milk tasted this good. I reached up with both hands to caress her breast as I sucked, squeezing ever so gently to help relieve her. I felt Jenna move slightly still holding my head to her breast. Then, I saw and felt Margo's face next to mine. Jenna wanted Margo to relieve the other breast. What a sight this must be -- a man and a woman sucking the milk from the voluptuous breasts of a new and beautiful mother.

An electric shock struck me as a hand reached for my groin. It must be Margo since I can feel both of Jenna's arms, unless there is someone else with us. I dutifully continued with my task straining my eyes to see Margo. Her eyes were closed, and she was still at work on Jenna's right breast. The hand was rubbing and stroking me. It did not take long for me to feel the pain of the swelling within my running shorts. The hand continued to stroke me in full recognition of the accomplishment.

From the corner of my eye, I saw Margo release Jenna's breast and back away from her. I stood straight up somewhat in shock when Margo pulled my shorts to the floor. Jesus Christ, what are these women doing to me? What the fuck is going to happen next?

Jenna smiled at me as she turned around with her back to me. She leaned over placing both hands on the stairs in front of her. I can't do this. I can't. I want to, but I can't. Maybe she wants something else. Maybe I'm thinking of the wrong thing. Jenna did not move. I waited hoping she would say something, or do something. She can't really want what I think she is trying to tell me.

Margo, the co-conspirator, must have reached the limit of her patience. She moved beside me without looking at me. She reached down to Jenna's skirt lifting it completely over her hips. The long, shapely legs before me were spread slightly apart with the round globes of her buttocks beckoning to me.

I don't think there is any doubt now as to what these two beautiful women have planned. Margo's hands touched my bare hips gently pushing me toward Jenna.

My hands moved to Jenna's hips. Her skin was smooth and warm like velvet to the touch.

My feet were outside of hers to accommodate the difference in height. I entered her slowly and carefully. Her wetness was physical testament to her purpose as she accepted me without resistance. I moved slowly with her. The agony within me was too great. If I'm not careful, this may be over before it starts. Slowly, Joshua, slowly, I kept telling myself. A fine wine must be sipped and savored, not gulped. The heat of her body was radiating through me uncontrollably. We were moving together. She pushed her hips in unison with me.

This is just too incredible. I must be dreaming. My fantasies were never this good. Why is this happening to me? Why did they choose me? I'm rising too fast. I must control this myself, pace myself, to prolong this ecstasy.

I moved my hands over her skin. She was so soft. The curves of her body were pleasure by themselves. Her blouse moved with our motion. Can I reach her breasts? There they are. Gently, Joshua. Touch them ever so gently. The curve of her breast was so sensuous, so fascinating, so addicting. Her nipples were still hard. Milk continued to flow. The wetness made her skin slippery, accentuating the smooth texture similar to that of wet, warm, polished marble. I could live my life just touching her and I am the chosen one to have joined with her. This must be heaven.

Jenna's groans from deep within her were becoming more audible, more pronounced and quickening. She was enjoying this as much as, if not more than, I was.

Fingers touched my scrotum. It must be Margo again. She is really into this also. I won't be able to hold out much longer. The caress of her fingers as I moved across her hand was like an injection of some magical drug that super-sensitizes your nerves. This isn't fair. These two women are working me over like veteran thugs. I've never felt these feelings before. Margo's caress produced an involuntary quickening within me. My body was moving faster and faster. The rocket has lifted off, and was climbing faster and faster to the heavens above.

"Oh, God. Oh, God. No. No. Oh, God," Jenna almost growled as her entire body trembled in climax. Salvation was so close as my legs began to shake. Don't fail me now. A slick, cool shaft entered me, which instantly exploded me like the trigger of a nuclear weapon. My convulsions were so violent I wasn't sure if my heart would continue to beat. The small snake stole every ounce of control and vestiges of reality remaining within me. I'm going to die. This is death. I'm passing into another world. I collapsed.

The next thing I remember I was lying on the landing in a near fetal position. My heart and lungs were racing to recover to some stable level, desperately trying to perform their duty to keep my body alive. The ache in my groin was undeniable, and yet so intoxicating. I could hear nothing other than my own heart and lungs. I could not open my eyes. There were groans off in some distant place within me that were felt rather than heard. I must look so silly just lying here on the stairs, but I don't care. If I am dead, it does not matter.

Motion, I finally heard movement near me. I still couldn't move anything. I tried. Not even my eyelids would open.

They were leaving. That must be it.

"See'ya later, Josh. Thanks," Jenna said to me from some far away place.

Well, I guess this is it. I've been used, abused and left for dead.

———

Margo

—

It was a quiet, beautiful afternoon. Pinks and violets of the approaching dusk were beginning to appear. The small, puffy clouds moved slowly across the background of the sky above. I could feel the coolness through the window. It definitely was not cold, but it wasn't warm either. The street below was nearly deserted. Only a few elderly people walking to some destination with a sense of purpose. The cars were so infrequent, they were barely noticeable.

What was taking him so long? He is usually out the door earlier than this. The impatience, or was it anticipation, was creating an unwanted tension – a stress of the moment. Where is he? Somebody ought to give him a push.

A bright red sports car of some type flashed by the cross street to the right. That guy is in some kinda hurry. What's that? Something moved below. There he is. Man, is he good lookin'. Those loose shorts and T-shirt do show off his body. Yes, indeedie.

Well, so it begins. I'd better call Jenna. Why did I have them install the telephone on the kitchen counter? He started his run and was soon out of sight. OK, let's give Jenna the call.

"Jenna, our man just left." None too soon I should add.

"Thanks, Margo. I'll meet you on the stairs in about ten minutes," she said.

"OK."

I wonder if she is really going to go through with this. We've done too much sex talk for our own good. I'll bet she chickens out. She won't go through with it. The real stuff is never as good as the imaginary. So, why are we doing this?

Walking over to the mirror, I needed to confirm my appearance. Jesus, am I getting big. I look like I've swallowed a small dog. This just isn't fair. Why did I have to wait? Jenna's so lucky. She's just about back to normal, which is probably why she's so horny lately. Well, I guess I'm about as good as I'm going to be in my present condition. I suppose there is no reason to postpone this. There is nothing I'm going to be able to do anyway. This is all Jenna's show.

I'd better not lock the door. Can't tell if I might need to make a quick exit. This is really risky. Why did I encourage her to do this?

Jenna's door opened as I approached. She closed the door behind her and then checked to make sure it was locked. She's not thinking ahead. Maybe I'd better say something to her.

"Hiya, Margo," Jenna said with her patented smile.

"I'm so excited, Jenna. What do you think he's going to do?" I lied. Why don't I have enough courage to tell her not to do this? Why am I still supporting her?

"I know what you mean. My heart rate has been a bit pumped up since your call. I kinda feel like a schoolgirl, Margo. I haven't felt like this since high school," she said.

The woman is really going to go through with it. She's nervous as hell. Look at her fidget.

She nodded toward the landing. "Why don't we wait over there?" Jenna said with clarity and conviction.

OK, OK, OK. Let's get on with it. I nodded my head in agreement.

We slowly walked toward the stairs. Jenna kept looking over her shoulder at me. The excitement is in her eyes. My God, I think she's really looking forward to this thing. Whatever happens I hope nobody surprises us while we're out here. It would be so embarrassing, verging on humiliating.

Jenna lowered James to the floor and carefully slid his carrier against the wall. She stood still for a few moments, and then sat down on the second step up from the landing.

This is crazy. We are both grown women, and we shouldn't be doing this sort of stuff. Maybe she'll back out and forget about this insane fantasy. Standing near the wall opposite Jenna, and seeing nothing gave me the peace and distance I needed for sober consideration. What if we get caught? What if he's a maniac?

The principle question on my mind needed to be asked. Turning to face my contemplative, sitting friend, I asked, "Are you scared, Jenna?"

"I wouldn't say I'm scared. I suppose I'm just excited and apprehensive. I've only talked to Joshua a few times. I don't know how he is going to react," she answered.

"Remember, they say that you should never act out a fantasy. Reality is never as good as the fantasy."

The boards that comprised the landing upon which we stood were the object of my sight. I couldn't look at her. This feeling must be like that sense of helplessness when you are paddling as fast as you can upriver and the roar of the waterfall is still approaching. I have contributed to her delinquency. I want to stop this, but there is an unexplainable force that keeps drawing me closer.

"Nothing has to happen, Margo. We're just going to talk to him. We'll just see what happens after that. OK?" Jenna said with a tone of solicitation for reassurance.

"Sure. I guess so," I responded. Why am I continuing to follow this charade? Why can't I say, no?

There's the door. Oh God, he's here. Well, maybe not. Maybe it's someone else. Now my heart rate was beginning to rise. The excitement took off through my body like a flood. I'd better check to see who it is. Jenna remained seated not even twitching to move.

As I looked over the banister, his powerful legs were all that could be seen on the first set of stairs. His loose green shorts identified the target.

"It's him. He's coming up," I said to Jenna.

"OK. Settle down. He's just a guy," she responded with some strange sense of inner calm. Her admonishment did not have the intended soothing effect.

The sound of each step was clear, distinct and coming closer. I stood back somewhat as he began the last large segment toward us. Watching the stairs, his face soon appeared above the edge of the landing.

"Hi, Josh. Did you have a good run?" I asked.

"Hiya, Margo. Yes, great. Thank you. How are you this glorious afternoon?" he responded.

"Oh, I'm pretty good. Kinda enjoying the clouds passin' the skylight and talkin' to Jenna."

"Isn't this a pleasant surprise," Joshua said. "It's great to see both of you." He looked over to Jenna's baby boy. "How is little James?"

"He's doing very well, thank you. He's been sleeping peacefully in his afternoon nap," Jenna replied.

Jenna was definitely attracted to this guy. It's written in big, bold letters across her face, across her whole body for that matter. We're past the point of no return here. I can see this coming. She's going to go through with this unless something or someone interrupts the proceedings.

"Great. He's a beautiful baby. Of course, what would you expect from such a beautiful mother," Joshua said with a broad smile on his face. And, he's attracted to her. He's got to sense the energy, the vibes coming from her.

"Thanks, Josh. You're such a charmer," Jenna said with an almost embarrassed expression.

He wiped his face with a small towel he carried in his waste band. Am I imagining things or has the profuseness of his perspiration increased?

"I'd better go get cleaned up. I don't need to be grossing out you two attractive ladies with my sweat," he said as he started to walk past Jenna and me.

"It certainly doesn't gross me out, Josh. Actually, I think it's kinda sexy. You certainly don't need to go on our account." Jenna glanced over at me just to confirm what she already knew, or at least wanted to think. I nodded discreetly.

"OK," he responded with some hesitation.

I nodded discreetly.

"We don't get a chance to talk to you very often even though you live just a few doors down from us," I said. Why did I get into this? Well, maybe she needs a little help. Plus, I don't want these two animals to get coupled up and forget about me.

Joshua communicated his acknowledgement with his eyes and broad grin. This guy is lovin' all this attention. I wonder what he thinks is going to happen? Does he even have a clue as to his fate? Hell, do I know what's going to happen? Nope. We're just kinda floatin' down this ol' river.

Jenna's facial expression changed slightly. Something distracted her. Holy cow, her blouse is turning transparent. You can see her whole nipples. She must be full. It's past feeding time for James, and she's letting down with all this excitement. That's her distraction; she can feel the wetness on her blouse. Let's see what she's going to do with this?

"You're leaking, Jenna."

Young Joshua just couldn't resist the temptation any longer. Jenna's predicament and her attractive breasts were an unavoidable attraction to this young buck. I doubt any man could resist such a sight. Did she have this planned? Of course not. If she did, she's better than I thought.

Will ya look at this. This guy is actually blushing. He's genuinely embarrassed by these events that are no longer within his control.

"Maybe I'd better take care of this. I'm sorry, Josh. Can I borrow your towel?" Jenna said so clearly.

"Sure," he answered with an odd tone, indicating his curiosity.

This is like leading a pig to slaughter. He still doesn't have a clue. She took the small towel with a slow deliberate motion.

Jenna unbuttoned her blouse opening it completely to reveal her entire chest. She sure does have nice tits even if I do say so myself. Starting at her lower abdomen, Jenna wiped up the streaming milk from her breasts. She cupped each breast with the towel squeezing ever so gently. I think she's doing this more for him than to dry herself.

"I think I'm going to need some help. My breasts are so full," Jenna said trying to intone her statement apologetically.

"Ah....what can I do to help?" Joshua said with considerable timidity. He's outta control.

"Well, James is still sleeping. However, there is something you can do to help," she responded.

She's not going to do this. This is too obvious. Oh God, yes, she is. Jenna raised her left hand placing it on the back of Joshua's head. Slowly, she pulled him down to her left breast. He's actually going to take it. This is incredible.

Shifting my eyes to Jenna's, the contact was instant. She motioned for me to come to her. She wants me to suckle her right breast along side the object of her seduction. What the hell, she does have a nice taste to her.

The milk flowed freely, almost effortlessly. The warm, sweet liquid was soothing to the spirits. She stroked my hair much as a mother strokes her baby. She was definitely enjoying this.

Well, if she is going to go the distance, we might as well do it right. I could feel the heat from his body as my hand touched his leg. Slowly, I moved up to the juncture. The thin, silky material of his running shorts could not disguise the details of his anatomy. Touching him had an air of forbidding that was enticing and inciting. There was a certain and definite feeling of power associated with my extracurricular activity. The swelling of a young, anxious man was unmistakable. In short order, he was fully erect and ready. I could feel every detail. This young buck is ready. So, let's move to the grand finale.

For the first time, I tilted my head to look into Jenna's eyes. The wink of my eye had the desired effect. She knew I was still with her. I continued to draw from her as I stroked him. I could feel his hand next to my cheek as he gently stroked the contours of her breast. His eyes were closed as if he was trying to pretend this was a dream. Maybe he thought that if he opened his eyes, this whole experience would be gone in a flash of realization.

It's show time. I rose from her breast. She did not stop me, although I could sense the question in her thoughts. Joshua continued with his task probably not aware that I was no longer beside him.

My hands hesitated at the edge of the loose material of his shorts. We'll see how he does with this. I clinched the material on both side and pulled down. His shorts hung up in front briefly, but soon came all the way to the floor. He reacted standing straight up. There was probably confusion and anxiety rolling through his consciousness right now.

Jenna took her cue without even looking at him. She turned around bending over to place her hands on the stairs now in front of her. Joshua did not move. He was frozen like the proverbial chicken on a white line. I guess I'm going to have to make the move toward her. Jenna's not moving and neither is Joshua.

Her long, loose skirt rose easily above her hips. I dropped the gathered material on her back. Damn, she doesn't have any panties on. She really was going to do this. There cannot be any doubt in his mind now with this perfect white buttocks in front of him.

Joshua finally raised both hands placing them on Jenna's hips to steady himself or hold her, it was not clear which was correct. He moved forward spreading his legs and carefully placing himself behind her. He disappeared into my best friend. They were now joined here on the stairs of our apartment building. What the hell, you only live once.

He moved with a slow, rhythmic, deliberate motion as they blended together as one. Jenna braced herself against him. Short soft groans of pleasure from both of them were barely audible as they mixed with the other characteristic sounds of their union. There was a strange, indescribable pleasure absorbing the sights and sounds before me. It was mesmerizing. The rest of the world ceased to exist.

Every muscle in his legs were taught and rippling with the motion they generated. The definition in his legs was incredible. The undulations of his tight little buttocks were fascinating to watch by itself in isolation.

The independent motion between his legs was like a pendulum hanging and swinging as if it was carrying a heavy weight. Just watching and listening to all this is making me horny. What am I going to do? Maybe I can use this guy when she's finished with him, if he's still alive. That's incredible watching those things move. I've got to touch 'em.

I could feel their weight as they moved across my fingers. The roundness and texture of the skin changed as I stroked them. The moistness from his exertion was pronounced and unmistakable. They seemed to draw up slightly at my touch. Their rhythm is changing. The sounds from both of them were confirmation of the approaching conclusion.

This is absolutely fascinating, watching his muscles ripple. The sights, sounds and smells of their passion were intoxicating, verging on addicting. There was magic to this event. An assemblage of unknown forces that were intriguing in their own right added to the intensity of the moment.

His legs were beginning to shake as the tremors of ecstasy began to envelop him. Jenna's chest was heaving in shallow, rapid succession, which made her breasts swing wildly. They were both climbing the peak together. Boy, this is going to be impressive. The anticipation was welling up within me.

The attraction of his body was irresistible. My fingers migrated from the stroking of his retreating sack to a new target. This ought to extract every last ounce of control he might have left. The distance was short. The effect was dramatic and predictable.

Jenna went first as her groans and moans were replaced by expressive words rising from deep within her. "Oh, God. Oh, God. No. No. Oh, God," she spoke aloud as her chest convulsed and her legs wobbled as the waves of her climax rolled through her body.

Starting as a light pressure against him, I pushed harder as his muscles finally released allowing me to enter him just as his groans transitioned into a strange, primeval howl. His buttocks twitched violently as his knees shook wildly with the muscles of his legs tensed to rock hardness. I could visually watch the electricity of his orgasm pulsating through his body. My finger wiggled slightly to make sure he knew I was there. His climax lasted for an incredible time.

As the convulsions of his pleasure peaked, young Joshua collapsed to the floor with a thud. His breathing was quick and shallow. His eyes were closed as oblivion enveloped him as his body struggled to recover. There seemed to be no awareness of activity around him. It was apparent that he was temporarily in another world.

Jenna finally stood up with her legs noticeably shaking. She made no attempt to lower her skirt, it simply returned to its proper position from the force of gravity. Turning to sit on the stairs, Jenna first looked at Joshua then she finally looked toward me. She had done it. Taken her fantasy all the way. I wanted to ask her if she was happy with the outcome. The question would wait until a later time, anyway we needed to return to the privacy of an apartment, hers or mine. I winked at her to reassure my friend I remained with her and nodded toward the stairs above.

She stood up again with her legs still shaking. I began to climb the stairs above us as she moved over to retrieve her peaceful sleeping son.

"See'ya later, Josh. Thanks," Jenna said to the struggling mass on the landing of the stairway.

Since she was the weakened one, I decided on her apartment. I waited for her to catch up. Without a word or even a glance, we entered the safety of Jenna's apartment.

Not bad for an afternoon of entertainment.

Byron

—

The excitement over the awards banquet and ceremony was contagious. It was a very special night for James – a just and timely reward for a friend that had done so much for others. To add to the specialness of the award, the foundation provided a beautiful, well-appointed limousine to transport all of us across town.

Fortunately for Amy and me, James asked us to join Megan and him for the night's celebration. Amy was excited as much for me as she was for James. It was his award, but he was my friend. The four of us have known each other for close to ten years, while we have been together as couples for less time. Amy and I were picked up last, which was also propitious since my lovely girlfriend was late as usual in her preparations.

Amy's full skirt and bodice dress were not particularly complimentary to her delicious figure. The black, long sleeves of the dress were still quite elegant. I was definitely proud of her. Amy's attire was in dramatic contrast to Megan's choice of dress for this special night.

Black was the only element that was common to both women. Her strapless, low cut dress was also hemmed rather short for a formal occasion. Megan's dress was an absolute tribute to a likewise beautiful woman. James and Megan had been together as a couple for nearly a year, although they had dated off and on for a little over three years. Every time we saw them together and especially when they were both happy and animated, I received a jab from Amy as an implicit reference to the way it should be.

"My, my, don't you ladies look beautiful tonight," I stated the obvious upon following Amy into the limousine.

"Thanks, Byron, just what a lady needs," Megan answered.

With all four of us seated, the driver resumed his task that entailed roughly 45 minutes of relatively easy driving to the other side of town each way.

"You look smashing, Amy. That's a spectacular dress," Megan said with a broad smile on her face.

"Thanks," Amy acknowledged the plaudit.

"It sure is except it doesn't show any of her beautiful body," I had to add which resulted in a squeeze of my thigh from Amy.

"Well, my friend, are you excited or what?" I asked James changing the subject from the volatile topic.

"Yeah, I suppose. I think I enjoy this chance to get together as much as the award. Hell, the award is a good excuse to get the four of us in a limousine."

"I don't know about the rest of you, but I'm so excited I'm wet," Amy said with some pride.

"Is that so," I said quickly in return. "Let's just see about that."

I ran my hand along the inside of her thigh. Amy tightened the pressure holding her knees together. The crease between her legs provided a perfect guide for my hand as it disappeared under her dress.

"Byron, this is not the place," Amy said with an almost playful tone to her voice.

"Why not? We're among friends. So, let's find the tru . . . ." I stopped in mid-sentence as I discovered Amy's secret. "Holy shit, you're not wearing any drawers."

Amy looked directly at me with a broad smile on her face and a sparkle in her intoxicating blue eyes as she release the pressure on her knees. My hand slowly drifted down the line of her body. The pounding of my heart must be audible, I thought, as my fingers discovered the truth of Amy's words. There was a devious expression on her face as she concentrated on my reaction. Leaning forward, we joined again as our lips touched. The passion within her was strong as her entire body responded to my caress.

The undulation of the roadway provided a gentle sway to the car. The well-equipped limousine was specifically designed and built for the privacy of its occupants, which added to the intrigue of the moment.

James and Megan. We've been carrying on. I didn't even think about James and Megan. Slowly, I released Amy's lips to allow my eyes to drift to the rear of the car. Expecting two shocked expressions from our friends, Amy followed my eyes. As our glance shifted from each other to our two companions, we caught them in the expression of their reflected passion. Megan's dress was over her waist exposing her curvaceous buttocks. She had straddled James and was in the process of lowering herself onto him. They had obviously responded quickly and in kind to the fountain of energy in this limousine.

"I guess we don't have to worry about them," I whispered to Amy.

"I think you're right."

Raising my hand to touch Amy's face, I kissed her cheek to carefully watch the words her eyes spoke. There was a brief flash of broken desire filled with a yearning to protect this moment.

"Let's watch," she said with a clear, effervescent and amused voice.

"OK," I said in acquiescence to the control she possessed.

Their motions were in unison with the movement of the car. The union of our friends before us held a certain, special aura of life. Their world had shrunk to the finite extent of their lust. They were oblivious to every-thing around them as they continued their copulation. The muscles of her legs danced before us as they contracted and relaxed taking him into her. The diffuse light from the exterior sparkled and flickered off the wetness between them. The fascination of this spectacle was alluring and addicting.

As my fingers continued to explore the subtleties of Amy's folds, her hands drifted along the inside of my thigh. Her discovery of my readiness did not alter her intentions. Her gentle strokes produced an incredible agony within me. There was a feeling of desperation as my desire grew.

"Shall we join them?" I whispered to Amy.

"No. We must watch and wait our turn," she responded softly, but with assertion.

My eyes returned with Amy's unbroken observation to witness James' hands fall from her shoulders to lower the zipper of her dress. The bodice of Megan's dress fell upon him as the tension was released exposing the delicate curves of her right breast under her raised arms. The combination of their motions along with those of the limousine and the lights from the street accentuated her white skin against the black background of his tuxedo jacket.

James caressed her breasts lightly as if to feel the motion of her skin over his hands. Occasionally, he moved to squeeze her prominent nipples that sent shudders of ecstasy throughout her body.

Amy's response to watching the pleasure evolving before her was equal to that of her friend as the motion of her hips changed. Sensing the desires within her, I began to stroke her with a rhythmic touch verging on vibration. Her breathing quickened, as her eyes remained fixed upon the magnificence of Megan and James. Amy's body reacted to the combination of her sight and my touch.

My need to join our companions was creating an internal agony that was difficult to deny. Amy's touch was becoming less controlled as it slowly transitioned from her gentle stroking to a sporadic squeeze. She was climbing with them to the impending eruption.

James began to rise against her as the tempo of their union grew. The welling of their approaching climax was manifesting itself in an obvious visual sense. The nearly spasmodic heaving of Megan's chest, the arching of his head against the seat, and the shifting of the preponderance of motion from her to him were definite precursors to the imminent conclusion. Amy was rising in unison with them as I began to concentrate on her pleasure. The spontaneity and cohesion of this event was too incredible, too phenomenal and almost too much to bear since I was the only one not struggling with the climb. I glanced over to measure Amy's stage. Her eyes were closed and her head arched back as she focused on her own pleasure.

It was James that was first to peak as the groans from deep within him blended with the sounds of their pounding flesh.

Megan followed soon after and prior to his fall with a more audible indication of her pleasure.

"Oh my god. Yes, yes. Oh god. Oh god," she spoke aloud clearly and distinctly as the warmth of her orgasm rippled through her body. "No, no. Oh god. No," she continued as if to command continuance of her pleasure.

Just as Megan and James began to come down from their mutual conclusion, Amy's body, her breathing and spasmodic contraction foretold her climax as she pushed hard against my touch. Her guttural growling mixing with the audible product of her labored breathing and the convulsions of the muscles of her body were the demarcation of her final rise to satisfaction. There was a sudden rush of warmth within me as I felt, listened and smelled her orgasm. She seemed to have several consecutive peaks that lasted an inordinate amount of time. I savored the involuntary contractions of her body around me. It was truly one of her best, and there was great pleasure in that for me. As she came down, her body virtually collapsed against me. I withdrew from her to restore her dress to its proper position, I finally noticed that both Megan and James were peacefully observing us for the first time, as she was still upon him, and they were joined.

As Amy began to recover to a conscious state, Megan and James separated and casually moved to restore their clothing. They cleaned up the products of their passion.

"We need to take care of you, Byron," Megan said, as the first to speak.

Amy looked up to my eyes and began to move her body.

"We are approaching Jefferson Hall," the voice of the unseen driver said over the intercom. I wondered if he was aware of what just happened back here. It was a thought that was instantly shared by all four of us, as we each smiled knowingly to one another.

"I'll take good care of him later," Amy said as she kissed my cheek and then my lips. The transmission of her commitment through her lips and soft tongue was extraordinary.

"Maybe we could just go around the block a few times. What do you think?" I asked in my own defense.

"Byron, this is James' night. I'll take very good care of you later," Amy answered.

"Sorry, Byron. How do we look?" Megan asked as she straightened her beau's bow tie.

We each looked to one another with a quick evaluation of appearance and crosschecked the findings. Everything was in order. There was a glow that seemed to fill the limousine as we approached the awning of the Jefferson Hall entrance. Well, I guess I'll have to suffer through this evening until I can collect my promised reward.

The car stopped. A doorman opened the curbside door. Megan was the first to exit followed by James and Amy. I was the last to leave. Without thinking, I glanced back to the driver who had a broad smile on his face, as he winked at me in confirmation of his knowledge. I wonder if this happens to him all the time?

———

Stephan

—

Damn, I hate the underground! Someday, I'll be wealthy and powerful. I'll have a permanent chauffeur and an elegant limousine to drive me around town to my exterior appointments. However, today I cannot expect much as a brand new graduate.

Having a pleasant but challenging job is a welcome change to the idealism and sheltered environs of academia. The unfortunate part is this damn commute each day. I can't afford to live downtown so I'm relegated along with the preponderance of humanity to this arduous journey each day.

I could kick myself for making this afternoon appointment with the landlord. This peak-of-the-rush-hour crowd is enough to try a wise man's patience. If I don't get back there in time, it will be another three days to get that damn plumbing fixed. What a racket those guys have got. The world is at their feet. They seem to be able to work when they want to work, or they have more work than they know what to do with. Either way, they are in pretty good shape. The rest of us slugs wait upon their schedule.

Only another twenty minutes of this jostling. At least, I don't have to change tracks. The downside being an appropriate number of my fellow travelers are also continuing passengers, which means I must stand. Good fortune must be with me today, I can lean against the wall of the car kinda out of the way for all the transfers.

One more stop. This sure is a popular stop. It must be Castlemaine Street Station. Why did they make these cars for short people? I have to bend over every time I need to read the station signs. Yep, I was right, Castlemaine Street Station. Half the car is unloading. Not enough to open up any seats, but we'll have a pretty good turn over.

Wow, look at that woman. What a magnificent creature! A fine example of God's creation. She looked right at me. What incredible emerald green eyes. A perfect match for deep, rich, reddish-brown, I guess most would say auburn, hair. She's going to stand right in front of me. Well, seeing the back of her is better than not seeing her at all, I suppose.

Now, that's an interesting perfume. This is almost intoxicating just seeing and smelling her. Too bad, it has to be winter, and we can't see more of her. Such is life. This is good enough right now.

Another stop. Nobody is getting off, but more are getting on. Now, this is a nice situation. The crowd is pushing her back against me. We're packed in here like sardines. If it must be this way, what better way to travel. She was now close enough for the fragrance of her hair to become noticeable.

This is quite intriguing. I've been riding the underground nearly a year since taking my first job after graduating from the university. A distraction such as this could make riding the underground almost enjoyable.

Yet another stop. They seem to be coming much faster now. It must be this woman just in front of me. More people crowd on to the brimming railcar. There's a shoulder. That must be her buttocks. She feels nice, even with these overcoats on. Why couldn't this happen in the summer time when there would be less clothing between us?

What was that? It wasn't an occasional bump. Now, that is her buttocks. Damn, this is getting me excited. Not now. My excitement was growing rapidly, and there was nothing I could do to stop it. This is going to be embarrassing. Think of something else quickly. Concentrate. Anything else. It's out of control. Oh well, what the hell, let it go. Full engorgement with the confinement of my clothing was beginning to produce a dull ache that made it impossible to ignore. Thank God, I have this overcoat. At least I'll be able to cover up if it lasts that long.

There it is again. Jesus, that's a hand. I looked around quickly, almost nervously. It can't be that guy, he's holding a newspaper. Her purse is between us. It must be this woman in front of me. She was rubbing my bulge gently but continuously. This is not good. Her touch is turning this ache into a sharp pain. I wonder what the hell she's doing, or what she's going to do?

She squeezed me as if to evaluate the tension of her victim. Her touch was light and purposeful enough for the desired effect. This is definitely not my imagination. Incredible, absolutely incredible! What is she going to do? What does she want? Fortunately, the crowded car and the combination of her coat and mine provide some protection for her molestation. Maybe this is her way of picking up guys, and I'm her choice for tonight.

I reached up to place my hand on her shoulder. Her body instantly tensed, and she withdrew her touch. She made no attempt to move away or look at me. What the hell is she thinking?

Well, I suppose I was wrong. I immediately removed my hand. It is to be a one-way affair.

Her touch soon returned to restore the pain she created. Just enjoy it. An incident like this doesn't happen everyday, so just enjoy it. Words formed within my thoughts. They were words I wanted to whisper to her. The urge to communicate with this rather attractive woman was overwhelming, but I also knew what the result would be.

Jesus Christ, she's going for my zipper. Oh lord, don't do that. Don't pinch me. Be careful with that thing. She's actually going to do this. What the hell is she trying to do?

Her hand began to work its way like a snake in a tunnel. It's getting real hot in here. I could feel the beads of sweat beginning to descend across my back. The coolness of her hand against the heat of my flesh added a near burning sensation to the pain she had already caused. Her fingers encircled me like a python around its prey.

At first, she did not move. She let the motion of the car take care of the movement she wanted. An occasional soft squeeze was sufficient to communicate her attention to the task at hand. The additional motion began slowly and purposefully. There was a strange feeling that she was measuring my response to her action. She's in control, that's it. She wants to control every action and response. This is absolutely incredible, actually more like insane. What the hell am I doing?

The stroking of her hand was becoming more noticeable, more obvious to me. Then, with a swiftness that startled me, she extracted her prey from the confines of my clothing.

My head and eyes moved sharply from side to side. Does anybody else know what this woman is doing to me? Is he aware? No, I don't think so. Does she know what's going on? Has she felt the movements? Maybe not. Why did I let this happen?

Oh God, another station. She held me in place with occasional combinations of strokes and squeezes. Holy shit, people are getting off. A lot of people. Please don't get of at this station. If she gets off or moves away from me, I'll be completely exposed. Please, please, don't move. Oh, thank you lord. Not as many were getting off as it seemed, and enough additional passengers got on to keep her in place as the shield for my embarrassment.

The train began to move again. Where are we? Court on the Green. Two more stops. How am I going to end this?

She began to stroke me with a new purpose. What does she want from me? Her fingers were magnificent. There was expertness to her touch. This was familiar territory for this woman. I wonder what she does for a living? She's trying to get me off! Why? The product will be all over her as well as me. Why is she doing this? Her motions were quite definite. There's no doubt in my mind what she is doing, but why?

The ripples of passion were beginning to roll through my body. The effect of her touch was changing the sensations within me. The pain and tension were growing with the sensitivity of my skin. I could feel the occasional texture of her coat brush against my flesh. She might actually succeed at the rate she's going, if that's her real purpose. Well, even if it's not, she might take this to its natural conclusion.

The world around me was beginning to fade into the distance. My awareness of the sights, sounds and smells of the railcar and the passengers it contained were passing away from me. My world was rapidly shrinking to the touch of a strange woman on the flesh of sexuality. I hope this is what she really wants to happen. There's no way she could be doing this without knowing what the result was going to be. It must be. She is good. She definitely knows what she is doing? In fact, she may be better at this than I am.

With suddenness consistent with her prior actions, she stopped, hesitated for a moment, and then quickly but carefully returned me to my normal place. No, no, don't stop. Finish, please, oh god, finish. This hurts too much. You've got to finish. She squeezed me one last time. What's happening? Why is she stopping now?

Lights. The light is changing. We're approaching another station. Where are we? The train stopped. People began to move through the open doors.

My friend began to move as well to join the rest of the departing travelers. This is her stop. I ought to get off with her. I want to finish what she started. What time is it? Maybe . . . . Damn, I've only got twenty minutes. I can't.

The woman stopped at the door across the car. She turned to look back at me. Is she trying to see if I am right behind her? Does she want me to follow her? There was a sparkle in her eyes. The expression on her face was a testament to her pleasure. She had fun. She couldn't have enjoyed it as much as I did.

"Have a nice night," she said with the sweetest voice as the doors closed between us. She stood on the platform. Our eyes were riveted to one another. The smile on her face was subtle but distinct as the train rushed away from the station. She winked as she disappeared.

This angel of the underground has changed my image of the commute forever.

—

Rebecca
___

"I'm Rebecca MacDougal. My husband was brought in about an hour ago."

"Yes, ma'am. We've been trying to locate you," the nurse said. "Just one moment, please. Would you please take a seat in the visitor's lounge?"

"Can you tell me what happened? What's the problem? How is my husband?"

"Please, ma'am. If you will wait in the lounge, I will get the attending physician right away. He'll explain the situation. We aren't allowed to provide status information," she said with a serious, but pleasant expression. This nurse was doing her best to help.

"OK. Yes. I'll wait, but please hurry. You're scaring the stuffing outta me."

The duty nurse did not respond verbally. She simply nodded and left presumably to find the correct doctor. Her departure left no one at the nurse's station.

Why did he have to work late tonight? What the heck happened? It must be an accident. He's had an accident, or, oh God, a heart attack? He's got to be all right. Why did it have to be tonight when I was out with Sara? Why is it that bad things always happen at the worst time?

The lounge was vacant. A surprisingly quiet night for a hospital emergency room. It's only a little after ten, and I'm the only one here. Well, at least, the medical staff didn't have a busy night. They were able to concentrate on John. God, I hope he is OK.

An attractive young woman dressed in a long, white coat entered the lounge. Her coat was open over the distinctive blue-green, loose fitting garb of an operating room medical person. This must be the doctor.

"Mrs. MacDougal?" she inquired.

"Yes," I said as if there were other women in the room who might pass for the victim's wife.

"I am Doctor Mary Hilton. I'm your husband's attending physician. He was involved in a rather nasty accident a few hours ago."

"I was told it was only an hour ago." I just couldn't ask the right question. A process of self-denial. If I did not ask and she did not answer, then everything would be OK.

"Actually, according to the police report, the accident occurred 2 hours and 24 minutes ago. It was a hit and run. Apparently, a truck ran a red light hitting your husband's car. Please, would you sit down?" she asked as she touched my elbow trying to lead me to the lounge chair. She had a very serious expression on her face which broadcast trouble.

Oh God, it is serious. Please do not let him be dead. Please, please, do not let him be dead.

"Your husband is in critical condition. He has multiple injuries, most of which are minor. Our most serious concern is the severe concussion he has suffered. He has several lacerations and miscellaneous contusions. There are no other internal injuries that we have been able to detect."

"Is he going to be OK?" I felt the blood drain from my head. Am I going to faint? I felt weak as though all my strength was flowing from me.

"It is hard to predict. He has been in a coma since the accident. We have no immediate means of determining the severity of the trauma to his brain. A patient's performance with an injury in this category is dependent on several variables. We are monitoring him continuously. We're looking at several significant parameters. We will know more in a few hours. However, I must tell you that his condition may not clear up for several days or weeks. Eventually, he will settle into one side of consciousness or the other. Until that time, we must wait."

The tears began to roll down my face. I fought back the urge to cry. I could not cry. He needs me to be strong, to help him. I must be strong. I just could not stop the tears. I wiped them away with my hand as quickly as I could. The doctor reached behind her to pass me a box of tissues conveniently provided for this precise purpose. They helped.

"Can I see him, now?" I asked.

"Certainly. I must caution you that he has extensive attachments as a precaution for the time being. Most of the equipment we are using is not mandatory, we just don't want to take any chances right now. Do you understand?"

I nodded in response.

The sign on the door was chilling. Intensive Care Unit. Authorized admittance only.

Doctor Hilton led me to a separate room. The curtains were drawn back revealing the glass walls that enabled the medical staff to quickly see all their patients. There he was in the third room on the right. He was lying with his head and torso elevated. There were tubes of various sizes connected to both arms, his mouth and nose. An array of wires was attached to his chest and head.

"Before you go in, I would like to tell you that he is probably not aware of anything right now. Coma is a very difficult condition to understand. We have never really understood what a patient in John's condition can assimilate.

We are convinced, however, that a familiar voice with sanguine words are the best medicine to help an individual fight off the fog of a coma. You are encouraged to touch him and talk to him, but please be as positive, supportive and upbeat as you possibly can. He needs your help."

I nodded again. Words would not come to me. Talking did not seem to be appropriate right now.

He looks so helpless just lying there. I reached out between all the tubes to touch his face. He was warm. I still could not talk. If I said anything to him, I would probably start crying. I did not want him to know I was crying. The tears were still running down my face. There was no reason to wipe them away. His left hand was resting on top of the sheet covering his bruised body. I took his hand in mine. Why did this have to happen to you?

Doctor Hilton was no longer in the room, or the ICU. Only three nurses, two females and one male, were at the far end of the unit. There was one other patient in the eight bed ICU. I was alone with John.

"I'm here, John. I'm with you, now. We're going to beat this together."

———

It had been eight days since the accident. John's medical condition had finally settled into a stable area. He was removed from the ICU five days ago. Most of the tubes and wires were removed from his body. A long-term venous catheter was implanted to insure that his unconscious body received nutrients and medication to sustain him. His cuts and bruises were healing nicely. Doctor Hilton's early assessment was quite accurate. There were no other internal injuries. The only task remaining was to bring him out of this coma.

"Rebecca, how are you doing today?" Doctor Hilton asked.

"I'm OK, Mary." Using her first name helped to personalize this traumatic experience. Mary Hilton was an unusual doctor who took great pride in the personal, human side of her profession.

"What have you been doing with him today?"

"I've been reading to him. Reading letters from friends and family. Reading some of Winston Churchill's speeches."

"Winston Churchill," Mary said with some astonishment.

Her amazement made me laugh aloud. I suppose it did seem a little strange reading Churchill's speeches to a man in a coma.

"Well, you said to do things that are special to him. Anything that is important to him. He's always admired Churchill."

"You are perfectly correct. It just struck me in a peculiar sort of way. Have you seen any reaction from him?"

"No. Nothing other than the occasional twitch of his hand which we talked about a few days ago."

"He's close, Rebecca. I can feel it. I can't show you evidence, but I can feel it. I certainly don't want to give you false hope, but the things I see tell me he's on the edge. All his physical signs are good. We've simply got to restart his consciousness."

"What should I do?"

"It's hard to say. I suppose what you have been doing. We've learned empirically that the best therapy for comatose patients is personal, pleasant exposure to things that are familiar and enjoyable. You could reminisce about special times together or important personal events. Your choice of encouragement seems to fit those prerequisites. So, it sounds like you are doing the right thing," she said.

I touched his hand, and then his face. He felt normal as if he was taking an afternoon nap. Unfortunately, his nap was now in its eighth day.

"I understand, Mary. I'll try to think of something else."

"Rebecca, please don't misinterpret my words to imply that you aren't doing the absolute best things already. I know this is a very hard time for you as well. I am equally concerned for your health and emotional well being as I am for John's recovery. Your strength and support are as important to his recovery as all the medicine we have at hand." Doctor Mary Hilton's sincere, soft voice was reassuring and comforting.

"Oh, by the way, I never have thanked you for helping us get this room and the roll-a-way bed for me. It helps me and I hope it is helping him for me to be right here with him. Thanks, Mary."

"You're most welcome, Rebecca," she said with a warm smile as she touched my shoulder. Mary Hilton was a special person. I am lucky to have her. John is lucky to have her. "I'd better be on my way. A doctor's work is never done, it seems."

Mary left the room to continue her appointed rounds. Her humility was one of the endearing traits she possessed. No matter how hectic things might become, she never made you feel as if she had more important things to do, or other patients she needed to see.

———

What?

Something woke me up. The room was quiet with the diffuse, dim light passing through the window blinds. John was lying in the same position I last saw before I drifted off to sleep. What time is it? Two in the morning. Looks like this night will be a tough one.

I rose from the small bed putting my robe over my favorite, long, night-shirt. With slippers on my feet, I walked to the door. The hall was quiet and dark except for the dim light of the small night-lights sparsely disbursed at the base of the walls. The nurse's station mid-way down the hall was also quiet. Neither of the night nurses nor the sole duty orderly were in sight. Everything appeared to be in normal order. What was it that roused me?

Returning to John's room did not alter the results of my reconnaissance. John's condition was the same. I walked over to the window to open the blinds. It was a beautiful, clear night. Buildings and signs obscured by the lights of the city. Very few lights cast their rays directly into the room. The stars were out in force tonight. The abundant portion of the Milky Way was spread across the evening sky. The city lights overpowered some of the stars, but the magnificence of the celestial display was still quite evident.

If I could just get John to see these stars... This is the kind of night he always gets emotional about. Maybe I could describe the stars for him. Maybe that might work.

I walked over to his bedside. Taking his hand in mine, I leaned over to kiss his forehead and then his lips. There must be a way to bring him out of this coma.

"John, this is one of your nights. The stars are spread across the crystal clear night sky. The bright band of the Milky Way is right outside the window. This is your kinda night, John. You've got to see it." Watching for the slightest twitch or flicker was hard. I wanted it to happen so much. Come on, John, fight this thing, I said to myself.

"Remember the night we made love under these stars? It's about that time of the night. It's the same stars. I'll never forget these stars. You were so gentle and thoughtful. That was one of the most enjoyable nights of my life. There we were out in the middle of that field under the black sky and all those stars. The air smelled so sweet and clean. I can still smell your skin mixed with the fragrance of the night air. The serenity of that time made me forget completely that we were stark naked out there for everyone to see.

"You were so slow and careful with each caress, with each kiss. I thought my heart was going to explode out of my chest. Lying there on your extra-large blanket with the coolness of the evening air was intoxicating. Touching each other as you talked about the stars. Oh John, that was a very special time for me, for both of us. God, I want you back. I need you, John. You've got to come back to me."

I could feel a single tear slowly falling across my left cheek. God, I want you back, John. I need to be loved again just as we did in that field that night. This is not fair for you to be like this. You have to come back.

There has gotta be a way. Maybe I ought to try something really radical. Mary said I needed to do things that were personal and meaningful to him. There is one thing that has always been important to him, and to me for that matter. I should have asked her, but then I really could not ask her something like that anyway.

Well, let's see what we can do. I walked over to the door taking another look for any activity on the floor. The scene was a virtual still life, nothing moved or changed. There were no sounds.

I closed the door, and then wedged one of the chairs under the handle to block any entrance. We will have no interruptions.

John was lying there so peacefully. I pulled the single sheet completely back to the foot of the bed. His magnificent body was showing some of his age. A little extra flesh and a few notable scars of past wounds were the principle indicators. His skin was smooth and warm which contributed to the image of quiet sleep.

Touching him was no different, I kept telling myself. He's just sleeping. This is no different from the many times I have awaken him from a nap, or when I could not sleep at night. I have no idea what works and what does not, but it never hurts to try.

"John, we are in a field lying here under the incredible stars, your stars. This is our night, John."

To my absolute surprise, his body began to respond. This is incredible. This is really crazy. I continued to stroke him gently as I had done so many times before. The progress was slow but definite.

"Oh, John. You're fantastic. I love you so much."

My heart was beating hard. All the nerves in my body were hypersensitive. I could feel every pump of blood rushing throughout my body. Watching and feeling his body respond to my touch produced the natural involuntary reaction within me. I could feel that change. This is crazy, I kept telling myself.

I gripped him firmly as my strokes became more purposeful. He's always enjoyed my touch. Maybe this will help you, John, I told myself. You always told me there was nothing a good orgasm could not cure. Maybe this will help you now.

The urge for something more was growing rapidly within me. Why not? If his body works like this, why wouldn't it work all the way? It's been so long since I've done this. What the heck? Let's go for it, John.

I took my robe and nightshirt off. There was a twinge of vulnerability standing in a hospital room completely naked. The door was still blocked.

Let's do it.

Fortunately, hospital beds were notoriously stiff, making my ascent of his bed much easier. For some strange reason, I stood straight up stepping across his body. If someone walked into the room, the sight of a naked woman standing erect straddling an equally naked reposed man would be quite a strange image. An instinctive glance over my shoulder provided the assurance that the door was still secure.

John looked so tranquil. I wanted him to have a smile on his face and a sparkle in his eye. I wanted him to enjoy this. Well, time's a wastin', Rebecca Ann.

I descended upon him guiding him into me. The feel of him inside me brought a chill, a shiver that passed through me. He felt so good as I began to move upon him. The portion of his body within me was working as well as it ever has, however the rest of his body remained limp and motionless. Supporting my weight on all fours allowed me to move my hips in the rhythmic motion of life. His face remained placid and expressionless.

"Come on, John. Feel this. Feel our union." I had to keep my sentences short. The exertion was taking my breath away. This has got to work. "Come on, John. Remember the stars...the open field...the smell of the trees and grass. Feel it, John."

This is hard work. I must keep going. The beads of sweat began to form. I could feel some of the streams beginning to descend to the low point of my body in this crouched stance. This seemed like a good idea when I started all this. My gosh, sex is hard work. Come on, John. Just give me a little reaction. Come on, John, come back to me.

I've got to take a breather. The muscles in my legs were burning with the pain of fatigue. I lowered my knees to the bed on either side of him. Raising my torso to rest my arms while I continued to move my hips although the strokes were short. Still no response from him.

"Please, John. Feel this. Fight back."

My entire body was wet from my exertion. He feels different. He's growing. He's growing. I'm getting him closer. I've got to keep going. I leaned over to kiss him on the chest. God, his breathing has changed. I've got to keep going. I've got him. I raised my knees to help my hips stroke him long and fast. My rhythm picked up. I could feel his body stiffen slightly. I've got him.

"Yes, John. Keep it comin'. Come on, John. You can do it. Feel me. Feel me, John."

The sweat was rolling down my body. The sheets were wet. I could see the drops from my body glistening on his body below me. The burning in the muscle of my legs was heightening the sensations I was feeling. A tingling shiver rolled through me. Pain and pleasure began to fade into one another. My sensations took hold of me. The pain was being transformed into pleasure even as the tempo of my hips was increasing. John's body stiffen ever so slightly. Or, was it my imagination?

"That's it, John. Keep coming." My breathing was heavy and labored. "Yes. Yes. Fight."

We were sliding together with the wetness of passion. Our passion.

Oh, my God, I'm going to get off. This is incredible. Come on, John. Oh God. John's head moved, first down, then arching back. A slight, almost imperceptible groan emerged from within his body as the convulsions of his orgasm shook his body. He continued to shake with his body stiff. Every muscle in his body seemed to be rigid. His reaction had the usual effect on me. My excitement was climbing rapidly. The world around me disappeared.

"Oh God. Oh God. Yes. Now. Now." I could hear my voice emanating from some distant source as the waves of ecstasy surged through my body. I squeezed him with the muscles that enveloped him. The warmth of the sensations continued to ripple across me.

I collapsed upon him as all the strength that remained within me rushed out as the peak of my climax passed.

My panting, heavy breathing continued in an effort to recover my strength. I could hear John's heart beating strong and vibrant in his chest. My entire body was dripping wet. The sweat continued to stream from every square centimeter of my bare skin.

A hand touched my shoulder. I screamed. Jesus, somebody slipped into the room.

I looked back at the door. The chair was still there. John. My head swung back around. John's eyes were open. His head rose slightly off the pillow as he looked into my eyes. A smile broke across his face.

"Oh, John," I said as I began to cry hard.

He stroked my shoulder gently. No words came from him, but he was back. I could not talk either as my tears mixed with my staggered breathing. I hugged him a strongly as I could.

The door shook as someone tried to enter. Fortunately, the chair held it in place, blocking the door.

"Mrs. MacDougal, are you OK?" one of the duty nurses asked.

"Yes." I struggled to catch my breath. "Yes. John has regained consciousness."

"Why is the door blocked? Open the door please, Mrs. MacDougal," she said with a stern, but pleading tone.

"Yes." My breathing was still labored. "Just a minute."

My body was very weak and shook with fatigue, as I rose from him. I kissed him before reaching for my robe. I kissed him again as I started for the door. Wait.

"I'd better cover you up, don't you think?"

John smiled back at me as I pulled the sheet back over his now relaxed body. I moved the chair away from the door and opened the now heavy door.

"What happened?" she asked. The nurse moved over to the bed and picked his right wrist to check his pulse.

"Well... He's regained consciousness."

"He's all wet," she observed as she felt his arm and the sheets, and then looked at me. "You're all wet as well. What happened in here?" she asked with a serious concern born from the unknown. Then, like a flash of lightning, an expression of recognition erupted on her attractive face. "I won't ask any more."

The quick medical examination including his vital signs was completed in rapid, efficient fashion. She seemed pleased with the results.

"How are you feeling, Mr. MacDougal?" she asked with a slow deliberate cadence.

"I feel weak and confused," John answered. The music of his first words was pleasing to my ears and heart.

"Your feelings are normal. You've been in a coma for eight days as a result of your accident. Do you remember the accident?"

"Yes. That's the last thing I remember until I woke up with Rebecca on me," John said smiling at me.

"John!"

"It's OK, Mrs. MacDougal. I understand. I don't think I've ever seen anything quite like this," the nurse said with a knowledgeable wink.

"I.. I.. I don't know what to say."

"You don't have to say anything."

The nurse took the electrocardiograph leads off his chest. She started to remove the catheter, and then stopped.

"Is something wrong?"

"No, I just think it may be a good idea to leave everything connected until Doctor Hilton can examine your husband. Please, excuse me, Mr. MacDougal. I'm afraid I should reconnect you," she said as the leads were reconnected.

"Thank you for checking on us."

"You're welcome. Everything looks normal. I think we can leave you alone. Well, maybe I shouldn't. Do you two think you can control yourselves?" she asked with a smile.

The heat of embarrassment flushed across my face. The feeling brought a sharp reminiscence of younger days. There was an element of invigoration in this moment.

"I just did what I thought was right."

"Mrs. MacDougal, you do not have to justify your actions to me. Whatever you did appears to have worked quite admirably, I would say. I congratulate you both. I'll leave you alone."

She offered a pleasant, friendly smile as she walked toward the door.

"Thank you again. We appreciate your help."

"You are most welcome. I'll check on you in a few hours."

The door closed behind her. The room was quiet again. As the door completed its travel, I turned back to John. He had a weak, but definite smile. His face displayed the telltale signs of fatigue.

"It's good to have you back, John."

———

Lydia

—

"You look like you had a tough day at the office, miss."

Cab drivers seemed to enjoy idle discussion with their passengers. It is a reality we have always accepted. They spend most of their day confined in an automobile, racing around town without much in the way of human interaction other than meaningless discussion with their captive passengers.

I don't feel much like talking after a day like today. However, there is no reason to deny a friendly cabbie just because I was having a hard day.

"Yes, I did," I finally responded.

"Well, we all have hard days now and then. A good workout will help settle the stress."

There was a flash of suspicion. How did he know what I was going to do? The address, he knows the gymnasium is at that address. My gosh, my mind is a bit too foggy. The reality of leadership is the price one pays for success. Fifty-seven people depending on my judgment for guidance to further success.

"You are definitely correct," I said. The thought of a good workout was sufficient to begin the process of unwinding.

"We'll have you there right quick. Just kick back an' let ole Roscoe take care of the hard work."

"Thanks."

The gray in his hair and the lines across his face were the telltale markings of age. He must be in his sixties. A congenial, extroverted old man driving with reasonable conservatism and obvious skill added to my relaxation. It would be easy to doze off with the undulations of the street and the security of Roscoe's taxi.

The buildings, the people, the cars and the other elements of Chicago were a blur of no interest today. The usual enjoyment of watching humanity was just not in me this day. Even the weather was dreary. The sky was low and gray, dark with the impending storm. The remnants of the previous snow were dingy with the sludge of city life and the extended interval from the last deposit. The winds had not yet increased, but would be here soon enough. This was supposed to be a big one. Only another month of winter and maybe we can see some sunshine. Pleasant thoughts of the fading vacation to Martinique were sustaining my daydreams on a generally depressing day like this one.

All the stoplights were in our favor, which was quite a contrast with previous journeys in this direction at this time of day. The relatively short trip took significantly less time than usual which was a tally on the positive side of the ledger. This is a good sign, I nearly said aloud. I will have a nice workout, relax a little, get a quick bite to eat and settle in with my book. No complications, no obstructions.

"Here we are, Miss," Roscoe announced with some flair.

The taxi was stopped with care at the curb in front of the main entrance. A few other women were entering the building, as I paid Roscoe before leaving the cab. I felt impelled to add a substantial gratuity as a modest bonus for Roscoe's expertise and extra concern.

"Thanks, Roscoe. You are a gentleman and an excellent driver. It was a pleasure to be with you this afternoon."

"Well, thank you very much, Miss," he responded with noticeable enthusiasm. Compliments must be rare for the elder man even though he probably deserved many more.

"You are quite welcome."

The late afternoon was still fairly orderly. The gentle breeze was barely noticeable which made the temperature feel less severe.

"Have a good night, Roscoe," I said, as I stepped out of his cab.

"And a good night to you, Miss," he answered as I closed the door behind me.

I walked to the entrance without hearing the cab depart. He must be watching me walk enjoying my legs since that's all he can see. As I opened the gymnasium door, I heard the cab's motor increase speed as the automobile drove away. There was no reason to look back.

The warmth and uniquely distinctive smell of the gymnasium enveloped me as I entered the sanctuary of the health fanatic. There was certain energy present throughout the interior. Several of the faces were familiar while some were new for both the staff and the clientele. The new faces and bodies always made the workouts more enjoyable. There was a definite beauty, attractiveness, to bodies of all sizes, shapes and colors for both genders.

"Good evening, Lydia. You pumped up for tonight's sweatfest?" The young male desk clerk was impressed with his own image and probably considered himself quite the ladies' man.

"Good evening, Jimmie. Not really. I just want to get this one over with."

"Bad day, huh?"

"Yes," I answered although the question did not deserve an answer.

I picked up the proffered towel without acknowledgement. Walking to the women's locker room door was thankfully uneventful. I checked my watch, and then the clock on the wall as if there might be some deception.

The aerobics class was scheduled to begin in slightly more than 15 minutes.

In a locker room, all the senses were activated and supercharged whether you liked it or not. There was something mystical about so many diverse women in such close proximity to one another.

The smells of the locker room were pronounced. Heavy with moisture from the showers utilized by the previous class, the air was rich with odors and fragrances. Perfume mixed with soap and deodorant did not mask the underlying tinge of human perspiration.

Sounds of inconsequential chatter intermingled with the serious banter of gossip between friends. Certain words jumped out of numerous conversations. Sex. Affair. Pregnant. Caught. They came from different parts of the large room spoken by unidentifiable people.

The most fascinating element of this evening's display of sensory shock was visual. The spectrum of humanity passing through this one locker room was incredible and strangely alluring. Often I considered sitting here simply to watch this snapshot of the population.

After finding an open locker, I began to peel off the layers of clothing required for winters in Chicago. There was space for each of us. No one seemed to be too close, and yet the room was crowded. The commingling of two aerobics classes, one arriving and one leaving, in addition to the usual solos made the transition more interesting. The breadth of this human spectrum was dramatic with excellent examples of the vast variety of female characteristics.

One woman was so fat that every inch of her jiggled when she moved. Her pubic hair was not visible underneath the layers of flesh and her breasts were swollen to an almost grotesque size. She obviously had an inner strength that gave her confidence to expose herself in all her glory without embarrassment.

Another woman was virtually a skeleton. The sight of her bones through a paper thin, and nearly transparent skin elicited a pain within me. She was sufficiently self-conscious to expend the extra effort required to transition from the protection of her towel to her loose fitting full slip without exposure of her torso.

An intriguing facet of this crowd was the various levels of modesty exhibited, and how each woman dealt with her own inhibitions. There were a few individuals that brought robes to assist in the protection of their propriety. The ingenious use of a towel to minimize the exposure of flesh was equally interesting to watch. The far extreme was occupied by those few that wanted a workout, but their modesty precluded a shower in front of strangers or even friends.

Then, there were a couple of rare specimens who were so proud of their bodies that they virtually paraded through the room repeatedly stopping in front of the full length mirror to admire God's creation and their hard work.

"Hi, Lydia. How are you doing," Samantha Greenville asked?

The white towel wrapped around her head concealed her full head of curly blond hair. Other than the towel, Samantha was stark naked standing directly in front of me. She was stroking her breasts as she waited for my response, as if she was making sure they were still on her chest. It was an odd habit of hers. Sometimes it seemed like she did it to draw attention to the outstanding breast augmentation surgery she was still quite proud of.

"I'm fine, Sam. Well, actually I'm really tired and I'd rather be in bed than here."

Samantha did have an impressive body in every respect even though her vanity felt the need for supplemental assistance. She was without question proud of her body and was by no means afraid to show of her physical attributes.

"Well, a good workout will make you feel better," she said. It was difficult to tell whether she was being facetious or sincere.

"You must have just finished." I couldn't think of anything else to say with her standing naked in front of me as I tried to complete my preparation. Her nudity and raw sensuality made me a little uneasy, although I tried hard not to show my discomfort.

"Yes, I should hope so." She leaned a little closer to me in an effort to whisper something. I stopped my dressing with my leg-tights half on to listen. "You're looking good, Lydia. You've got a nice body. The workouts are helping, I should say."

A flush of embarrassment rolled across my body and mind. A naked woman complimenting me on my naked body was quite alien to me. The synergistic combination of resentment and gratitude produced a strange feeling that was difficult to control.

"Thanks, Sam, but I certainly don't look as good as you."

"Well, thank you, Lydia. I didn't mean to embarrass you. I've been watching your progress, and I just wanted to compliment you."

I quickly completed dressing including the requisite adjustment of my colorful leg tights and French cut leotard to ensure a good fit and proper placement of body parts. Samantha continued to watch me as I finished although I refused to look at her. I didn't know what to say, and she was making me quite restive, now. I closed my locker checking to make sure it locked.

"Have a good evening, Sam," I said as I turned to leave.

"I will. Enjoy your workout. I'll see'ya later, Lydia."

The confusing jumble of emotions was difficult to sort out. The thoughts racing through my mind about Samantha's explicit, and maybe implicit, actions or intentions was a sufficient distraction to block my awareness of reality. It wasn't until I thought I heard my name that I comprehended the extent of my distraction. Somehow I had moved through the halls and several doors, and was now in the middle of the workout room in a sea of colorful women.

I looked around the room to ascertain the source of the unrecognized call.

"Lydia, where is your mind," Colleen asked.

I turned to find her voice. She was standing directly behind me.

"Oh, just some thoughts clogging up my consciousness, Colleen. How are you doing this evening?"

"OK. I'm ready for a little punishment, though," she responded with a broad smile.

Before I could answer, we heard, "Here we go ladies." It was the dreaded command of commencement.

Susan James, our highly competent and accomplished instructor, began the workout as usual with the necessary stretching movements. The music she chose was always pleasant and yet stimulating. Beginning slowly, she expertly increased intensity with the shifting tempo of the music. There was always an undercurrent of anticipation leading to the crescendo of a block of songs often like the Rolling Stones' "Jumpin' Jack Flash" or the Eagles' "Already Gone." She was definitely of our generation.

Tonight's exercise routine was progressing at the usual pace. Stretching gave way to low impact aerobic events joined in a graceful sequence. The tempo of the music took the rhythm of the exercises to the level of a pounding heart rate, heavy breathing and rivers of sweat. The large fans moved the air to produce the contrast between the heat within and the chill of evaporation. There was a clear satisfaction in the accomplishment as Susan concluded the high intensity portion of the workout. She was slowing the action to bring each of us back to a level of relative calm.

As the routine approached the inevitable cessation, I looked around the room to gage my exhaustion. Colleen was hunched over trying to catch her breath. Her leotard was just as wet as mine. There was some small comfort in the comparable depiction of exertion. The variety of colors and the relationship to the bodies underneath were subtly erotic with an intriguing combination of physiological responses to exertion and the chill of the circulating air over the wetness of the fabric.

"That was a pretty good workout, wouldn't you say," Colleen asked rhetorically. She was still breathing hard.

"It most certainly was. I needed it."

"I know what you mean." She took a couple of deep breaths. "Do you want to get some juice while we finish cooling off?"

"That sounds like a good idea," I answered without a clear sense of commitment.

Colleen slowly began to move toward the door. It was part of the sequence of steps leading toward the lounge and the juice bar. I followed a few steps behind her without words. The towel helped to dry off the droplets rolling down my face and arms. Each step brought an incremental reconsideration of the agreed to respite.

"Colleen, wait. Please excuse me. I think I'll pass on the juice."

She stopped as she turned around to face me.

"What? Do I smell bad or something," she asked with a slight smile?

"No. Of course not. I'm just tired and I need to get home."

"I would say that is a reasonable excuse."

"I think I'm going to take 20 minutes to unwind on a tanning bed, take a good hot shower and go home."

"That sounds like an even better idea. Maybe I'll join you," she said.

"OK," I answered as we walked the short remaining distance down the hall and into the lobby. This health club was quite popular, which was readily understood with the sights and sounds of people in motion.

Colleen and I waited for a man and a woman to check in and receive their towels. The two desk attendants had changed during our workout. Both of them were young, attractive women I did not recognize. Having completed whatever administrative task they were working on, the two women looked up nearly simultaneously without saying a word.

"We'd like two tanning booths, please," I stated for both of us.

"Ahhh. Let's see. Oh yes, we have just two left. How much time would you like?" the desk clerk asked.

"I'd like twenty minutes," I said as I looked over to Colleen. She nodded her head in agreement.

The woman keyed in the desired time on the master control panel for the tanning rooms.

"Room 7 and room 9 for twenty minutes each," the black hair woman said as she raised a key in each hand.

I took the key in her left hand as Colleen reached for the other key.

Room 7. Each of the booths was the same. A long, ultraviolet tanning bed, a washbasin, a small stack of towels, a chair and several full length wall mirrors.

"Thank you," I responded with a definite tone of fatigue.

"Thank you as well," Colleen added her own statement.

We walked across the lobby to the far set of doors which led to the ten tanning booths and additional offices. I glanced up to catch the number seven on the appropriate door.

"See'ya later, Lydia," Colleen said as she passed me on her way to room 9.

"Enjoy," I responded simply as I entered my assigned booth. I locked the door behind me although I felt no threat of intrusion.

The rooms were pleasant and well kept. Extra care was taken by the staff to insure that the booths were clean and not offensive to the senses. This room had a delightful scent of jasmine. The light rock music over the public address system added a nice touch to the small room.

Removing my shoes, wet tights and leotard felt good. The dull ache of fatigue produced a simple serenity and sense of satisfaction.

The diffuse light of the tanning room reflected off the wet sheen of my skin. It's not such a bad body for 36 years of age. The light brown tint of my skin was the last vestige of my Caribbean holiday, supplemented by a few sessions of artificial tanning to retain the color. I cupped my breasts before the mirror as I made my own personal assessment. The recent image of Samantha flashed before me. The soft strokes even from my own hands produced the usual pleasurable feelings. My breasts didn't stand up like they did when I was a teenager, but they were all mine. Fortunately, I felt no need to alter my appearance. These tits are plenty nice enough for me.

I turned nearly around to survey my posterior. The extra weight I carried occupied two sites, my breasts which was OK and my hips which was not. Still, all in all, my tush was not too bad I told myself as my hands traversed the skin of my buttocks.

Turning back around, I could see the slight bulge on my hips. A little extra work and I know I can get that off. It's just that as each year goes by, it gets a little harder to accomplish.

The dark brown triangular patch of hair between my legs caught my eyesight. Well, it's about time to give her a little trim I'd say as my hands brushed across my pubic hair.

I can't stand here all night, I'd better get on with this, or I'll never get home.

Out of habit, I pulled off a couple of paper towels and picked up the spray cleaner. It always seemed like a good idea to wipe down the tanning bed before reclining upon it. The task took only a few seconds and did give me some peace of mind.

There was a slight chill to the glass surface of the bed as I lowered my body on to the bed. The digital readout on the controller indicated twenty minutes as requested. The eye protection goggles were hanging from a hook on the controller box. I pushed the start button, which quickly immersed the room in the characteristic blue light of the ultraviolet lamps. With the goggles in place, I pulled the full-length cover of light over me.

The warmth of the light felt so good. There was a miraculous quality to the blue light that engulfed me. I could feel my whole body relaxing. The double benefit made the time expenditure more acceptable. Relaxation and skin color were positive products.

As the tension of my body continued to wane, my mind began to drift. Initially, the thoughts roamed over impending events and tasks at work. Then, odds and ends of little errands I needed to accomplish for me. The sensations slowly began their inevitable transition. The change occurred no matter what my initial state of mind was. With the shifting feelings, my thoughts likewise underwent a metamorphosis aided by the knowledgeable touch of my fingers. Maybe I'll conjure up a good fantasy to go with the touch.

My imagination rummaged through several of my usual scenes until the thought of the Caribbean sun and its effect on me possessed sole occupancy of my meditation.

The sun in all its brightness and heat fondled my naked body as I lay on the desolate and secluded beach. The murmurs of the small waves crossing the shoreline were the only audible sounds in the afternoon. The sun touched me in an erotic way that enhanced the sensuality of the moment. The tingling within my groin rose up to the level of awareness. God, the sun on my naked body always makes me horny.

What was it about the sun that produced these sensations?

He approached directly out of the water like a magnificent creature born of the ocean. There was only one purpose for his very existence. He was there walking toward me with the ebb and flow of his well-muscled body. There was a simple and primordial beauty to his naked and aroused physique.

Without the slightest hesitation, he descended to me. I could feel the jerk of my lungs as he entered me. He was large and long. His entry hurt me in a pleasurable way as my body adapted to him. The low-grade pain gave way to the inexorable seduction of the flesh.

His strokes were slow and deep as he rode high between my legs, which surrounded him and drew him into me. The drag of his taught skin across me amplified the grand sensations of sexual pleasure.

He kept his arms straight sustaining his position above me. His eyes consumed me, sucking my only remaining inhibition from me. Occasionally, he would glance down to the sole point of our physical connection as if to confirm his periodic disappearance within me. There was naturalness to this act without the slightest regard for intrusion or observation by others. We were alone in this small part of the world, and if we weren't, I didn't really give a damn. There was too much pleasure in this moment to be concerned about what might be.

The contrast of my light brown skin against his ebony black added to the eroticism of this instant. Rivers of sweat lacerated his skin as the sparkle of reflected light accentuated their presence.

The rhythm of his hips was slowly increasing and with him my own climb toward ecstasy. The cyclic tensing of my muscles raised my hips to meet his. The rubbing of our flesh heightened the pain of pleasure that tormented me. He filled me with his black flesh. The near brilliant, obsidian shine of the driving piston of this powerful locomotive was a clear, distinct image of this erotic experience.

The muscles of his body tightened as his breathing became more pronounced and erratic. Even his nipples were erect and prominent. The hardness of his entire body was increasing as I became aware of the droplets of his exertion hitting my skin. With each movement, the sensitivity of my body was ratcheting higher, producing a tingle, verging on a chill. The sphere of my awareness was shrinking rapidly to the boundary of our union. The rush toward my own climax was breathtaking. I felt my body tense as I stopped breathing entirely.

The waves of orgasmic relief rolled throughout my body, as I strained to contain the audible reflection of my pleasure.

His climax was equally as strong as mine and virtually in unison with me. His hard, well-defined body shook as he struggled with his loss of control. I could hear the barely audible, primitive groans from deep within him.

He drew his knees up underneath me to support himself as he rose up off the support of his arms. He looked down upon me with the undeniable expression of contentment and satisfaction upon his face. The luminous white of his teeth shown like a beacon against his black skin and the sapphire blue sky above him. His chest billowed rapidly as he worked to recover his strength. He reached forward to caress my breasts with tenderness not consistent with his massive, rippled musculature.

Without a word, he withdrew from me, leaving an unwanted emptiness and stood erect between my outstretched legs. He nodded his head to indicate his respect and to acknowledge our union. The magnificence of his anatomy was clearly apparent as he turned to walk away from me. His return to the sea from whence he came was uninterrupted as he slowly disappeared below the waves.

The sting of the buzzer startled me.

I raised the right side of the goggles to see that the lights of the tanning bed were no longer on. My allotted twenty minutes were up.

The well-balanced cover of the device was pushed away without much effort. There was coolness to the room that was not present prior to my session. I was never sure if the apparent temperature change was due to the process of artificial tanning or my orgasmic flight.

The weakness in my legs was dramatically accentuated as I stood for the first time. My body did not look particularly different in the mirror before me other than the erect, hardness of my nipples, which were still taught from my arousal. I could feel the wetness between my legs as I reached with a probing finger to confirm the reality I already knew. There was a unique pleasure in feeling the products of my fantasy from the swelling of my flesh to the warm, velvet wetness within. This was a good one, a really good one. I should be ready to go to sleep now.

There was a definite revulsion to putting my damp leotard back on to make the trek to the locker room. The towel was not big enough to make the journey and show respect to the decency of others. The urge was to walk the distance, as is, was nearly irresistible. However, I had no desire to offend others so I grit my teeth to don my leotard for the trip to the showers. I gathered up the remaining items I had entered with, unlocked the door and opened it to see Colleen waiting for me on the other side. She had dressed completely.

"You look like you had a good time," she said with an interrogatory tone.

"Yes, I most certainly did."

———

Justin

—

"That was a delicious dinner, Justin," Lisa said as we entered my apartment.

"Yes, it was. The food was enhanced with your company, Lisa. I thank you for joining me."

"What a nice apartment. It's almost perfect," she said as she started laughing. It was the hearty laugh of a confident woman that brought a good feeling to the room. I liked to hear her laugh.

"What's so funny?"

"Oh, it's just a thought. Your apartment looks so well kept, I considered the possibility of an absent wife."

"I suppose that is a compliment. Actually, I have no reason to mess up the place and I have a housekeeper that comes in once a week."

"Yes, but, are you married?"

"No, I'm not. Never have been."

"Well, that settles that then doesn't it," she said with a chuckle.

The spacious couch situated in front of the large balcony window was apparently inviting enough. Lisa walked delicately over to the sofa and sat. She was not the slightest self-conscious about the position of her short skirt revealing even more of her exquisite legs. There was an unequivocal presence about her that added to the appreciation of her intellect and physical attributes.

"Would you like something to drink?"

"Sure. Do you have a little white or blush wine," she asked?

"I think so."

The contents of the refrigerator were characteristically scarce. However, a small carafe with the remnants of a bottle of Beringer's White Zinfandel adjacent to the two gallon iced tea dispenser was all that was required. There was enough wine for just about two glasses. I poured one glass for her and a small glass of iced tea for me.

"Here we go," I said as I handed the wine glass to Lisa.

"What are you having," she inquired?

"Ice tea."

"You know, that sounds much better. Would you mind if I have what you're having?"

"Actually, no, I wouldn't mind at all. Your wish is my command."

Returning the wine to the carafe was easy enough and the iced tea equally effortless.

"That ought to do it."

"I'm sure it will be just fine. Is it a home brew?"

"No. Boiled water and a few bags of Constant Comment for fifteen to twenty minutes."

"Tastes great," she said with her first sip.

"Thanks."

The feeling of restraint led me to sit farther down the couch about an arm's length from Lisa. As was usually the case, I put my feet up on the coffee table. She had a pleasant smile discreetly, revealing her perfect, white teeth.

"I forgot. Would you like some music?"

"Sure."

"Any preference?"

"Not really. I appreciate any good music," she said with sincerity.

I always wonder if it's a woman's true feelings or acquiescence speaking in situations like this. Mozart was my choice of the moment. The delicate chords and intermingling of the notes represented the feelings toward Lisa tumbling deep within me.

"That's nice," she said with the music's commencement.

"You like Mozart?"

"Absolutely."

Returning to the couch brought the desire to ask the lingering question suppressed until now.

"What exactly do you do over at David Taylor?"

"I'm a hydrodynamist for the Navy," Lisa stated simply.

"How did you get into that field?"

"I've always enjoyed the sea and sailing. It just seemed like a natural extension."

"What areas do you work on?"

"Well, actually, the most I am allowed to say is, I work on submarines."

"Classified stuff, huh?"

"Yes. It's kind of like your work at State."

"I suppose so. It's just very interesting to me."

Lisa looked quickly around the room a few times as if she was trying to find her escape route.

"It's such a pleasant night. Would you mind if we went out on the balcony to look at the stars and the lights of the city?"

Lisa looked back toward me for concurrence. She obviously needed to change the subject of the discussion.

The cool spring evening provided relatively good atmospheric stability for viewing the stars despite the city lights. Nights and situations like tonight made the extra effort to obtain this apartment and the monthly expense worth it. A nod and smile acknowledged my agreement with her.

I led Lisa to the sliding glass door for access to the balcony. The evening air was refreshing. The lack of any wind made the evening temperature quite comfortable.

"What a view," Lisa acclaimed!

"I certainly agree."

The view across the Potomac River was unusually awesome with a clear line to the Jefferson and Washington Memorials. Only part of the Lincoln Memorial was visible behind the adjacent apartment building. The golden glow of the Capitol dome was one of the most distinctive features in the panorama.

"You can see just about everything in Washington. This is great."

"I've found this view to be restful and relaxing. After a tough day, these nights can usually work out the knots."

"I'll bet," she said. For the first time she scanned the remainder of the balcony. "A telescope. Are you an amateur astronomer also?"

"Just a hobby star gazer."

She walked over to the device of my space curiosity satisfaction. The survey of the knobs and adjustments was accomplished with ease.

"May I?" she asked. Respect for another's property was a proper trait of Lisa's character. She wanted to move the telescope toward her own target.

"By all means."

A quick glance skyward established a respectable enough object for a closer look. With a deft, graceful dexterity of a swift learner, Lisa utilized the sighting glass to aim the primary telescope. Shifting her eye to the main sight glass brought the expected response.

"This is fantastic. What star is this?"

"Let me take a look."

I used the wide-angle sight to place the star in the star field and compared the relationship with the amateur astronomer's ready reference star finder.

"I would say that is Vega, a magnitude 1 star. It is beautiful, isn't it?"

"Absolutely."

Lisa trained the telescope on another stellar object.

"Wow. This looks like a cluster of stars. Do you know this one?"

Another rapid comparison established the identity of the object in question. "I would say that is the M3 cluster."

"This could become quite addicting, you know. How do you breakaway from this thing?"

"Some nights, it is hard."

Her head rose from the eyepiece to look upward, and then lower as she scanned the horizon.

"I wonder what else you can see with this thing?"

"It's not something I've used it for."

The optical power of the telescope was certainly capable of bringing earthbound objects closer as well. The temptation occasionally reared its ugly head, but a sense of propriety confined the urge to the realm of random thoughts. Using a powerful telescope to spy on other people has always seemed to be an intrusion on the privacy of others.

The barrel of the telescope began to come down. Once pointed in the general direction of the adjacent building, Lisa peered into the wide field acquisition sight.

"Oh, come on now, Justin. Do you mean you never used this thing to discover earthly delights?"

"Actually, no, I haven't."

"You've never been tempted?"

"In that respect, I suppose I would have to say, yes. However, I have a rather antiquated feeling that powerful optics like this telescope are an intrusion into the privacy of others."

"Maybe so. However, just think about it. This is totally passive. It can't see through walls, or even curtains for that matter. If you observe something, it is because the other person allows the observation."

"I suppose you have a point, although I still have misgivings."

"It doesn't look like there is much to look at anyway. Nearly everyone has their curtains drawn. Well, not quite. There's a guy barbecuing a couple of hamburgers for he and the little woman," Lisa said with some levity in her voice.

While her attention was focused on the image of the distant building, I could not help taking a good look at the well-turned body standing at the telescope. A superb set of legs, a gentle curve of her posterior were complimented by the rather tight, short skirt. Her torso was sufficiently camouflaged by the loose fitting, peach colored, lace blouse she wore.

"Oh my, there's a woman hanging out her panty hoses. She must have just done the wash. She's wearing a robe." There was a mischievousness in her words. Lisa was undoubtedly having fun peering into the lives of others. "I wonder what she has on under the robe?"

There was no driving reason to interrupt her exploration especially since I was having just as much fun watching and listening to her enjoyment. Lisa was certainly an attractive woman in so many ways.

"An old man and woman having a late night snack. Johnny Carson must be coming on shortly." She laughed with a mixture of giggle and belly laugh. "He's wearing boxer shorts and a tank top, and she's in a long robe. Oh my God, he just pulled his genitals out of his shorts. She didn't take to that too well, it looks like. I'll bet that would be an interesting conversation to listen to." The excitement in her voice was a positive indication of her enjoyment.

The telescope moved again without an accompanying narration. The old couple must have left the intruding stare of the telescope. Several potential targets failed to produce a worthy subject. Lisa eventually raised her head from the telescope to look at me.

"Do you want to have a look," she asked?

"No thanks. I'm having fun just watching and listening to you." Somehow it did not seem appropriate to truncate her innocuous spying because of my idiosyncrasies.

"Does this bother you?"

"No." I lied.

"Are you sure? This is really such innocent fun."

"As I said, I have my own misgivings, but there's no problem."

"You ought to try it. It really doesn't hurt anyone."

She smiled then lowered her head to the eyepiece.

"Maybe I just need to find something interesting for you," she said returning to her search.

"Don't you get the feeling you're a peeping tom?"

"Not really," she said as she continued her search. "I think a peeping tom takes an active step toward intrusion, such as, going up to a window to peer through a crack in the curtain."

"I see what you mean. You have a point, I guess."

"Sure I do," she responded. The movement of the telescope indicated that she was being rather methodical in the observation of the distant building. The angles gave her about 70 apartments to check.

"Here we go. I just may have something here. A nice, well endowed, young woman in her bra and French cut panties. She's probably going to get undressed. No. Sorry. She's getting dressed. She must have a late night date. She's in a hurry, too. She must be late. Oh, well, that one was close. I wonder why some of these people don't close their curtains or something. I am glad they don't in this instance, but it is still a curiosity."

Lisa returned to her search without further conversation. Actually, I wasn't talking much so it was hardly conversation. The telescope was pointing down now which was near the limit of her height unless she changed the adjustments on the tripod. She was on her toes in order to point the telescope and see what she was aiming at.

"Ah, ha! Eureka!" she exclaimed with excitement. "We have a winner." Lisa looked up from the telescope again to motion me silently toward her. She looked back into the sight one last time to make sure the scene was the same.

It apparently was unchanged so she moved aside. I walked up to the telescope, looked in the direction of the line of sight, but couldn't see anything of note. The building was probably a little more than a kilometer away. The telescope was definitely pointing toward the building so she must have found an interesting apartment.

I looked at her sparkling green eyes that were full of excitement, enthusiasm and anticipation. Her eyes and face had an expression portraying foreknowledge of what was about to happen. Lisa was unquestionably a person of intriguing character.

"Go ahead. Take a look," she encouraged.

Looking down into the sight glass was easy and comfortable since it was almost to my height. The image startled me.

"Holy cow," I said as I rose up from the sight. I looked back toward the apartment building without the telescope and still could not see the specific feature the telescope was aimed at.

"Not bad, huh?" There was a mischievous quality to her intonation. "Look back down there and tell me what you see."

"You know what I see," I said without looking at her.

"Yes, I know, but tell me what you see," she said with emphasis.

Returning my right eye to the eyepiece confirmed that the scene had not changed.

"Go on now. Describe what you see," she admonished.

The words were difficult to bring out. My embarrassment between the scene and concern for Lisa's sense of propriety were choking off my response.

"Come on, Justin. Describe what you see."

"There's a naked woman doing exercises," I said plainly. What did she want from me?

"Describe what she looks like and her motions."

"She's relatively young, probably in her twenties. Dark hair, possibly brown. Nice body, good tan especially for the long side of winter. She's doing the splits, and then lowering her torso to the floor. It's a strange sort of push-up."

The image was crystal clear and the powerful optics enlarged the woman's image to nearly full frame. Watching the woman move was fascinating. Her moderate size, well-shaped breasts moved in consonance with her actions.

I could clearly see her fully erect nipples. She continued to alter her position as her exercises changed.

Lisa placed both her hands on my hips. I rose from the telescope to look at her face highlighted in the reflected lights of the night. Her gentle smile and jubilant eyes were delightful to absorb.

"Continue to describe what you see," she said softly.

I nodded my consent and returned to the telescope.

The woman was now performing some form of oriental control exercise. She was raising her legs and arms, stepping and moving in a slow, graceful manner as she turned and twisted.

"Talk, Justin, talk," Lisa whispered to me.

"She's moving around the room in an oriental exercise of some type. Her moves are smooth, slow and graceful. She's stopping to face the window. She's raising her arms. Her body is glistening with sweat. She must be doing some sort of breathing exercises to cool down."

The woman's body was quite beautiful from her face to the shape of her body, her moderate but firm breasts, her delightful legs and the small, thin, triangular patch of hair above her legs. She moved around the room without concern. There was a curiosity and seduction to watching this woman move across the room. The apartment was simple and yet elegant. I wonder what this woman did for a living. How did she afford a high-rise apartment of that type?

"Justin, please."

"Do you wonder what she does?"

"Sure. She's either a kept woman or an executive with some company, I would think."

"That sounds reasonable."

Lisa was stroking my back and shoulders. Her touch felt so good. She had strength with gentleness to her touch.

"Jesus. I think she's..." The image of the woman beginning to touch herself stopped me short.

"What?"

The woman's touching became more purposeful.

"I think she's going to masturbate. This is incredible. She is certainly not self-conscious, is she?"

"Now, isn't that interesting," Lisa added as her stroking continued. "Talk."

"She is kneeling facing the window. Her knees are spread widely for good access. She's stroking herself. She's stopping and getting up. She's left the room. Maybe somebody rang the doorbell, or the phone rang. No, she's back. She's brought something back with her. Oh my gosh, you won't believe this. She's got a dildo. It's like a floor pad with two phallic protrusions. She's kneeling over it. She's guiding both posts into her. One front and one back. Oh my, this is incredible."

Lisa moved her touching around my hips to discover the direct evidence of my arousal. I stopped. I started to raise my head.

Lisa stopped me saying, "No. Keep going. Let me play a little. You've got to continue to talk."

"She's moving up and down slightly as she strokes herself. Her breasts are moving noticeably. She must be breathing fairly hard."

The zipper on my trousers opened with the deftness of her hands. Freedom from the confines of my clothing relieved the ache and raised anticipation for what might be down the road. The touch of her soft hand was firm and experienced. It was quite obvious this was not the first time she had held a man. Her movements were purposeful and well paced.

The combination of the sights before me through the telescope in concert with the delicate stroking by Lisa produced never before experienced sensations. Control was difficult verging on impossible. I wanted the feelings to last forever.

"Talk," was the whispered word from Lisa.

"She changes her motion occasionally as she moves on the dildo. Sometimes she rocks back and forth, and then side to side. It must be to change the sensations she is feeling as she strokes herself."

Lisa's rhythm increased.

"She's going up and down now as her pace is quickening."

Lisa stopped her stroking and her touch left me. My thoughts immediate jumped to wondering what she was doing. I knew her admonishment was coming.

"Her motions are becoming..."

My sentence stopped short as I felt the warmth and wetness of her mouth. My God, this cannot be happening to me. This only happens in books or porno films. The feelings, the sensations Lisa created were absolutely exquisite. The last vestiges of control were rapidly disappearing.

"I think she's..." Somehow I could not talk.

The woman in the window of the distant apartment appeared to be experiencing her own pleasure. Her motions were random and somewhat hectic as she approached her own climax.

"I think she's going to..." I whispered as I fought against the clouds of my own climb.

"She is. Her body is convulsing. Oh my God. Oh God. Here it comes. Oh God."

My eyes closed to the world as the tremors of ecstasy rippled through my body and my legs shook in the climax. Lisa continued to draw the juices from me like a maid milking a cow. My breathing was uncontrolled. I could not tell whether I was breathing or panting like a spent male dog.

I wanted to sit down. I wanted to fall down, but Lisa supported me with her arms as she continued. The textures shifted from subtle, soothing and soft to intense, sensitive and verging on pain.

"What is the woman doing?" she asked.

For a moment, I could not remember what she was talking about. The telescope. What is in the telescope?

"She is folded over on the floor. Her knees are still spread wide," I said fighting for words.

Lisa's motions were slow and delicate now. Her actions were like she wanted to experience the aftermath.

"She's not moving. I can see her breathing hard. She's still on the floor. Oh now, she seems to be slowly removing herself from the phallus. Actually, phalli, I suppose. Lisa, my God, what gave you this idea? Why? That was absolutely incredible."

Her right hand rose to remove the residue of our passion from her lips. She had taken all of me. Lisa remained kneeling in front of me looking up with an impish grin of personal satisfaction at her accomplishment. The soft, delicate beauty of her face, eyes, full lips and auburn hair were a powerfully seductive image.

"It just sort of happened, I guess," she said at last. "I've been attracted to you for some time. I'm glad we finally were able to get together. I've wanted to make love with you. This was something that was very much spontaneous and different."

"You can say that again." I wanted to say more, but I felt almost clumsy with the words rolling through my mind. "I've been attracted to you as well, Lisa. I guess I've been afraid to ask you out. This is certainly a nice compliment to our first meeting."

Lisa stood, looked into my eyes, and then gave me a strong hug. There was an inner feeling between us that was difficult to explain. There was a connection that transcended the physical, the sexual.

Upon releasing me, she turned to the telescope. "Is our friend still there?" Her observation was short lived. "Nope. That must have been incredible just to watch."

"It was different. I have never seen anything quite like that before in my life. The image coupled with your actions nearly caused a sensory overload. I am amazed my heart didn't stop."

"I'm glad you enjoyed it, Justin. It was fun, giving you pleasure," Lisa said with her seductive smile.

"It's late, Lisa. Why don't you stay the night? Anyway, it's my turn to bring you pleasure."

"OK," she responded with a near whisper.

I took her warm, soft hand and led her inside.

———

Megan

The day had started abruptly with a louder than normal squabble between two of the children. It was not clear which of the four had been involved but it was enough to terminate my sleep this Saturday morning. With children ranging in age from seven to fourteen, undisturbed sleep was more often than not difficult to obtain especially on the weekends. Every time they woke me up there was an element of anger that fortunately subsided before I could get to them.

For the most part, they were good kids. We were quite proud of them as individuals and as a group. However, kids will be kids. It was times like these that made all parents yearn for the freedom of life without children living at home. It was the fictitious nirvana of all parents. We were no different.

After the usual admonishment for the disturbance, breakfast was prepared for the entire crowd. The burdens of a mother and wife were relentless. My inner benevolence was dominant on this particular Saturday. With waffles, eggs and bacon, the favorite morning cuisine of our family, the early feeding of the crowd was complete.

As I cleaned up the utensils of the meal, Jack began to fulfill his family work obligations by performing and supervising the boys in the yard work and vehicle maintenance. The daughters completed their assigned tasks throughout the house in relative quick order.

One by one, the children certified the completion of their chores, provided their requisite location for the day and departed. Little Jimmy was the youngest and the last to determine the nature of his personal activities for the day.

"I'll be over at Jeff's house or the school. See'ya, Mom," he said in his usual cheerful voice.

"OK, Jimmy. Be careful and have a good time."

Jack had also completed his assignments for the day. In the mêlée of children beginning their flight from the nest, he had made the move from the garage to the bedroom without me noticing. He appeared in his swim suit with a towel.

"I'm going to take a quick dip to cool off, hon," he said as he passed through the house.

"OK. I may just join you in a bit."

"Now, that would be nice," he said as he continued his ambling movement toward the backyard door. "Where are the kids?" he asked.

Was there an undercurrent of intent? It was difficult to say sometimes with Jack.

"They have all departed. We should have some quiet time I hope."

"What a pleasant thought that would be," he added closing the door behind him.

Jack was a good man, but the intensity of his professional life often made him quite dull on the weekends. I understood the pressures of the week and the need for relaxation on the weekends. Success always has its price.

The silence of the house and the first moment of solitude for the day helped me decide to join Jack in the pool. Who knows, maybe with the kids gone, Jack and I could simply enjoy each other for a change. Shedding my robe and donning my smallest bikini did not take very long. Maybe a few curves and lots of exposed flesh would encourage Jack.

The hot sun of summer had begun its relentless torture of the earth below early on this particular summer day. The lack of even a meager breeze made the heat more intense. At least, the children were off with their friends for a few hours. Somehow that made the heat more tolerable. Peace and quiet were just what the doctor ordered despite the timing near the apex of the sun.

Jack was already sound asleep in the lounge chair strategically situated in the shade of the large orange tree.

A quick glance to both gates confirmed their closed and locked condition. Privacy, even with Jack not too far away, made the enjoyment of the pool that much sweeter. There was a luxurious feeling to the coolness of the water, which enhanced the pleasure of the brief respite from the rigors of everyday life.

Once more, I looked toward Jack. He was definitely asleep and probably would remain so for the next hour. I'm not sure what inspired me. I suppose it was the combination of the quiet, the heat, the attraction of the water and Jack's slumber. The pleasure of the water was certainly better without the confinement of my bikini. Removing the small patches of cloth was simple and quick.

Although the water was warm as indicated by the reading of the thermometer, the contrast with the hot air made the water feel closer to cold. I stepped slowly into the pool, bending over to splash water on my legs. A little further into the water and the slap of water on my hot abdomen. My heart rate quicken as my breathing became short and rapid. I always felt a little silly entering the water this way in the heat of the day. At last, the final plunge under the surface immersing my entire body provided the sought for relief.

I stayed perfectly still for a few moments to savor the soft, smooth texture of the water against my skin. The coolness all around me was withdrawing the heat from my body. The water always made me feel light. I could not feel the weight of my breasts although their presence was affirmed with the slightest motion.

The air felt noticeably cooler to my skin as I floated, gently caressed by the water. This was a natural state where all my joints and limbs were free. There were no pressure spots however diffuse they might be.

As I propelled my body slowly, the flow of the water over my skin, around my breasts and buttocks, and along my legs became the thoughtful gentle caress of a lover. The sensuality of this weightless, total body condition was undeniable. The combination of the cool water and the warmth of the sun compounded waves of pleasure that began to build within me.

If this continued, I would have to do something about the growing tension mounting in my groin. Jack was still asleep thoroughly enjoying his moment of quiet. Drifting near the edge of the pool, the filtration system recirculation flow caught my attention. Now, there was an idea....the jets.

I moved toward the pulsating stream of water bursting from the side of the pool. Placing my arms on the pool deck above, positioned the stream exactly where I wanted it. The smooth side of the pool felt like sandpaper against my erect and sensitive nipples. The desired effect was immediate. I needed just a few minutes of solitude to accomplish my objective. It was simple. I had to relieve the carnal tension building inside.

It was quite easy to let my mind drift to other thoughts, to enhance the pleasure of the moment.

The young man who came once a week to clean the pool and its equipment would be the object of this fantasy. He couldn't be more than a year out of high school. He was probably working his way through college by servicing pools and the women that owned them. His background and the depth of his character were not areas I had explored. His body, however, was something to be explored.

He had a well-defined, moderate musculature. Nary a drop of fat obscured the movement of his muscles as he walked, lifted, twisted and stooped. His hands were quite large and the bulge in his shorts left little to the imagination. His sapphire blue eyes and golden blond hair accentuated the chiseled features of his face.

There he was above me watching my movements against the pool jet. Instinctively knowing what to do, he entered the water and moved behind me. I could feel the caress of his strong hands envelop my breasts and squeeze my nipples. Shots of pleasure raced through my body. The coarseness of his calloused right hand sent little jolts through me as it moved along the contours of my body toward its target. Slowly, he moved until his hand was nestled between my legs. His fingers were gentle and methodical as he probed the folds of my flesh to find what he was looking for.

At first, he circled that part of me, as if he was outlining his target. The sensations were so pleasurable they were on the verge of crossing the line into pain. The hurt of desire was strong within me as he continued his rhythmic stroking.

He pressed his body against me continuing his purposeful touch. His arousal was undeniable with the evidence rising to fill the crevice of my buttocks. I wanted him. I wanted him desperately to enter me, to fill me with his life. I pressed back against him to signal my readiness, my willingness, my desire.

He did not move other than the rhythmic pulsation of his right hand. The contrast of emotions was stark and yet dramatic. From the frustration of his hesitation, to take me to the near agony of his pulsating hand, the feelings were consuming me.

The tempo of his movements noticeably began to change. He must be sensing the erratic surging of my chest with my breathing reflecting the onslaught of sensations confronting me. There was no longer the discrete stroking of his fingers against me. Now, the movements were more akin to a vibration.

The world began to disappear. All of my extracorporeal awareness was fading into the distance. The only consciousness was the fireball growing rapidly underneath his hand.

The first tingling signs of the approaching ecstasy began to permeate my body. The intensity of his motion seemed to be in complete unison with the climb to the peak before me. He was an extension of my own body, my wishes, my needs.

The convulsions of the orgasm rocked my entire body. The release was powerful and fulfilling. The warm waves of my climax seemed to roll through me continuously as though there would be no end. These were the sensations of life, the substantiation of life that made the world a more tolerable place.

"Whew, that was a good one," I said aloud with my inevitable return to reality. It was probably the best orgasm I've ever had, I said to myself. Of course, the last orgasm is usually the best, I chuckled within.

Looking around the backyard confirmed that everything was just as I left it, including Jack still sleeping in the shade.

As the warmth of the orgasm receded, the heat of the air and the coolness of the water returned to my consciousness. I moved away from the side of the pool submerging to swim to the other side. The cool temperature of the water on the hot skin of my face felt quite good. It was a pleasant finale to the heat of the moment.

An itchiness seemed to well up within my genitals which brought the inevitable question. Maybe I wasn't as fulfilled as I thought. I looked over to Jack once more. His continued slumber was the only encouragement I needed, moving to the side of the pool again.

The magic of the pool jet was seductive. The simplicity and effort-lessness of the small stream of water flowing back into the pool added to the attraction. This was just so easy. Orgasms with no fuss and no muss, what more could a woman asked for?

The feel of the water was not the same. Heightened sensitivity per-sisted from the previous episode. The rush of the water soon overcame the exposed nerve ends as I began the return to the fantasy world of my imagi-nation. Stimulation of the physical with the freedom of the intellect enabled unbounded journeys into the world of the sensual.

The effect of the pool jet was working much more quickly this time. I needed a different fantasy.

The examination table was cool to my skin when I first lay down on it. Initially, the placing of my legs in the leg supports had the usual result. Embarrassment, or vulnerability, or regret, they were all emotions that tended to mix with each one alternately appearing at the top like clothes in a washing machine. As soon as the doctor entered the room and touch me on the leg, the emotions disappeared in a flash.

He was so young and beautiful. The attraction to him had been unde-niable from the very beginning. Everything about him was perfect, his face, his hair, his eyes, his voice and his body. Oh yes, his body, even under the attire of his profession, was something to behold.

Words never seemed to pass between us. If he was talking, I could not hear him. He knew what he had to do and what I wanted him to do. He was unique in so many ways. Not least of which, he never placed a sheet between us. I could always see his face and his eyes.

His examination was short, purposeful and gentle. He always took great care to warm his tools, worked slowly so I could relax and touched me gently. The extra care was special to me.

He was nearing the end of his assessment of my reproductive and sex-ual health. The anticipation was growing within me. The first portion of the examination was a necessity, a requirement, to gain the reward. It was rapidly approaching reward time. The anticipation was almost painful. I wanted to feel his touch not as a doctor, but as a man. This is the part I needed the most.

After quickly completing the annotations of findings, he returned to his position between my legs. Looking directly into my eyes, as if he were assessing my mood, his expression changed from the neutral features of the professional to the warm and caring features of a man.

Placing his warm, smooth hands on my knees, he slowly moved his hands along the inside of my thighs toward the juncture. The sensation was like small electric shocks that made my breathing erratic and quick. My legs instinctively tightened against the supports. His nimble fingers caressed and moved the folds of my flesh until he had a clear view of the object of his desire and my pleasure. I watched his head move toward me, and thought I was going to lose control of myself.

The warm, softness of his tongue touched me like a magic wand spreading ripples of pleasure and warmth rolling throughout my body. His technique and skill were as polished and effective as his medical expertise. The tempo of his touch quickened with the movement of my hips. The pleasure was becoming unbearable, overwhelming and consuming. It felt so good I wanted the sensations to last forever. And yet, the feelings were in brilliant contrast to the need to relieve the carnal tension within me. I wanted him to continue, but I wanted him to stop. I wanted him to enter me, but I did not want him to stop. The emotions rolled through me like massive, speeding freight trains.

My rise to the climax was a rocket rising from the launch. The first bursts of convulsions of life shot through me like lightning from the storm cloud. The waves of relief were huge and violent. I could feel all of my muscles twitching from the pulsations of the orgasm. I could feel my chest heaving rapidly, then stopping, then repeating. I could hear the quiet primordial groans coming from deep within me.

He continued to stimulate me to the point very near pain. I wanted to reach down and make him stop, but I could not. As the waves receded, my sensitivity became even more apparent. It felt like I was going to split right down the middle of my body, but I could not stop him. The tempo of his caress continued verging on a vibration.

The second peak hit me so quickly I was not sure what was happening. This climax was not as high, however it was more prolonged. Each warm wave was discernible and appreciated. The pleasure rolling through me was a celebration of the joys of life and the enchantment of being a woman.

I opened my eyes returning me to the real world. Moving away from the pool jets brought a deep, dull ache, the remnant of the recent events. Once again, I submerged to cool off the heat enveloping my head. The water felt so good.

A light breeze was now adding some cooling to the hot air. The leaves of the trees were moving to the rhythm of the wind.

I looked over to Jack. He had missed the personal inner events of my satisfaction. Contentment belonged to me.

Leaving the coolness of the pool, I picked up my discarded bikini and returned to the house without drying my body. The breeze and evaporation of the moisture covering my skin made the air seem almost cold. A brief chill shot through me partially from the coolness, but also from the relief. The course of the day had improved substantially.

—

Tad
—

"That was a great game, wasn't it?" my Uncle Nick said with some pride and satisfaction.

"It sure was," responded Brad, my cousin and his son.

Although neither of us were in high school yet, or even in junior high school, we all enjoyed the Grover Cleveland High School football games on Friday nights.

"How 'bout let's get somethin' ta eat?" suggested Uncle Nick.

"Yeah," my cousin and I said in unison.

The drive from the school stadium to his favorite diner took the usual route and time. The stoplights were a bigger pain on this evening. Sitting in the middle of the back seat, gave me a good view. Each time we stopped, Uncle Nick reached into the console compartment between the front seats to extract a plain, brown paper bag. Unscrewing the top enabled him to drink a deep swallow of the contents. I was never quite sure why he did this. Brad and I both knew what was in the bottle. We weren't sure what he thought he was hiding. The effect on him was always the same. I didn't like it when he drank. He left us and it made us feel alone. But, at least we had each other.

"Here we are," he said with mushiness to his words as he hit the curb jolting all of us.

Brad and I looked at each other as we followed his father into the diner. The wavering steps were not uncommon, but we always looked around to see who was looking and might notice Uncle Nick's affliction. Only Betty, the usual waitress on Friday nights, saw us walk in. The diner did not have very many people. In fact, there were only two other people, one man at the counter with his face practically buried in his plate and an elderly lady in the booth by the front door.

We chose one of the booths midway back against the wall opposite the counter. Uncle Nick sat on the end of the U shaped booth facing the door. Brad sat in the middle and I sat opposite my cousin's father.

The talk between us stopped and started. It was mostly about the football game and different plays each of us remembered. Several comments by Uncle Nick about a couple of the cheerleaders brought back immediate images of flowing hair, slim white legs and bouncing breasts. Brad and I couldn't help but laugh a little as Nick's observations mixed with our memories and whispered agreements.

Betty took our orders. Brad and I both asked for a cheeseburger. Uncle Nick ordered scrambled eggs and bacon as he usually did. I often wondered if he thought it was breakfast time, but I couldn't ask him and I didn't want to embarrass Brad.

While we waited to return with our meals, three bikers, two men and one woman, walked in. They were talking about something and didn't seem to notice anyone else. They sat in one of two booths at the far end of the diner. The woman sat down very close to the man in the middle. She kind of rubbed up to him and he did not react to her at all. They were each wearing black leather clothes. For the first time, I saw that the woman's jacket was unzipped almost to the bottom and she was not wearing anything under the jacket. I couldn't believe it. The smooth white space between her breasts was like a magnet to my eyes. The curves of the sides of her breasts were out in the open.

After Betty took their orders for food, the woman reached up to stroke the man's hair. Her right breast came out of the jacket. The reddish-brown circle around her raised nipple was incredible on the smooth round curve of her breast. She just left it there, out in the open for anyone to see.

I looked around and no one else was watching her. Even the other guy had his head leaned back and his eyes closed. I quickly looked at Uncle Nick who was quite, solitary and concentrating on his fork and spoon. Brad was doodling on his napkin when I nudged him with my knee.

"Look at this," I whispered to him and signaled him with my eyes.

The woman's breast was still plainly visible.

"Wow," Brad whispered in response to the view.

For the longest time, her breast remained exposed to us. The beautiful mound of flesh was like a huge magnet that we could not pull away from. Our treasure was eventually taken from us.

Her eyes acquired our unflinching attraction. Without looking down to see what was so interesting to us, she lowered her arms, but the seam of her jacket hung up leaving her breast exposed. Again without looking, her left hand rose to cup her right breast and return it to the confines of the leather covering her body.

The expression on her face did not change. It was like she either didn't realize we were watching or didn't care.

Brad leaned back against the cushion of the booth, rolled his eyes, and then leaned toward me. "That was really neat, and she didn't even care if we saw her tit," said Brad.

"I know. Wasn't it great," I responded.

"Here we are," announced Betty as she placed the appropriate plates in front of Uncle Nick, Brad and me.

"Thank you," we said together.

"Is there anything else I can get for you?"

"Sure. How about a shot of vodka," Uncle Nick said without clarity.

Betty released a strange coarse laugh. "Oh, Nick, you are such a card," she said with a wave of her hand toward him.

He did not smile. Betty returned to the kitchen. Uncle Nick returned to his thoughts and the plate of breakfast food in front of him. The cheeseburger and fries were good, real good, even without all the catsup Brad smothered things with. The mumbled words between Brad and me didn't really amount to anything. Our real concentration was on the rich, full taste of the cheeseburger complete with ripe tomato, hot onion and crisp lettuce. Repeated glances toward the trio in the end booth yielded nothing of interest.

The man in the middle and the woman occasionally kissed and touched their tongues. The other man must have been asleep. His head continued to rest on the seat back with his eyes closed. In fact, I hadn't seen his eyes since he entered the diner.

The change in the scene didn't come until . . . well . . . maybe, the tenth look in their direction. At first, the change did not catch my eye. It was the movement and the small flash of white in the shadows under the table and in the field of black leather that demanded attention.

I was mesmerized by what I saw.

Her right hand moved in an up and down motion over the rigid white shaft protruding from his black leather pants. The motion was not fast and it was not slow, but it was continuous. Most of the time, she kept her head on his shoulder as she kissed his neck, cheek and ear. Occasionally, he would turn to kiss her on the lips or the forehead. The scene was absolutely incredible.

The line that was the tabletop seemed to split the scene in two. The affection above the table did not match the action under the table. It was so strange and yet so fascinating.

Several times I saw her stop to stroke the shaft with her fingertips giving me a clear view of the erect organ. I had never seen a penis so large, even that was incredible.

The reaction in my own groin was undeniable. The uncontrollable and rapid growth made it hurt verging on serious pain. There was a deep, but hidden urge to join them.

My heart rate increased even more with the impending confrontation as Betty carried the tray of food to their table. Balancing the tray on her shoulder and planning her step to the booth probably prevented her from seeing the action under the table. As Betty served the meals, the middleman's expression did not change. It was as if everything was perfectly normal. In fact, it appeared that he thanked Betty for the service while the continuous motion of her hand continued without stopping. I couldn't believe what I was seeing.

I looked at Brad who did not return my eye contact. He was lost in his own thoughts, and it looked like Uncle Nick was asleep over his plate.

The motion continued.

"Is everything OK?" asked Betty who sneaked up on us.

The startled expression on my face must have given me away. Betty looked directly at me. She winked her eye, shifted her eyes toward the back of the diner and winked again.

Oh, my god, she knows what's going on under the back booth and she knows I have been watching.

Uncle Nick grunted, but did not raise his head.

Brad looked up and said, "Sure." He then returned to the fries without even meeting my eyes.

My face flushed with embarrassment at being caught. Betty must have noticed my condition.

Again, she looked at me, and then leaned slightly toward me. In a near whisper, she said, "It's OK as long as no one objects." Without waiting for a response, she turned to return to the kitchen.

Did she mean my watching or their activity? I watched her retreating figure. She was very shapely even for an older woman. I couldn't look back at first. Then, it was like a huge vortex. My eyes were being dragged back to the scene.

The left man was now eating. The motion continued. The middleman was trying to pretend nothing was out of the ordinary as he slowly ate his food. The motion continued. The woman used her left hand to eat a few bites of food and mixed her eating with kisses on his neck. The motion continued.

I began to wonder if she was ever going to stop. My short experience with this particular activity told me there had to be a volcanic conclusion, but the motion just continued. I couldn't eat and Brad still didn't know what I had been watching. He was mopping up the remaining catsup with the last of his fries. I still had half my meal and the motion continued. Then, the scene changed.

With her left hand, she reached for the napkin on her lap. The middleman's fork in his right hand was lowered to the seat beside him and his head stretched back to the seat back in a strange, contorted way. For the first time I saw them since this whole show began, the left man looked over at his companions and either did not know what was going on under the table or he didn't care. The napkin covered up the now frenzied pump below the tabletop. The middleman's body became rigid as a board for just a few moments, and then slumped. That must have been the climax as they say in the books. The thought was confirmed when the woman used the napkin to wipe her hand and the object of her efforts. The middleman's head rest on his chest and she left him exposed while she returned to eating her meal.

As I looked from under the table to her, the woman was looking directly at me with a large, friendly smile on her face. She winked and nodded her head at me. She knew I had been watching them. For some unknown reason, I returned her smile, but averted her eyes several times although she continued to look at me.

The expression on her face changed as the middleman moved. She reached under the table to return the not quite fully limp organ to the confines of his pants. The middleman never looked at me or anyone else in the diner.

The half eaten cheeseburger still in my hand was cold when I tried to complete what I had been distracted from doing. It took me several moments to realize that Brad was looking right at me.

"What have you been thinking about?" he asked.

I didn't know what to tell him at first. I simply couldn't tell him about what I had just seen with his father sitting near us. I'd have to tell him later when we were alone. "You won't believe it," I responded with quiet excitement. "I'll tell you later."

"Tell me now," Brad demanded a little too loudly.

Uncle Nick woke up. "Are you guys ready to go?"

"Not yet," I answered as I sped up my eating.

He had not finished his meal although it did not appear that he cared much. He motioned to Betty for the check.

As I hurriedly ate, the trio at the back of the diner got up to leave. The left man had the check and led them toward the door. He stopped to pay the bill. The other man and the woman walked out holding hands. As they past our booth, the nice smile returned to her face and she winked at me one last time.

Wow, no one is ever going to believe this.

———

Jessica

—

The journey had been a long one and not particularly pleasant. I never really like flying, but there was no choice if I was to take a reasonable vacation. This was the first time I would be separated from my husband. My sister's beachfront home was a welcome change having completed my master's degree as well as full time employment. Unfortunately, my husband, Carlos, could not come with me and I missed him already, but I needed this break from the strain.

The ride from the airport to their home was likewise a welcome change from the internal trauma of air travel. Both Linda and Jon picked me up as I debarked from the airplane. Jon's driving was steady, cautious and quite enjoyable as the abundant pine trees and green grass passed by the car windows. The scenic contrast was the most dramatic when compared to the browns of desert Nevada.

"Here we are," Linda announced as Jon pulled into the driveway of a larger than expected house. The trees and shrubbery surrounding the house brought a grand smile that I could feel to my ears.

The tour of their home confirmed the peaceful image of the exterior. Even my room assignment was out of a storybook with floral wallpaper, shuddered and curtained windows, and a large, canopied bed. The ocean air permeated the house and added a wonderful touch to the idyllic residence.

My first meal at the beach was equal to the setting. The laughter and reminiscence mixed well with the wine. It was good to be in a comfortable home, in a comfortable locale with my sister and brother-in-law. They were good people.

The safe arrival call to Carlos was punctuated with the jubilation of the evening. I was happy and he was happy for me. The buzz of the alcohol was not what he wanted to hear, but he was still glad that I was finally able to relax. I was pretty far long and failed to note his slight irritation over my inebriated state. It was good to talk to him nonetheless.

While I was on the phone, Linda and Jon had exchanged their clothes for bathing suits.

"We're going in the spa. Want ta join us?" said Jon.

"Sure. That sounds like a great idea."

Jon looked a bit odd with his bright red Speedo brief containing his manhood tucked under his accumulated beer paunch. Linda was wearing a simple yellow bikini, not too brief and not too big for her age.

"We'll be waitin' for ya out there."

I went up stairs to change as well.

The cool night air felt good on my skin. The flush of the wine made the coolness even more pronounced.

The backyard was full of various shrubs, vines and other vegetation among the trees. The spa was set into a redwood deck off to one side of the porch. The steam from the hot water of the spa produced a wafting, breezy image without any detectable wind. They were both in the water on opposite sides of the round tub. Jon had opened another bottle of wine. Actually, it must have been a second bottle since there were three full glasses and the bottle was full.

"Come on in," Jon offered.

"Looks pretty hot."

"Sure it is. It gets the blood flowin'," Jon added.

As I slowly moved into the hot water, I took a few sips of my wine. The combination was relaxing.

"You are lookin' good, sis." Linda contributed.

"Hot body, I'd say."

"Thanks," I responded with some measure of self-consciousness.

The reminiscences continued as we talked about a broad range of topics from life on the beach to the state of the economy. Eventually, the topics inevitably moved toward sex as it always did with Linda and Jon. The most pleasurable of human activities was an important part of their lives as it was for Carlos and me. I couldn't help but remember the lack of interest from Linda not too many years ago. Jon helped change that. My sister was definitely a different woman, much more alive and fun to be around.

The greater surprise was the revelation of their apparent mutual consent to sharing one another. Their words staggered me even under the influence of the wine. Their reasons were somewhat unclear. Their first experience was with Jon's brother and sister-in-law. They spoke with flowery, glowing terms about the concept others reviled. Their extramarital affairs were not common or usual, but also not solitary. What a puzzle?

With the course of our conversation and the relaxation brought on by the hot water and the wine, it did not take long for the confinement of cloth to be broken. Actually, Linda was the first to remove her suit. Her small but well shaped breasts were a tribute to her age. They were not large, but she was proud of them.

At first, I stayed immersed as I removed my suit. The effects of the environment continued to work its magic. The temperature of the water induced raise up with expected attraction of Jon's and Linda's eyes.

"Nice breasts," said Linda with a genuine complimentary tone.

"Thanks again." I placed my hands under both breasts. "You can thank my bank account and my surgeon."

"You're kidding," Linda exclaimed.

"Actually, no. I decided I wanted a change . . . to tighten them up and thought, what the hell, I'll make 'em a little bigger. I've always admired big tits."

"They look great," Jon added. "You can't see any marks."

"There are some very thin lines, but they are difficult to see. He did a pretty good job. I like 'em."

"I probably ought to get a set like yours," Linda said with lightness to her voice.

"Oh sweetheart, your tits are just fine," Jon added.

All three of us were sitting on the edge with our legs in the water to cool off slightly before returning to the warmth of the steamy water. The discussions about breasts and their virtue continued.

"What do the implants feel like?" asked Linda.

"Well, they feel like normal, tight, young breasts," I responded with a good laugh. I reached up to squeeze both breasts.

"Can you feel the implants?"

"No, not really. You can't feel them from the outside or the inside."

My breasts were obviously a point of fascination for both Linda and Jon. They both seemed to be captivated by my modified mammary glands. In a weird sort of way, I enjoyed the attention and the admiration of my breasts, which I was duly proud.

"Can I feel yours?" asked Jon without even looking at Linda.

I couldn't believe what I heard. I immediately looked at my sister who only smiled and said, "Me too?"

My heart rate shot up as I felt my whole body flush with embarrassment. I wanted to hide. The protection of the water was inviting, but I did not feel threatened or offended. Linda obviously agreed and consented to Jon's request. Her smile and their patience were disarming.

"I don't agree with swapping," I responded in defense of my inner feelings.

"We're not asking you for sex, Jessica," Linda said. "You have such beautiful breasts, and we just wanted to admire them more . . . more intimately." Again, they waited.

The wine took its toll on my inhibitions. I nodded my agreement.

Linda was the first to move followed shortly thereafter by Jon. His hand was the first I felt cupping my left breast with a soft but complete touch. Linda's hand was smaller and slightly lighter in touch.

"So soft and round with nipples so hard," Jon said.

Both of them fondled my breasts in their own ways. Their compliments on the shape and feel of my breasts were appreciated, but I was still feeling a little uneasy. The effect on Jon was quite obvious and unmistakable. I could feel him against my leg. He showed no embarrassment or self-consciousness. I was scared. My heart pounded and my brain raced through all the possibilities. What was I going to do if he tried to take me? What if they both tried to do something more? Should I stop them now? Except for Jon's erection, their fondling was innocent enough.

They looked closely at the bottom of my breasts to observe and feel the pencil thin incision. Their continued compliments were interspersed among discussion between them. The examination ended when Jon decided to test my nipples by suckling and gently biting my right nipple. I wanted to pull away. This was going too far.

I looked at Linda. She just smiled and winked at me. The concern in my eyes must have changed her mind. For the first time, her awareness of Jon's excitement was evident.

Linda grasped his erection. "Come on, Jon. Fuck me."

The words were sufficient to terminate his intimate assessment of the breast. As Jon turned toward her, Linda settled back into the water facing me with her arms resting on the side of the spa behind her. Moving between her spread legs, Jon raised her hips toward him.

"Yessss," she exhaled as he entered her.

I couldn't believe what I was seeing. I had seen other people making love, but never my sister. The difference was strange and yet quite intriguing. In fact, watching Jon's rhythmic motion and listening to their intimate sex talk was intoxicating and addictive. Linda occasionally looked at me. I did not move. The image before me was having the expected effect. The ache in my groin was becoming undeniable.

The heat of the water must have been getting to them, or at least Jon. He lifted her while they were still joined. After taking a few strokes in the air, Jon placed her on the edge of the decking. He continued his stroking. Linda moved her legs in different positions from wrapped around his waist, over his shoulders or pulled back nearly against her chest. The shaking of her breasts and the flexing of his buttocks were a broad contrast of the visual.

With Jon's back to me and their increasing absorption in their own sensations, my hand moved with a will of its own to the soft patch of hair between my legs. The touch of my own fingers shot bolts of electricity through my body. Listening to Linda's changing sounds established the reality of her approaching climax. Why was watching and listening to them fuck any different than watching other friends? The effects were obvious.

"Oh yes," she cried. "Fuck me, fuck me hard, Jon. Oh, my god, yes, oh yes." The words of passion continued as the waves of her orgasm rolled strong waves through her body. And, I always thought she didn't like sex.

She began to come down as Jon's motions continued unabated. I caught her watching me and her eyes shifted between my hand and my eyes.

Softly, with the satisfaction of her climax, she said, "You want Jon to help you with that?"

He stopped to look over his shoulder and caught my hand between my legs.

I froze. What was I going to do? What was I going to say?

"It's OK, Jessica. He won't mind doing you too." There was a strange, but sincere smile on her face and in her eyes. "I'll share him with my sister."

Jon looked at me for consent. The enormous conflict within me must have been obvious to them. I wanted him inside me. I almost didn't care who it was. I just wanted to have a big cock fill me up, to bring me off. The lust of my loins was fought by the image of Carlos. I couldn't although I wanted to. The struggle was great and also increased my heart rate.

"I can't," I finally responded.

"It's OK," Linda said for reassurance. "I don't mind and I know Jon won't mind." There was a jolly chuckle in her voice.

For an instant, the sensation of giving into my lust washed across me. I started to lean back and began to raise my knees. Then, instantly, Carlos' face came to me and I stopped. "No, I can't."

"OK," both of them said simultaneously.

"You go ahead and finish, Jon."

"Yes, Jon," Linda laughed. "Do finish."

To my relief, they returned to their carnal pursuit. The conclusion did not take long. In fact, his orgasm came fairly quickly. He absorbed his ecstasy in silence. With only slight tremors of his orgasmic convulsions, their primal motions ceased.

Then, with a fascination of a distant and yet intimate observation, I watched them separate. His still erect member was glistening with their combined juices of passion. The bright pink lips of her womanhood were full and spread like shell lips of a hungry clam among the soft patch of her brown pubic hair. The light reflected off the moisture of their union.

I wanted to finish my pleasure, but I no longer could. We each returned to the water. We did not talk about what had just happened. They wanted to talk about the pleasure and excitement of sharing. I could no longer join in the conversation.

I left them in the spa and returned to my room. The lust of the flesh was replaced by a new urge. "Hi, Carlos."

"How are you doing, sweetheart?"

"I'm pretty good."

"What's going on?"

"I just wanted to hear your voice and tell you, I love you."

———

Scott

—

The bright spring day brought the warm caress of a light breeze among the enveloping leaves of the shrubs and trees of the park. It was a good day and I was excited about meeting Jenny in our special place. The shadows danced among the leaves bringing softness to the matt of pine needles and leaves.

She was not there yet, so I decided to sit down on the short stump near the small clearing. I was excited about this meeting with Jenny. Somehow I knew this would be a different time.

I remember a lot of things about Jenny and every time I have seen her. She lived several miles away from me. She was the daughter of a man who worked with my father, and she had been my sitter since I was ten. Jenny had always been a person of considerable interest to me. I enjoyed being around her for as long as I could remember.

My relationship with her changed a few months ago when she kissed me for the first time. Jenny was the first girl, actually a young woman, other than my sister or mother, I ever kissed. I have no idea why it happened. In fact, I can't even remember the circumstances, but it did happen. Her soft lips gave me the most incredible feelings. Every time I kissed her, my heart began to pound in my chest.

The last time Jenny was at our house, she let me touch her tittie. Her's felt different than my sister's. I liked touching my sister's tit, but I loved feeling Jenny even through her shirt and bra. Jenny had larger one's than Susan, and they were more round.

I had shown her this place several times over the years I had known her, and now it was a special place for us. I was a little afraid about this meeting, but I also couldn't wait to see her again. Things were happening and feelings were rushing through me faster than I could understand. I did not know why I wanted more, but I did.

The steps in the leaves made my heart beat faster. Through the spaces among the branches and green leaves, the yellow of her clothing bounced in and out of view.

"Scottie, are you there?" came the confirmation of her approach.

"Scott, Jenny! Scott!" I protested. "Yes, I'm here."

"OK, OK, Scott. I keep forgetting," she answered with a laugh among her words.

Seeing her curly, blond hair and her brilliant blue eyes were like a sun on earth. She was wearing a flowing, yellow dress with lots of folds, but the mounds of her chest could not be hidden. Jenny was so beautiful although not everyone agreed with me. She had a blanket rolled up under her left arm and held a small, carryall, picnic ice chest.

"What are those for?" I asked motioning with my eyes to the blanket and chest.

"Oh, I just thought we ought to be comfortable, and I decided to bring a few sodas and some cookies."

"Great."

"Have you been here long?"

"No. I just got here a little before you."

"It's good to see you again, Scott," Jenny said, and then leaned over to kiss me. The kiss was short and on my lips. She started to kiss me again and stopped. "Let's put these down."

I helped her spread the blanket on the leaves and she put the box beside the stump.

"I've been looking forward to today," Jenny began as she sat down on the blanket. She motioned for me to join her. Her legs were crossed such that her knees were apart and her dress was taught across the space. "You know I've always liked you. In fact, I think it's a lot more than like. You are the sweetest boy I know."

"Thanks, Jenny," I answered. I was almost afraid to tell her what I really thought. I loved her. I loved her more than anyone I had ever known. I had never known anyone quite like her.

"I kind of wanted to do something special with you, and you have chosen the perfect spot."

I didn't know quite what to say, so I just smiled at her. The brightness of her blue eyes and the whiteness of her teeth answered me.

Without another word, Jenny leaned forward on her left arm moving her head toward me. I knew what was coming and my heart began to race. I wanted to feel her lips on mine.

As we kissed, she opened her mouth slightly and her soft, wet, dainty tongue touched my lips and parted them. Our tongues danced together as I responded to her lead. This was not the first time our tongues had touched, but every time seemed like the first with her.

After several moments of wonderful, she reached to my shoulder with her other hand and pulled me toward her as she lowered us to the blanket. Lying next to her felt like home. Like a place I was supposed to be. I certainly didn't know what was going to happen in the near future, but I knew whatever it was, it would be nice.

We continued to kiss as our lips and tongues became more excited.

There was a strange enjoyment to her exploration of my mouth and mine of hers. The closeness to another human being was not something I had ever felt before and it was incredible.

Without realizing what was happening at first, I found my hand resting on her right breast. She did not react so I kept my hand on her although I didn't move it. Her breast felt different than the other times, flatter and a little harder. But, what was really different was, I couldn't feel a bra. Jenny wasn't wearing anything under her dress. The thought that I was one step closer to the soft flesh of her breast brought a new urgency to my excitement.

Jenny slowed and then stopped our kissing as she raised her head slightly from me. I froze. Had I done something wrong? She looked into my eyes with a strange expression, a sort of mixture of enjoyment and expectation. She grasped my left wrist. I knew I had done wrong. She lifted my hand from her. She didn't want my hand feeling her tit. Oh god, why did I do that? Now, she was going to stop.

I started to apologize for offending her when she moved my hand to slide it under the material covering her breast onto the bare skin of her right breast.

My heart practically came out of my chest as I felt the velvet soft skin and cushiness of her breast. Jenny's lips descended upon mine. Then, against the edge of my hand, I felt the hard rise of her nipple begging to be squeezed. I didn't know if I should or not, so I didn't, but I wanted to. God she felt so good. This was the most fantastic thing in my entire life. I knew nothing could feel better.

Jenny's free hand stroked my shoulder and back, and occasionally touched my head, my cheek and my hair. I squeezed her breast to feel the softness under my hand, and slowly began to knead her flesh like my mother kneaded bread dough. The curves, the textures, the softness felt so good. No wonder my dad and other men seemed so concerned about women's' breasts. Now, I knew.

"Not so hard," Jenny said suddenly.

The shock jolted me like a slug to my face. "I'm sorry," I said as I drew back from her. "I'm so sorry." I withdrew my hand from her dress.

"No, don't stop," she said with a soft, warmness of her words. "Just be gentle. Don't squeeze so hard." She kissed me a couple of times in quick succession. "If you want to squeeze something, squeeze my nipple. I like that." The smile on her face seemed to confirm her words and give a little reassurance.

My hesitation must have convinced her to change the situation. She sat up and I thought she was going to leave. Then, without any warning, she pulled at her dress. The elastic gave way. Her entire body, at least from her waist up and that's all that counted right this moment, was naked. I couldn't believe my eyes. Her two, round breasts with their brownish-red circles in the middle and prominent raised nipples in the center of those were like huge, powerful magnets for my eyes. I couldn't take my eyes off of them.

"You like 'em?" asked Jenny.

I finally looked into her eyes. The smile on her face took some of the bite out of my embarrassment. "They're beautiful, Jenny. I've not seen anything so beautiful, anywhere, not ever."

She laughed a little with my words. I wasn't entirely sure if she was laughing at me or with me.

Jenny cupped both breasts with her hands. "I like them to. I think they have the neatest feeling," she said as she squeezed them a little herself. "Here, feel them like this," she continued as she raised my hands to her breasts. "Feel the curves, the heaviness. Doesn't that feel great?"

I nodded my head. I couldn't speak.

"Squeeze my nipples."

I complied.

"A little harder. Harder. Kind of roll them between your finger tips. Yeah, that's it," she said as she squirmed a little. "Don't twist them too far. Just a little, back and forth. Yes, that's it. Jeez, that feels so good."

I simply could not believe what I was doing. I couldn't believe she was letting me do this to her. I also didn't want to stop.

"Do you want to suck on them?"

My hand withdrew involuntarily. "No. I can't."

She smiled. "Sure you can. Go ahead. Try it, you might like it," she said as she reached to the back of my head and began to slowly pull me toward her waiting breast.

I didn't think this was right. Sucking on tits was what babies did with their mothers, not what big guys like me did. She kept pulling me toward her. I couldn't resist.

I took her right nipple in my mouth. At first, I did not suck. I kind of squeezed her nipple with my lips. Without thinking, I reached up to hold her breast with my hand and squeezed it gently as I began to suck on it. I wondered if anything was going to come out of it, like milk. Nothing did, but what I was doing was obviously making Jenny feel real good. I could hear her groan a delightful groan. She stroked my hair on the back of my head as I continued to suck on her tit. For some strange reason, I like doing this. I didn't feel like a baby. I felt good. Maybe it was because I was making Jenny feel good, but I really think it was because I liked it. I liked sucking on her tit.

After a while, Jenny stopped me and began to kiss me with a new intensity. There was a weird sensation of a fire building within me; a feeling the fire was out of control. I had no idea what it meant, or where it was going, or what was going to happen next.

She lay back down bringing me with her. Her hands moved quickly over my upper body from my head to my hips. She must have felt a fire similar to mine because that was what her movements reminded me of.

I had not been aware of my own excitement until her hand touched me. Then, like a flash, I felt this incredible pain in my groin under her stroking hand. The pain subsided a little as she released me from the confines of my Levis, but she also released a surge of fear within me. She wrapped her fingers around me like the handle of a club. I was afraid like I was falling into a deep well and I didn't know where the bottom was.

This was going way beyond anything I had ever imagined or even thought I could imagine. I wanted to stop, but the feelings wouldn't let me. It was like my mind knew I should stop, that I shouldn't be there, but my body and the sensations I was feeling wouldn't let me stop.

She finished unbuttoning my Levis and began to pull my pants down. I didn't mind her being naked outside, but I didn't want to be naked out where someone could see me. I tried to resist by not moving my hips to help. She was very determined. I stopped.

"I can't," I said.

"Sure, you can," she responded.

"No, I can't. I don't want to," I returned without thinking about the words I was saying.

"Why?"

"I'm scared."

Jenny laughed. "Don't be scared. There's nothing to be afraid of. This is what boys and girls do," she said. There was a peculiar sort of wisdom, an eternal logic, to her words, or the meaning of her words.

"No, Jenny, I am afraid. I don't know what is happening, what is going to happen, and I am afraid."

"Scott, listen to me. There is nothing to worry about. These feelings are the greatest feelings in the entire world. I love you so much I want to share these feelings with you. Just trust me you will like what you feel. Just trust me."

My resistance began to break down, but my fear did not go away. She returned to kissing me and returned my hand to her breast while her hand returned to my penis and testicles. I liked the feelings her hand brought to me, and my hand derived from her body, but it was the unknown, the unexplored territory.

Well, pioneers had to start somewhere, I told myself. I did trust her as much as I loved her. So, I figured I might as well go along with her. She seemed to know what she was doing and what she wanted.

The frenzied activity between us began to change after she got my pants, undershorts and T-shirt off. I was completely naked lying on the blanket next to her.

Jenny took another quick break as she took her dress and panties off. Now, she was completely naked as well. The dark brown, triangular patch hair between her legs had a new attraction for me. Again, she pulled me toward her.

Our hot skin seemed to melt together. She was so soft. All of her was so soft. There must have been steam rising from us, but I couldn't see any. Her skin felt like it was on fire.

She kissed me all over always returning to my mouth and reinserting her tongue between my lips. Without the slightest hesitation, she grabbed my hand from her breast and placed it on the brown patch of hair between her legs. I didn't know what to do, so I didn't move. Jenny moved her hips probably as a signal to do something, but I didn't know what.

"Touch me," she whispered in my ear. "Feel me. Explore me."

I still didn't know what I was supposed to do although the idea was beginning to develop in my mind. Jenny continued to move her hips under my hand.

Slowly, with a great deal of caution, I began to move my fingers. I felt a crease of skin under the hair and began to move down it. I touched a smooth, but hard knob of flesh in the crease that produced an instant groan and sigh from Jenny. She pushed up against my hand. Whatever this was, she liked my touching her at that spot. I moved around the knob of flesh several times and with each movement, Jenny's reaction changed.

My curiosity forced me to continue the exploration of her groin. I knew nothing about a woman's body, but this was an area I wanted to know more about.

My fingers continued to move among the folds of skin I felt. The fascination with the touch of this skin attracted my eyes. I wanted to see these features, to see what my fingers were feeling. Then, I felt the wetness among the folds. It was a wetness I had never, ever felt before. It made the skin soft and slippery. It was slippery like ice and yet hot like nothing I had ever felt before. Her hips moved in a crazy gyration with every action of my fingers.

The feelings were so incredible. The urge to see what my fingers were feeling was overwhelming. There was a hole among the folds of hot, wet flesh that literally sucked my finger into it.

"Oh, yes," came to audible words from Jenny. "Yes."

My middle finger entered her as if it was supposed to be there. The hole felt tight around my finger and yet it felt so soft and smooth all the way in as far as my finger would reach. My fingertip just barely touched a round knob about the size of a quarter with a recess in it.

Suddenly, Jenny removed my hand, pulled me closer to her and rolled so that I was lying on top of her. She spread her legs further apart so that I was between her legs. She reached down between us to grab and guide me to the spot I had just left. I thought I knew what she wanted me to do, but I wasn't sure.

"Put it in here," she said with an almost desperate urgency.

It was quite obvious she knew exactly where she wanted me to be. She moved me to a point where I felt the wetness and the hole again. With her legs now wrapped around my waist, she used her legs and arms to push me into her. Once I felt the wet, hot tightness around me, a supernatural force of unknown origin and power took over as I pushed all the way into her as far as her hips would let me go. For some strange reason that I absolutely did not understand, I felt like I was home, like this was a place I was supposed to be.

"Oh my god," she said aloud. "Oh Jesus, I can't stand it. Move. Pump it."

I began to move in and out with her. It was a natural motion like it was supposed to be, like I had done this many times before, and it was definitely what she wanted me to do.

The in and out motion produced an absolutely mind-boggling friction between us. Her hips moved with my hips. The feeling of unity, of oneness, of a unique union between us was born in the heat of our melding.

Each time I stopped to shift my weight or try to catch my breath; I was greeted by her words.

"No. No. Keep going. Don't stop," she said. "Don't ever stop."

I rose up on my arms above her and my hips continued to move into her. With each trust of our hips, her breasts would jiggle like little mounds of jelly. Her nipples were so big they looked like cherries on top of huge mounds of vanilla ice cream. Her eyes were closed, but I knew she could see me. Her mouth was open ever so slightly, and her lips moved continuously whether words or sounds passed through or not. She was so beautiful.

Then, as if a strange disease entered her, Jenny's body was becoming rigid. Her chest began to heave in a sporadic, pattern-less way as her back arched and her head drew back, tightening her slender neck. Her movement demanded a new urgency to our motion as a strange tingling sensation began to grow from the point of our union.

Jenny's body shuddered and began an odd set of convulsions. I wasn't certain what was happening, but somehow I knew everything was as it was supposed to be. The air rushing in and out of her mouth made an odd panting sound like an overheated dog. Whatever it was she was feeling, it was without question pleasurable to her. She liked what she was feeling.

Her sounds, her motions and the combinations of everything increased the spread of the tingling sensation, spreading from my groin. As my motions continued with their own renewed urgency, warm waves of electricity began to surge through my body. The sensations were so powerful; my arms almost buckled which would have sent me crashing down on her. An unusual series of pulses passed between us through our combination. Jolts, shakes and shudders accompanied the pulses.

When I opened my eyes, which I really didn't realize were closed, Jenny was smiling the biggest smile. There was a new sparkle to her eyes I had never seen before. I returned her smile from deep down inside me.

Her arms reached up to my shoulders and pulled me down to her so we were chest to chest. I could feel the hardness of her nipples against me. My gosh, did she feel good.

For the first time, I became aware we were all wet. Completely wet. We were both covered from head to toe with the wetness of our exertion together. The wetness was not the same as the wetness between Jenny's legs, but it was a pleasant, satisfying wetness. I liked it.

We stayed together, joined at the hips and intertwined in each other's arms. A certain, quiet peacefulness overcame both of us. As I drifted off into a distant solitude, I didn't recognize or realize that my young life had moved into a different more broad stage of existence. My life changed forever with my first union with Jenny Finch.

———

Kevin

—

"How long have we been together?" asked Debra.

"About two and a half years, I'd say."

"Would you say we have a pretty good relationship?"

"What kinda question is that?" I protested.

"Well, would you?"

"Of course, we do. I don't think I have ever been happier. We laugh together. We cry together. We have the greatest sex I've ever known, and besides that you have great tits." I said accompanied by a hearty laugh to insure some levity came with the answer to her loaded question.

Debra seemed to ignore my attempt at levity and was preoccupied with thoughts of her own as she pushed the remnants of her meal around the plate. Something was on her mind.

Her failure to respond brought concerns for a problem, an abnormality or an issue. "Is something wrong?" I asked.

The pearls of her teeth displayed between her full red lips softened the disquietude. "I was just thinking..." she stopped before completing the sentence. Looking around as if to establish who might be listening, Debra continued, "Are you content with our sex?"

"Jesus, Debra. What is with these questions? What's wrong? Is it something I did?"

"No, Kevin, it is not something you did," she responded with a touch of frustration.

"Then, what is it? What's botherin' you?"

The expression of her determination shot from her eyes. She was definitely serious, but about what?

"Are you content?" she persisted.

"Sure, I am."

"Really?"

"What do you want me to say, Debra?"

"Do you want to try something new, something different?"

"I'm always ready to try something new. You know that."

"This is really different," she said conjuring up all sorts of brief bizarre images in my mind.

"I suppose it depends on how different."

A serious expression returned to her face as she focused on some spot on the table in the vicinity of her plate. "John and I were members of a special group." Memories of her deceased husband always brought a certain melancholy that I was becoming accustomed to.

"What kinda group?"

She looked directly into me with her stunning emerald green eyes. "It's a sex group," she stated succinctly for maximum impact.

A hundred thoughts blasted into my head. Group sex. I didn't know what to think. My desire for new experiences was crushed under the steamroller of my own imagination. I had never had sex with more than one person and especially not in front of other people. A little sex in public places was OK, but I had never been seen or discovered. So many images ran through my brain, it was difficult to understand them all.

"What exactly does that mean?" I asked with some trepidation.

The hesitation and her lowered eyes provided the poignancy for the moment. "I'm not sure I should continue."

"Oh yes, I can't wait," I responded with some anticipation. "You have piqued my curiosity."

Debra picked up her forked and pushed some of the remaining morsels around her plate. She still could not look at me. "We don't have to do it."

"I don't even know what it is that we don't have to do."

"Well...it's a group of select people who enjoy sex."

"So?"

"They enjoy sex together."

"Together meaning all in the same room?"

Debra looked directly into my eyes to see what reaction there might be. "Yes," she answered softly and with some anticipation.

I tried to remain stoic and somewhat detached, although it was quite difficult. Here was the woman I had grown to love telling me she was into group sex. Comprehension was challenging. "You're kidding."

Her rich brown hair shimmered, as she shook her head.

"Oh yes, you are. You're just trying to test me, to see what I'll say."

"I knew it was a bad idea," she responded with frustration. "I shouldn't have said anything,"

She began fidgeting with the contents of her purse.

A torrent of thoughts, images, ideas and what-if's blasted through my consciousness. Did this mean she was unhappy with our sex life together? Did it mean she wanted something else? What was bothering her? Wasn't I doing the right things? The thoughts and questions kept coming, but my curiosity took control. Things like that were fiction for books and movies, not real life.

"Tell me more, please," I said as tenderly, patiently and considerate as I could possibly be.

The struggle with the decision to proceed was obviously causing some conflict within Debra, but she eventually overcame the obstacles. She decided to take the chance. Before she continued with her explanation, the proper suggestions were made and actions taken to leave the restaurant and return to her apartment.

Once comfortably inside and sipping a leisurely brewed cup of elegant coffee, Debra began the description of a moderate sized mansion in the country that was the private location for a carefully selected group of people, mostly married couples, who absorbed themselves in all facets of human sexuality. There were no imposed limits other than mutual consent. Heterosexual couples had to enter, but there were no restrictions beyond the front door. A detailed medical examination was required periodically to insure safety and the women were required to use the necessary contraceptive. The mansion had a permanent staff that was not allowed to partake in any of the festivities, but simply to serve the members. The description Debra provided was almost too wild to be true.

"Why?"

"Why, what?"

"Why did you do this? Why take that chance?" I asked.

"'The Club', as we call it, brought an excitement to our lives, a certain element of adventure that was also very pleasurable."

"Wasn't there jealousy watching each other do it with other people?"

"At first, we didn't do anything with others. We were both scared in our own ways."

"You mean you can go to this place and just watch?"

"Well, that's not the idea, but it is perfectly acceptable as long as you don't interfere with the pleasure of others. As I said, there are no rules other than mutual consent and respect for others."

"Did you have sex in front of other people?"

"Again, not at first, but eventually we did. It was a little tense the first few times, but we quickly warmed up to the environment and the people."

The discussion about sex and various aspects had the expected effect on us both. The carnal fires were lit and the flames were being fanned by our thoughts. The talk continued as we made our way to the bedroom, and the most energetic and exciting sex we had together. Debra had elegance to her mature body, and she knew how to use the assets she had. The night was long and filled with the pleasure of the flesh as well as a variety of topics and words of love. We learned a lot about each other. In the end, we agreed to try the club, at least once.

———

We arranged to go together to a specific doctor who supported 'The Club.' Several technicians took our vital statistics, drew blood for the appropriate tests and collected our other bodily fluids. It looked as if it would be a complete physical examination. Debra indicated the doctor could examine us each together. It sounded like a good idea since we could hold hands and be joined while we were examined. I had never seen a woman's examination before.

After the medical technicians completed their tasks, we played a little with our open frocks while we waited for the doctor. Debra was one of those rare people whom you instantly felt comfortable with no matter where you were, or what you were doing. This situation was no different although I knew the purpose of this medical examination was quite serious.

The doctor entered the room alone. She was a middle-aged woman with grey speckled, dark brown hair, chocolate brown eyes, medium build, and an average face beginning to show the signs of age.

"Good to see you again, Debra," she said with a course, gravelly voice that had a sexy deepness to it.

"Good to see you, Raye," Debra responded. "I'd like to introduce my boyfriend, Kevin," she continued motioning toward me.

"Nice to meet you, Kevin."

"Likewise," I answered not knowing quite what to say.

Looking directly at Debra, she said, "You have explained 'The Club' to Kevin?" Debra nodded. "He knows why we are doing such a thorough examination?" Again, an affirmative nod.

"Well, let's get to it, shall we? Who's first?"

"I'll go first since this is Kevin's first time," Debra offered. I felt a little silly, but my curiosity kept my mouth shut.

Doctor Raye Worthington began a methodical, no nonsense examination from Debra's scalp working her way down. Eyes, ears, nose, mouth and every square centimeter in between were examined carefully. I could see the questions of reservation in Debra's eyes as the doctor removed the examination gown to evaluate her breasts. There was a certain excitement, a quickening of my pulse, watching the manipulation of her body. The reservation disappeared as Debra watched my interest grow. A short wave of embarrassment washed over me as Debra lay down, placing her legs in the waiting fur covered stirrups for the examination of her genitalia. Every small crease was examined with great care. Every orifice was closely checked.

"With the results of your lab work, Debra, I would say you are in pretty good shape. You have no problems I can find," the doctor pronounced. She turned to look at me. "Your turn, Kevin," she said patting the table still warm from Debra's body.

A female doctor had never examined me, but she appeared to be very professional and thorough. The process for me was virtually identical. I wondered what she was going to do with my genitalia. The question did not take long to answer.

"OK, Kevin, lay back on the table and place your feet in the stirrups just like Debra did."

"Those are for examining women," I protested.

"Well, that may be," said gently in response to my near sexist remark. "But, what's good for the goose, is good for the gander," she added with a smile, touching one of the stirrups.

Being spread out like that was embarrassing to me, but convenient for the doctor. Her examination was gentle and meticulous. She worked quickly without missing anything including a complete rectal exam that added to my embarrassment. Debra and I had a creative sex life, but this was different.

"Everything looks pretty good, Kevin," the doctor offered. "You two can get dressed and meet me in my office. Most of the lab results should be back about that time." With our consent, Raye Worthington left the room.

Debra and I compared thoughts and a few laughs regarding our thoughts about watching and being watched. There was an element of thrill to the process. Partially dressed, Debra grabbed me fully and said, "I want you. I want you right now." My heart beat hard with excitement at the thought. Before I could say or do anything, she added, "Let's get out of here as quickly as we can. I need to feel you inside of me." The words added to the pressure in my veins and under her hand. My God, she was an exciting woman, and I wanted her desperately.

By the time we arrived at Raye's office, the doctor was reviewing pages of data provided by her staff technicians. After a quick glance at us, she continued her study of the information. Both of us sat in the chairs before her desk. It was a warm, well-kept, academic office ripe with books, medical visual aids and elegant artwork.

Looking up from her papers with a broad smile, she said, "Both of you will be happy to know you are in perfect health. There are no detrimental indicators nor signs of communicable diseases."

"Thank you, Raye," Debra said standing to shake her hand. "Will we see you tomorrow night?"

"You certainly will. It is my turn to be host," she responded with a knowing expression on her face and in her eyes.

"Thank you, Doctor Worthington," I offered.

"Raye, if you please, Kevin. It was nice to see you, and I look forward to our next meeting," Raye added with a wink to Debra.

We departed her office holding hands. The day was bright and warm with the smell of spring blossoms in the air. The walk back to Debra's apartment took about twenty minutes and was filled with more questions and intimate words. Upon arrival, there was no restraint as we threw ourselves into each other with reckless abandon. There was a utopian feeling to our union that brought a constant stream of renewal and contentment. Debra was simply a fun person to be with.

———

The drive to the country was longer than expected, although Debra's directions were precise. We did not talk as much as we usually did. Both of us were lost in our own thoughts. Debra's were probably of knowledge and anticipation, while mine were more of expectation and apprehension of the unknown. It was only because of my trust and love for Debra that I even consented to try this experience. She was not a careless person.

The early evening's dwindling light masked the expansiveness of the mansion and the grounds. It was much more than I expected and was more like a large estate than a large house. The building was surrounded by dense trees and well manicured shrubbery. The high wall that marked the front boundary presumably circumscribed the property limits. There was considerable elegance beyond my imagination.

The car park was off to the right side of the main building. There were spaces for about thirty automobiles and the area was roughly half full when we arrived. No other people were visible as we walked to a covered entryway. Debra motioned for us to go inside. The door was not locked. A large coatroom was the first room along a long hallway. After depositing our coats and umbrella, we proceeded down the hall. The additional doors, all on one side of the hallway, were all closed. The building was very quiet except for our footsteps.

A large, carved, wooden door marked the end of the hallway. Opening the door revealed a well-appointed waiting room complete with fine chairs and several sofas, a high ceiling with a splendid chandelier, and framed mirrors and paintings on the walls.

Debra looked into my eyes partially searching for a reaction as well as conveying her love. I loved her eyes and what they said. Our wait was not long as one of several other doors opened and in walked none other than Raye Worthington with one major difference from their last meeting. Her light green medical frock was replaced by a minuscule lingerie outfit that left her breasts and pubic triangle exposed. White hosiery complimented her shapely legs. She was not particularly self-conscious about the sag to her breasts since they still had an appealing form and large hard nipples, quite attractive breasts for a woman her age.

With a broad smile noticeably different than she gave us in her office, she said, "Welcome to Mirabel, Debra and Kevin. It is a joy to see you again."

"Hi, Raye," Debra answered with a light, but less jubilant voice.

I was speechless. This was already way passed my imagination despite the talks with Debra.

"I am sure Debra has already explained what we are about, Kevin. However, as a first time visitor, we have a policy of briefing you on the house rules and etiquette."

I could barely manage a slight nod of my head to acknowledge her statement.

"Mirabel is a wholly owed partnership of its members with the expressed purpose of allowing a free, uninhibited enjoyment of all things sexual." The words possessed an element of adventure as well as an inner terror. What was going to happen? What would I do? "The primary rule of the house is mutual consent. There can be no unwanted force. Interference is discouraged although mutual attraction is the prevailing emotion." Raye paused to let me absorb what she had said. The process was a bit overwhelming with my brain in sensory overload as the combination of reality and imagination resulted in a volcanic eruption of synergistic thoughts.

There was no obvious direction to the images racing through my head. Her pause seemed to ask for some response from me. Debra just watched me with a mixture of curiosity and concern.

"Does that mean you're supposed to do it with more than one person?" I asked feebly.

A patient, knowing expression washed across Doctor Raye Worthington's face. She had been here before. "First, you are not supposed to do anything. You are permitted to do whatever you want with or without a consenting partner. Second, you do not have to do anything. Only what you want to do. The direction, pace and duration are up to you."

"This is too incredible to believe," were the only words I could say. Looking directly into Debra's waiting eyes, I said, "And, I thought you were kidding."

Debra shook her head. "We don't have to do this, Kevin. We can leave right now, or anytime you want to go."

"I don't know. I have never done anything like this in my entire life, not even remotely similar."

"There is no pressure," Debra added.

"That's right, Kevin. At Mirabel, you control what will happen, it's that simple," said Raye without the slightest concern that she was virtually naked and we were still fully clothed. There was an irresistible fascination with the movement of her breasts commensurate with each motion her body made.

My curiosity was beginning to wiggle its way to the forefront. "Anything with anybody?" I asked inquisitively.

"Correct. There are no restrictions with whom your partner or partners might be, nor what you may do with those partners."

"You mean homosexual stuff is allowed?" I asked with some protestation.

"First, we call it same sex activity. There are no restrictions."

"This is too incredible to believe," was the only thing I could say. Both women waited patiently for me to indicate my intention. "Well, there's only one way to find out. If you're still willing," I said looking at Debra, "let's get on with it."

Debra smiled her agreement with a certain sparkle in her eyes.

"Well, then, the first step is a final inspection," Raye said with a chuckle, "just too make sure everyone is safe."

I thought I knew what she meant, although I had no idea what to do. Debra resolved the dilemma by moving to the only dining height table in the room. Without any prompting or hesitation, she lay down and raised her legs forming a 'V.' For the first time, I saw she had no panties. Without gloves this time, Doctor Raye Worthington examined Debra's genital region in a decidedly different manner checking every fold. She signaled the conclusion of Debra's examination by extending her tongue to flicker the exposed and now swollen clitoris several times. Debra squirmed with the sensation as her eyes remained fixated on me and an almost chiseled grin stretched across her face.

"Very good," pronounced the hostess raising herself from Debra's groin and turning toward me. I was frozen like a block of granite. My heart was racing, and I thought my veins would pop from the pressure. This examination, if that's what you would call it, was a world apart from the previous event, two days earlier. The fact was quite evident with what I had just witnessed and my own involuntary response that was soon discovered by Doctor Raye Worthington. She stood before me, looked directly into my eyes and touched me as a woman would, not a doctor. "My, my, I'd say you like what you see, Kevin Armstrong. Let's see what this thing looks like in its proper state," she said as she stroked me, and then unzipped my trousers. "There, much better," she continued looking down for the first time at my exposed erection. Raye knelt before me carefully examining every portion of me. I was still frozen stiff.

"Relax, Kevin," offered Debra. "Enjoy it. This is a night of pleasure."

There was a strange primordial fear pumping through my body standing in a strange room with the woman I loved watching another woman handling me, and then taking me into her mouth. I thought I was going to die from exploding blood pressure. All I could see was Debra's smiling eyes, and all I could feel was Raye's warm, moist mouth. It was a sensation like none other.

The hostess stopped her extracurricular activities and stood up leaving me with a throbbing erection. Without looking at Debra, she said to me, "It is a bit of a tradition for the hostess to take the first load of a first timer. If you have no objections, I would like yours."

I must have been transported to another planet or deep into a wet dream for this to be true. This does not happen in real life. It was simply too incredible to be true. The situation became even worse when I looked to Debra for a sign of resistance, and all she gave me was a wink, a smile and a motion with her head to go ahead. I looked back to Raye and the expression on my face and in my eyes must have been a sufficient clue. She turned around and placed her elbows on the table in front of her exposing the dark hair and red lips of her waiting body. The two attractive halves of her buttocks beckoned to me like some exotic fruit.

With some hesitation, I entered her from behind. She felt hot and very wet probably from others she had taken this night. After a few strokes, I looked again to Debra who was watching intently with apparent pleasure. I could feel Raye squeeze, as if to signal me to return to my duty.

"It's OK, Kevin," Debra said. "This is what Mirabel is all about." She walked toward us.

I moved a little although I did not withdraw and I could feel Raye squeezing me again. Debra leaned over to kiss me as I was joined with another woman, and then proceeded to fondle Raye's hanging breasts. Raye seemed to be appropriately appreciative as I could feel her body respond. I returned to my portion of the task. The conclusion did not take long when viewed in the light of the preceding events. I felt my legs grow instantly weak as my body shook in ecstasy. The rippling waves of orgasm lasted for an incredibly long time.

"Now that was a pretty good one," Debra observed. "Wouldn't you say?" Her left hand continued to play with Raye's left breast.

All I could manage to do was stand there with my hands on Raye's hips and wait for the pleasure to subside. Raye was patient to wait for me to withdraw, but was also quite content to enjoy the kneading of her breast. Eventually, after an indeterminate amount of time for me, I became aware of my contracting organ. Slowly, I withdrew from her to be rewarded with the dull pain of pleasure past.

Raye stood and turned toward us. "Thank you both for your participation." She smiled at both of us. "Kevin, since this is your first time visit, you are welcome to dress or undress whatever suits your fancy. You may proceed to the main rooms whenever you are ready."

Again, I looked to Debra for some hint of what I or we should do. It did not take long for her to recognize my expression.

"I'd recommend we get naked," she said with some exuberance. With my affirmative response, we both proceeded to shed our clothing.

Raye decided it was time for the next stage. "I'll leave you two to your evening of enjoyment. If you don't mind, I'll just sit over here to wait for our next arrivals and finish myself off."

I felt a certain failure. "I'm sorry," I said apologizing for not thinking of her pleasure.

"No problem. This is part of my duty tonight," Raye said with joy in her voice. "Besides, I got what I wanted."

As we continued to undress, Raye lay back into a large chair, spread her legs slightly, and began to stimulate herself. We placed our clothes on hangers in an adjoining coatroom. The variety and quantity of clothing were definite indicators of what lay ahead. As we walked back into the reception room after a rather short absence, Raye was obviously well into a good orgasm as her arched back, heaving chest and soft groans confirmed. The inhibition and exhibition were exhilarating, refreshing and enervating, all at the same time.

As we walked toward the entry door, I watched Raye's breasts move to the still somewhat spasmodic expansions and contractions of her chest. Her eyes were closed as she reclined with her hand resting over her groin. She seemed totally oblivious to our passage.

Beyond the door was yet another long hallway. This one was dimly lit although it was illuminated enough to see several men and women, some moving as a couple while others appeared to be solo. All were naked. Each was unique. There were some with young, tight bodies and others with various levels of indications associated with the aging process. The spectrum of people during our short walk holding hands was fascinating from a detached, clinical observation. This was humanity without its façade.

Debra led me through a large set of double doors into a large room with low, indirect lighting. My eyes took a few seconds to make the adjustment. What I saw was staggering to my consciousness. The room was filled with large beds, and mattresses on the floor interspersed among the various beds. A seething sea of people occupied most of the beds and mattresses. All were engaged in one form of sexual activity or another. It was a veritable cornucopia of human physical interaction. Debra continued to lead me slowly through the room as if she were conducting a walking tour of a living library of sex. Several people noted our presence while most ignored us. None of the participants showed the slightest sign of inhibition or embarrassment. The acts being carried out before us were so graphic, animated and sensual a corresponding involuntary response was impossible to prevent. I was unaware of my own reaction until Debra placed her hand around me as if she were grabbing a handle.

A sharp jolt of embarrassment rocketed through me and passed quickly with Debra's reassuring eyes. I surmised the common male reaction was normal. Debra continued to lead me through the room until she found what she was looking for, an open bed.

"It's my turn," she said softly. "I want you inside me."

My heart pounded with excitement. I looked around to the adjacent places. No one seemed to notice our presence. Debra sat down, shifted her position to the middle of the king size waterbed, and lay back raising and spreading her knees, inviting me to join our bodies. The invitation was simply too hard to deny even though I still felt a twinge of embarrassment. The radiating warmth of her body and the casual, almost matter of fact, expression on her face dissolved my only resistance.

As I entered her receptive body, she said, "There. This is how it should be."

All I could muster up in response was, "I love you, Debra." The sound of my own words seemed virtually apologetic, as if I knew we were not supposed to be doing this, but there were forces beyond our control.

"I know," responded Debra as if she knew what my mind was thinking.

We continued our copulation with an energy and passion of incredible proportions. Positions changed. Motions changed. The exertion for each of us was enormous. Rivers of sweat ran from our bodies and intermingled before soaking the soft sheets beneath us. Debra was the first to go over the top of the unique mountain of human pleasure. Her stiffened and thrashing body broke down the last of my resistance as I joined her in orgasmic ecstasy.

As the warm waves of physical relief subsided, we lay together joined at the hip and intertwined with our arms.

"How do you feel?" asked Debra.

"Drained."

"I'll bet. That was another real good one for you and in such a short time."

"It must be the atmosphere."

"It is." Debra paused looking deep into my eyes. "I feel a new closeness to you, Kevin, like we have taken down a final barrier to a total commitment. There is nothing more withheld."

"I know what you mean. I have the same feeling."

We kissed with our tongues dancing about among the soft, warm wetness of our mouths. There was indeed a new closeness, different from anything I had felt before. An honesty between two giving people.

"Do you want to try something else?"

"Well, I guess that's why we're here."

Debra led me again toward a door at the opposite end of the room. I looked back only to notice two naked people who had come from nowhere changing the sheet on the bed we had just vacated. It was a nice touch and probably necessary in this place.

"I'm taking you to the bath room. It's a combination sauna, hot tub refreshment room. People usually go there in between events to share their experiences and talk about whatever they want. Mostly sex as you can imagine."

"Sounds interesting."

"It usually is. We call it the bath room since it's mostly water and steam, but also in the European tradition of a common bath house meeting place."

We walked through several more rooms. One was probably an equipment room with a plethora of sexual aides being used by men and women. Watching was intoxicating and addictive. Activities I had never imagined let alone seen before. Another room appeared to be more group oriented with numerous bodies of both sexes intermingled in several pulsating mounds of flesh.

A short passage way brought us to the bath room. A large, white tiled room with four round steaming and bubbling hot tubs, two pools that were noticeably cooler, and three doors at the far end for entrance to the glass walled sauna. The room was by no means full with about an even number of men and women using the various facilities.

"Hey, Debra, it's been a long time," a woman said standing up in the hot tub and moving toward us. She was an attractive woman in her mid to late thirties with light brown hair drawn up into a clipped bun on her head and green eyes. The woman had small breasts and a well-kept body with no hair on her body other than what was on her head. The front cleavage of her groin was plainly visible along with her swollen clitoris protruding from the folds.

"Hi, Maggie," Debra responded to her friend as she stepped out of the hot pool.

"It's good to see you," Maggie said boldly reaching to touch the side of Debra's left breast and kiss her on the lips. The continued inhibition or effervescent openness was difficult to absorb.

"It's good to see you. Maggie, I'd like you to meet my partner, Kevin Armstrong."

"A pleasure to meet you, Kevin," Maggie said extending her hand.

I grasped it firmly and said, "It is nice to meet you, Maggie."

"Welcome to Mirabel, Kevin. It is always nice to see a new face and experience a fresh set of ideas."

I did not know quite what to say, so I simply nodded my head in recognition of her statement. Standing in plain view of numerous strangers talking to two naked women with no clothes on myself was more than my now diminutive experience could deal with.

"Why don't you join us?" Maggie added. With a nod and a sheepish grin, Maggie turned to the people in the closest tub. "Hey everybody, Debra's back with us and she brought her new friend, Kevin. Kevin, this is Ginny, Brian, Betty, Joel, and that's my husband, Jim."

"Nice to meet you all," I said with full knowledge I would not be able to remember any of the names.

Maggie returned to her spot next to Jim, and Debra and I slowly entered the hot water. Debra sat next to Jim and I sat on the end slightly more than an arm length from Ginny, a stunningly beautiful blond with sky blue eyes. The bubbles and layer of steam masked any view of the bodies, which was just fine with me. I noticed Debra when she looked at Jim and shook her head. She must have denied his advance of a hand on her thigh. The talk soon picked up where it had apparently left off.

This friendly bunch certainly reflected the mood and attitude of the Mirabel group. The casual, almost humorous discussion of some of the most intimate and private details of human sexual interaction was yet another shock to my senses. Techniques for stimulation of a reluctant male organ, for heightening the peak of an approaching orgasm, among so many other topics that blossomed in a barrage on my private thoughts. The one element of reassurance was Debra's hand grasping mine. Neither of us contributed to the discussion and our lack of participation did not inhibit the conversation. One couple, or at least I thought they were a couple, rose without additional words to go to the sauna. He had a full erection and no self-consciousness. She had enormous breasts that swayed back and forth with each step. Their names were Betty and Joe, or was it Joel, I could not remember. The discussion continued unabated.

Debra was probably feeling some empathy for the assault I was experiencing and decided to make our connection closer. She looked into my eyes briefly, as she released my hand and ran her hand up my thigh. The gentle stroking had the desired reaction as I felt some protection from the bubbling water. Maybe other activities were also well underway beneath the surface, but the only one that mattered to me was under Debra's skillful hand. Her slow, rhythmic stroking felt so good.

When my mind returned to the conversation, the group was well into a debate about the uniqueness of female genitalia. Before I could determine what the direction the discussion was headed, the woman named Ginny stood up.

"Attention. Attention, please." Ginny waited until the various conversations died down. "How many of you men feel each pussy is unique?"

Most of the men raised their hands. I abstained from the vote based on my own reluctance to participate in such a personal debate.

"OK. That's most. Now, how many of you feel you could recognize your lady's flower without sight or smell?"

Just about every man raised their hands along with some hoots and hollers. Again, I abstained.

"Well, then, what do you say about a little contest? We'll blindfold your eyes, clip your nose and let you use only your tongue to test each of us," she said pointing to several of the women. "Let's see how you do?"

After some discussion over the rules, five women and their partners decided to participate. At first, everyone wanted to disqualify Maggie since all her hair was removed, but with reluctance she was allowed to join the contest.

"Do you want to try?" asked Debra.

"No," I answered quickly. "I can't. This is still too much for me to comprehend."

Sensing the pressure I was feeling, Debra added, "It's OK, Kevin. There are plenty of things for us to do."

"Debra, since you and Kevin aren't participating, would you please keep track of the results?" asked Ginny.

Debra agreed, leaving me and my erection, to sit on the edge of the contest pool. The men were prepared using a swimmer's nose clip and a thin towel. After the contestant was checked, the five women arranged themselves on the edge of the pool. As the contestant was guided to each woman, she would spread her legs wide exposing the most private parts of her anatomy. I felt shots of embarrassment they apparently did not. The rules prohibited any movement or sound, which was a difficult requirement for some of the women. The women switched places for each man to insure no other means of recognition could be used. The laughter and joking were clear indicators of the mutual enjoyment everyone, whether participating or not, seemed to be deriving from the contest. Four of the five men were successful in the genitalia recognition. The fifth man took a little, light hearted, teasing.

His partner said loudly, "George, you obviously need some practice." The woman sat back down on the edge of the pool and spread her legs. "So, get to it."

George did not need any coaxing and immediately proceeded with his task. The woman was now allowed to be more animated, responsive and appreciative of the intimate attention. Several other couples liked the idea and joined in.

Debra returned to me, taking my hand and said, "Let's try something else." We dried off with large towels provided for the purpose and deposited them in the appropriate hamper.

We walked out into the hallway in another direction. I stopped. She looked at me with questioning eyes. I needed to kiss her. Drawing her close to me feeling her body press against mine, we kissed.

"I love you."

"I love you, Kevin," she answered. "I hope you're enjoying yourself. I know this is a lot to experience, but it does make you think."

"I am, it is, and it does," was all I could say as I released her and we continued to our next destination.

As we walked, Debra said, "I want you to meet a woman that can answer one of your questions."

"What's that?"

"You'll see."

We continued down several more associated hallways to an open set of double doors. It was another room filled with large beds. Several large screen televisions displayed erotic videos for the entertainment and enjoyment of numerous members. Only a few were engaged in sexual activities. A few, one man and two women, masturbated as they watched, and most were content to watch and talk.

"Jennifer, I'd like you to meet my partner, Kevin Armstrong. Kevin, this is Jennifer Johnson."

"A pleasure to meet you, Kevin." Jennifer had dark hair. It was difficult to tell the color. She was fairly young with moderate size full breasts and an average country girl sort of appearance.

"Are you still giving?" asked Debra.

Jennifer smiled at her and answered, "I think I've still got some for you."

Debra looked at me. "You said you wondered what breast milk tasted like, now is your chance," she said motioning toward Jennifer.

"Debra, I can't do that," I said in a barely audible whisper. "It's not right."

"It's OK, Kevin," Jennifer offered. "I do this for everyone. I'm the house cow," she said with a coarse laugh. "Besides, it's a quick way for me to get off." Her smile seemed warm and inviting. Jennifer stretched out her arms as if she were going to accept a swaddled baby.

With a few nudges from Debra, I moved toward her, and again with some physical urging I bent over to sample the natural fluid of life.

"No, no, Kevin."

I stood straight up with a start. What had I done wrong? I hadn't done anything yet.

"Come down here. Make yourself comfortable," Jennifer said with a broad smile and pleasure in her eyes. "You can take a good drink, plus I need to get something out of this as well."

Reluctantly, I lay down on the bed beside her and took her left nipple in my mouth. The product did not take long to arrive. It was warm and sweet with a thick, rich taste. I found myself reaching for the flesh of her breast to stroke it, caress it and feel its fullness.

"Come, Debra," Jennifer said. "Would you be so kind to take my other breast?"

A moment later, Debra was at her right breast.

"Oh, yes. That's good. Just keep sucking." Jennifer's body began to respond as if she had an itch she could not scratch. She squeezed her legs together rocking from side to side gently. She released an almost purring sound of contentment as Debra and I continued to enjoy our drink at the fountain of life. There was a certain inescapable attraction to the breast of this new acquaintance and giving woman. "John, please, give me a lick. I'm just about there." I started to look up. "No, don't stop now." A firm hand at the back of my head held me to her breast. I could feel the presence of yet another person and the back of a head descending into her crotch. She was right. It did not take long as her grunts and groans signaled the arrival of her reward.

We all stopped at about the same time. Debra leaned over to kiss me with her wet, smooth, warm lips.

The man who had accommodated Jennifer's request waited until we completed our kiss. "Hi, I'm John."

"Kevin," I answered as I awkwardly shook his hand. He was a young man, attractive, with light brown full hair and brown eyes.

I felt a hand grasp the organ of my excitement.

"Well, Kevin, since you have such a good erection, would you mind slipping it into me and give me yours?" Jennifer asked me without even looking at Debra.

I was somewhat taken aback by the request especially with Debra only a short arm's length away and another woman holding me.

Debra smiled and answered for me. "Go ahead. Enjoy."

With that pronouncement, Jennifer laid back and opened herself to me. Slowly, with my eyes mostly on Debra to see even the slightest indication of resentment or adverse reaction, I moved between her legs. I felt the slippery wetness of her cum and the warmth of her body surround me, draw me in, and absorb me completely. My arms remained locked above her as I began to move with her. A soft, gentle touch enveloped my scrotum. Debra provided the extra stimulation. I thought my rise to an almost painful orgasm was rapid, but Jennifer was able to climax twice with a third virtually simultaneous with mine. The responsiveness of the woman was incredible, so incredible I had to ask myself the question, were they real? Then again, what reason would she have to fake multiple orgasms with me?

"Isn't she something?" inquired Debra with a casual conversational tone and I was still inside of her.

"Debra!" I protested.

"This must be your first time at Mirabel," stated Jennifer, looking up at me with appreciative eyes.

I nodded my answer to Jennifer and looked to Debra still with protestation in my eyes.

"Well, she is. Jennifer is the most orgasmic woman I have ever known."

"Debra!" I said with a low growl as I withdrew from Jennifer. The sensation associated with my withdrawal was difficult to differentiate between pain and pleasure. In my entire life, I had never experienced so much sex and intercourse. I imagined the feelings were from overuse.

"You did good, Kevin," Jennifer added. "Some men have trouble taking to the breast. They don't mind looking at 'em, but they sure don't know how to handle 'em or use 'em properly. You're a natural."

Strangely, I felt the hot flash of embarrassment blast through my body like a kid caught with his hand in the cookie jar.

Debra smiled and nodded her head like a proud parent. "He sure is."

Another wave of embarrassment washed over me. My sense of propriety had never undergone such an assault as it had this evening. I had always thought of myself as a relatively uninhibited, sexually enlightened male, but in this group I felt like a novice, and yet my curiosity was intense, almost uncontrollable.

Jennifer sat up between Debra and me, and began gently stroking my back. "The first time is always the hardest," she said. "You are never quite sure what to expect nor do, and the sexual freedom comes on you like a lethal intoxicant." Jennifer paused, and then kissed me on the cheek. "You'll get over it." She paused again still rubbing my back. Her warm, soft hand felt good. She reached up pulling my chin toward her so she could look me in the eyes. "Debra's a good woman. You be good to her," she said as friendly advice, but also with a strange warning tone.

"Thanks, Jennifer," Debra said as she stood up. "You were great as usual."

I took the cue quite well.

"You're welcome. Have fun you two."

We walked out of the room. I took one last look at Jennifer who was sitting in a quasi-lotus position already back talking to other people near by. She was an intriguing woman.

"How long has she been doing this?"

"You mean giving milk?"

I nodded.

"About four years. She had her third child nearly three years ago and since her children don't need the nourishment and she enjoys giving, she just kept it going."

"Three children? She looks too young for three children."

"She loves kids and she started early," Debra added.

As I pondered her words, we continued to walk down a hallway arm in arm. Debra matched my footsteps so our bodies were in unison. Occasionally, I would look down at her breasts moving with our motion. They were truly fascinating and wondrous anatomical organs, so versatile and yet so attractive.

"There is one more thing I would like you to experience tonight."

"I don't know if I can. I am almost numb from the onslaught of sex in this place."

"We all felt like that our first time. You'll be OK. I'd really like you to try this."

"What is it?"

"Before we go any further, we need to talk," Debra said seeing a hall couch and stopping to sit down.

My curiosity was being poked at again with a sharp stick. I sat down beside her and waited for her to gather her thoughts.

"First off, let me remind you that no one makes any value judgments at Mirabel. Anything is possible." That was a heck of a lead in. "During some of our sex talks, you have wondered what it would be like to be a woman in sex." I nodded reluctantly, trying to anticipate where she was headed. "I want you to listen to what I have to say before you react." I nodded again. "One of the members who I know is here tonight from the register specializes in anal intercourse, and..."

My God, she wanted me to be fucked by a guy. The struggle to hold my facial muscles and eyes in neutral while she continued her explanation was almost too demanding of a task. There is no way. This is sick. It is not right. Aren't there any limits in this place? What else happens here that I have not seen or heard? I felt Debra's hand touch my thigh.

"...We'll do this together. What do you think?"

I couldn't remember anything she said after the initial shocker. I tried to appear contemplative, but finally decided to admit my distraction. "I'm not sure I heard what you said after anal intercourse," I stated softly.

Several naked men and women walked down the hall offering a friendly glance and slight nod of the head in recognition of our presence. Watching naked people had a certain fascinating element to it. Fortunately for what was left of my sensibility, Debra waited until the people passed before continuing the discussion.

"If you can get passed the image in your mind and give it a try you might find your curiosity fulfilled. He's really very gentle and it's much better than using a dildo."

"What a relief!" I could not believe we were talking about this.

"Your resistance is understandable, but if you truly want to take the journey toward understanding what women feel in sex, I can think of no better way. Several heterosexual men who have tried it have said that once they get passed the image problem they learned a lot. Some have said they even enjoyed it."

"I can't imagine." Just, the picture of some Brutus doing that to me was almost more than my stomach could handle.

"Did you hear what I had suggested earlier?" Debra asked patiently. I think she sensed the trauma this topic was causing me as if she had been there before, probably with John.

"No."

"We can get a private room upstairs so you don't have to worry about other people seeing us or watching us. We can do a little 69 with you on top and Jimmy will take care of the rest. Kevin, he's really very good and quite gentle."

"Is he...a homosexual?"

"No. If anything, he's probably bisexual. He just has a long penis that is very difficult for most women to take in vaginally."

"Oh great," was all I could say.

"He's really quite good with the back door," she said with a smile. She knew the struggle within me. "I'll be with you the whole time. We'll go through this together. It won't hurt to try, if you keep an open mind."

The thought was revolting to my consciousness, and yet I began to realize the telltale presence of my growing curiosity. Debra was right; I had sincerely wondered what it would be like. In our conversations, it was meant to be more of a catalyst for discussing the intimate details of feelings and emotions associated with sex, but there was still the curiosity.

"OK," I said feeling I was giving into a relentless and irresistible force.

"Good, Kevin. We'll take it slow and easy. Just try to keep an open mind and absorb the feelings."

Debra stood pulling me by the hand as we walked through more of the mansion. We passed a couple of familiar areas. We stopped at a small sitting area where several people were eating, drinking and talking. One couple had on matching bathrobes, which was the first time I had seen clothes of any kind since our entry. Debra signaled me to wait outside while she went to a dark complexioned man and whispered in his ear. The man nodded, finished his coffee or tea and excused himself from the conversation.

He was tall, about six inches taller than me, and slender. He had medium dark brown skin with chiseled, almost Caucasian, facial features. His flaccid penis was longer than any I had ever seen. My stomach turned over a few times, as I regretted my acquiescence.

"Kevin, this is Jimmy Standard. Jimmy, this is my lover, Kevin Armstrong." I liked how she said, lover. There was a definite sensuality to the way she said it.

"Nice to meet you, Kevin," he said extending his hand. After some hesitation, I shook his hand and acknowledged.

"Let's go find a room upstairs," Debra said, leading me by the hand again. Jimmy loped along with us. Small talk about odd things filled the time to finding an open room.

The open door was the indicator. It was a relatively large room for what was presumably a bedroom in its earlier days. The furnishings were simple, functional and quite tasteful. An enormous bed dominated the room. Jimmy closed the door behind us. A strong feeling of being trapped came to me. Uncertainty about what was going to happen raised my heart rate. Debra kissed me and moved close, so I could feel her breasts against my chest and her pubic hair brush my left thigh. She was trying her best to help me relax which was a very difficult task indeed. She moved us to the bed pulling me onto it with her. We knelt together holding each other as we kissed. She reached down to delicately, and yet purposefully touched my reluctant organ. The warmth and softness of her hand eventually began to have the desired effect as my mind moved away from Jimmy's long penis to Debra's sensual body.

At the appropriate time, Debra laid down with her feet toward the headboard of the bed. Her beautiful eyes and inviting smile broke down the last of my resistance. I slowly moved into position over her and began to savor the pleasures of her genitalia, as she took me into her mouth. The sensations were more ragged than usual, very strong and sharp. I could feel her body respond, and I joined her.

Debra's dainty fingers stroked me with her usual care and sensitivity. As I began to focus on the feelings both giving and taking, I felt larger hands on my hips. I began to raise my head, but Debra thrust her pelvis up at me to keep me at the task of her pleasure. I tried to keep my mind on Debra. The task became more difficult when I felt one hand leave my hips to be followed a short time later by a warm slippery fluid in the crevice that was soon to be the pinpoint of every nerve in my body. Debra's hands moved to assist Jimmy by spreading my cheeks.

I felt him against me pressing lightly waiting for me to relax my muscles. I remembered Debra's description of this particular activity, when our positions were reversed. The thought of running flashed to me. I could still avoid this experience. Debra's fingers worked on the areas immediately adjacent to the point of Jimmy's contact. The fact that Debra was probably working harder than either of us along with the expert touch of her fingers accomplished the task. I felt him slowly slip inside me. I could feel the sensations in my throat. My body froze, and I could feel the groan well up within me.

Once he was all the way in, Jimmy stopped just as I had done the occasions Debra and I decided to try something different. Debra continued to work hard on helping me relax. Jimmy slowly began to move. His motion combined with Debra's movement gave me an eerie sensation of filling up

Debra and being over-filled by Jimmy. A bright, hot sun began to form in my groin as the pace of our collective activity began to increase. Several times Debra had to thrust her pelvis up at me to keep my tongue busy bringing pleasure to her. The combination of all the feelings I was giving and receiving were causing the sun to grow quicker.

Jimmy's motion became more purposeful as he worked his way to his own pinnacle. The heat of the sun began to turn to pain as though I was being split apart directly in half. My tolerance level slowly decreased as Jimmy's intensity increased. I could not imagine what it would feel like to take this to the conclusion.

Finally, I reached the point where none of the little activities provided any pleasure or satisfaction. I waved my hand, as I raised up. I could not speak. Everyone stopped, frozen for a moment until the direction became clear.

"Do you want to stop?" Jimmy asked.

All I could do was wave my hand again and nod my head. Words would not form. Ever so slowly, Jimmy began to withdraw without protest or further pressure. I knew what he must be feeling, but I simply could not continue. We sat on the bed separately. It was the first time I saw his enormous erection. He had an upward curve that made it look like a bow. He took a few wipes, conveniently provided, to clean himself.

"Come here, Jimmy. I'll finish you off," Debra said, with a clear measure of confidence. "Lay down here, Kevin. I'd like you to suck on my breasts while I take Jimmy."

I did as I was ordered. Debra moved over me dangling her right breast over my face. Before I took her nipple, I watched Jimmy move behind her. Debra's body responded to his entry as she struggled to relax her muscles and accept the large man. As their motion became regular, I performed my part of the *ménage à trois*. Sucking on one nipple, I caressed her other breast and squeezed her other nipple. I moved my free hand down her swaying body to the patch of hair at the top of her legs. The wetness of her empty vagina was incredible, which made the stimulation of her swollen clitoris easy and pleasurable to me.

Jimmy was the first to reach a climax. The only indication was the quickening, short strokes and erratic frequency of his motion. He made no sounds. Debra probably felt other signs, although I could feel nothing or sense nothing from her. I continued to work on her pleasure. Jimmy moved very slowly trying to dance between what service he might be and his own pleasure which must be transitioning to pain. Debra's orgasm took longer than I expected, considering the signs from her body, but it was a strong and powerful event causing her to almost scream as her peak rocketed up. Her body shook violently and continued for what seemed like a long time. As her shaking began to subside, her arms gave way, and she collapsed onto me.

Eventually, we separated again. This time, Jimmy rose from the bed to clean himself, again. Debra brushed against me, and then looked to confirm my renewed arousal.

A smile grew across her face with her eyes showing signs of the fatigue that enveloped her body. Out of the corner of my eye, I saw her knees rise and move apart. Gently, she pulled me toward her.

"I want you to fuck me," Debra whispered to me through her smile.

Although part of my anatomy was capable, my mind was cloudy and there was a dull ache that pervaded my pelvis. I did not know if I could do it. Debra persisted. Finally, I gave in to her demands.

The feeling of her around me dissolved the lingering ache, or at least masked it behind the pleasure of our union. As the pleasure continued to build, I rose up on my arms to see her luscious brown hair spread out across the bed, her now brightened green eyes and drawn pink lips of her smile. I watched with irrepressible pleasure as her breasts moved with my motion. It was an absolute gorgeous sight that contributed to my pleasure. The pinnacle came with a suddenness that was frightening and wavered on the fine line between pain and pleasure. The climax took the last vestiges of control from my body as I collapsed onto Debra. She lay underneath me smothered by my weight for an indeterminate amount of time. She lasted as long as she could, then I felt her pushing me to the side to relieve the pressure on her chest.

We moved to a more comfortable position, laying side by side. I took a quick glance around the room. Jimmy must have left quietly and closed the door behind him. Both of us remained together and passed rapidly into the realm of unconsciousness associated with deep fatigue sleep.

———

Ashley

—

It was approaching midday, although there was no way to tell the time of day from the available light outside the window. The low, thick overcast and the dripping sky provided a depressing pallor to the first totally free weekend I have had in several months. Friday night, the thought of a do-nothing weekend brought pleasure and relief. Less than 24-hours later, the weather altered my feelings from light to dark.

Even a good romance novel with a moderate fire would not mitigate the suppressive mood of the weather and the moment. Times like these were the great equalizer. All the money, fame and opulence of success could not affect the scourge of intelligent human lives - loneliness. Many predatory animals thrived in solitary activity, but humans rarely prosper as solo entities. Artists tended to be the most solitary among humans, and yet they needed people at one level or another.

Something had to change. I had to shed the heavy, wet blanket that was suffocating me.

The strange element that colored the morose mood I was in was the essence of my maturation. Success breeds success. Achievement brings happiness. Here I was a young woman in my early thirties, or at least close, with an MBA and an MS in computer science from Stanford, the owner of a very successful, interpret that as a profitable, software applications company and already a widow. It was the last part that seemed to give me the most trouble.

I wanted to feel the presence of a man, and yet another side of my consciousness would not allow me to seek the company of a male. The thought to trying to date again contributed to the depression I was feeling. Several friends made valiant attempts to help me move past the loss of my best friend and husband, Carl. Work provided the most solace, more from distraction and absorption of time than companionship. My friends were married couples, Carl and I had known. A few of the men exhibited their liberal attitudes offering their physical services, with one even having the consent of his spouse and one of my close friends.

The depression was totally uncharacteristic of me, but I suppose it should not have been unexpected. Carl's death in a freak automobile accident was approaching four months old, and I missed him. This was probably the first real alone time I faced since his passing, which permitted the remembrance to surface, but I did not want to miss him. I wanted to remember him as he was.

Rita, I'll call Rita. She was probably my best friend. She was certainly my longest friend. We had been together since high school and shared many, if not most, of our mutual as well as singular life experiences.

"Hello," was the neutral but buoyant answer.

"Rita, this is Ashley."

"Hey, Ashley, how are you doing?" Rita asked with love and sincerity.

"Well, I suppose that is part of the reason I called." I didn't want to jump right into my own emotional valley until I understood Rita's receptivity.

"What's wrong?" Rita was always the worrying one in our interesting partnership.

"I suppose I'm lonely."

Raucous laughter on the other end of the line signified Rita's typical response to her release of inner tension. "Excuse me for laughing," which is what she said every time, "I thought something serious was wrong. You sounded so heavy."

There was no need to comment on her quirks. "This is the first weekend I've had to myself in a long time." I could not bring myself to mention Carl's name, since I was on the verge of tears already, and I always portrayed myself as the strong one of the two of us. "This house is so big. I guess I'm just lonely."

"Ashley," Rita's voice took on a more somber tone, "you have lost Carl and you are a workaholic. No wonder you feel lonely."

All of a sudden, I did not feel like talking even to Rita. "I've got to go. I'll talk to you later."

"No, wa..." I had hung up the phone before she could respond.

The kitchen seemed like the place to be at this particular moment. The emotions and sensations coursing through my body and brain were strange to me. Challenges, obstacles, energy, success, accomplishment and fulfillment had characterized my adult life. Carl had been the perfect complement as the owner of his own company, specializing in finding or making unique parts mostly for vintage car or airplane, owners or dealers. Our lives had blended very well as complementary would indicate.

The best stimulation I could think of at the moment was food. I searched the refrigerator, the cupboards and the pantry for anything that was ready to eat. Preparation did not fit within my defined constraints. Crackers, tortilla chips with some dip of some kind, two cups of yogurt, and then the mother lode....a large bag of M&M Almonds.

I situated myself on one of the stools placed around the preparation island so that I could stare out the window at the wall of green foliage interspersed within and defining the boundary of the back yard. The textures, smells and tastes of the sundry edibles accomplished the objective I had established.

Added to the physiological stimulation, I was treated to a display of nature with a variety of birds dancing among the trees along with several squirrels playing an energetic game of tag. It was fascinating to watch the animals move effortlessly and without a care in the world. How nice it would be as one of those carefree creatures?

The melodious bonging of the doorbells terminated my desultory observations. I tried to ignore the signal, but the perpetrator was persistent, and the bells were becoming quite annoying. With a strong touch of anger and resentment, I proceeded to the foyer to stop the disturbance.

"Why did you hang up on me?" Rita barked at me as she pushed past me. With further protestation, she added, "What is wrong with you?"

The twinges of resentment over her intrusion fueled my growing anger, but I fought to control the hostile emotions. "I didn't want a lecture on why," I responded simply.

"Ashley, Ashley, Ashley," Rita said with a smile and bubbles to her voice, "I was just trying to help you understand what you were feeling."

The anger was growing. "I know what I am feeling. I didn't want to feel it."

"You can't avoid it."

My frustration with her persistence was compounding my anger. "Look, Rita, I appreciate your concern, but I think I just want to be alone."

The conversation did not end there. Rita continued to probe and I began to open up a little as my anger subsided. She was trying to help and eventually I admitted to myself her presence and interest were beneficial to me. A few strings of laughter penetrated my depression as I felt the burden gradually lifting. Unfortunately, the void was still there. As was usually the case with Rita and me, our talk made its way to sex.

"I know just the thing for you," she said.

"Oh yeah. What's that?"

"I know these twins I see occasionally."

"You what!" I exclaimed. "You're having an affair with twins." Rita and Sam, her husband, had one of those quirky relationships where discrete, extramarital activity was permitted.

With some coyness to her face and voice, Rita responded. "Well, they are kinda special. Even Sam doesn't know about these two."

My curiosity was in afterburner, as I demanded more details from my best friend. Sensing the change in my mood, Rita spills her guts onto the coffee table of my living room.

These guys, simply referred to as Bill and John, were identical twins, a little less than ten years younger than Rita and me, apparently gorgeous male specimens, and they were both quiet, unpretentious librarians who had been sexually awakened by Rita. Even if I filtered out some of Rita's inherent exaggeration, the picture she presented was absolutely incredible.

"I'm going to invite them over here just for you."

"Don't you dare!"

"No, really Ashley. These two will be good for you."

"Not on your life. I don't even know these guys."

"Don't be so prudish. These guys work as one. They're like a sexual tag team, and they will leave you a satisfied woman."

"No way."

"Yes, way. It'll be good for you. Guaranteed to rocket you out of this hole you're in."

"I can't, Rita." The pause brought our eyes together again. Even though she was my best friend, I was not particularly comfortable talking to her about my rather narrow spectrum of sexual partners.

A smile gradually grew on her face with her full lips drawing back to expose her perfect, white teeth. "OK, so you're a little shy and apprehensive," Rita recognized my expression. "How about if I join you to break the ice, so to speak?"

"Rita!" I protested. I had only seen her naked a few times, and I had never had any sexual experience with anyone other than one heterosexual male at a time.

"Loosen up, Ashley. A great, fun filled, evening of sex will be good for you. I was just offering to be a familiar bridge between you, and Bill and John." Rita grinned twisting her head around several times. "Plus, I could get a little myself."

My heart was pounding so hard my entire body felt like it was going to burst from the pressure. I was repulsed, and yet seduced by Rita's suggestion. The long suppressed, carnal part of my psyche won out. "OK. I'll give it a try."

"Do you want me with you?"

After a moment's pause for further contemplation, I responded, "Yes, if you don't mind."

From that point until well into the evening, my best friend, Rita, took control of events. She made several telephone calls, to Sam telling him she would be with me, to Bill and John who were not doing anything else and would arrive in about an hour, to a specialty food establishment to arrange delivery of a variety of finger snacks. All the time, she talked with me mostly about miniscule or trivial events in our mutual past. Occasionally, the conversation would migrate to sex.

We talked about our experiences of the flesh more that afternoon than I think we had in all the previous years of our relationship. Rita was an amazing woman, and she was doing an incredible job of keeping my mind off my personal tragedy and depression.

As the anticipated moment of their arrival approached, I could feel the level of tension rising within me. It was agonizing. Here I was the owner and CEO of a successful company, and I was getting as fidgety as a schoolgirl.

"Relax," Rita soothed. "They're just two nice guys."

"That may well be, however I haven't been with another man since I met Carl."

Rita expelled a provocative and devious laugh. "Now you will get to see what you've been missing.

The doorbells chimed their now dreaded tones. Rita jubilantly floated to the door. In a moment, she returned to the living room with two moderately attractive young men. They were virtually identical except for their clothes. Light brown hair, intriguing light blue eyes with full lips, perfect teeth and slightly tanned skin. They were not big men, being only slightly taller than Rita and me, but it was obvious they took good care of their bodies.

I could sense a certain uneasiness in both of them although Rita was doing a great job trying to settle everyone. It did not take long for her to change the course of this gathering.

"Now that the introductions are complete, let's get naked and go for a swim," she said as she stood up and shucked her clothes without the slightest sign of self-consciousness.

This was the first time I had seen her body in years. Her body was still rather tight, and she was definitely not ashamed of her moderate features.

The two men looked at me, and then followed her lead. Both men looked even better without clothes, but the most distinctive feature was their rigid erections. Neither man appeared to be the slightest bit concerned. I was frozen in my chair, unable to even breathe. There was an element of surrealism to the scene, as I watched three nude people walk toward the backyard.

I sat alone in the quiet of the house wondering whether I should just run, leaving my house to these hedonists, but for some strange reason, I was drawn light a moth to the fatal flame. There was no way for me to judge how long it took, but I eventually found myself on the rear deck overlooking the pool.

"Come on, Ashley, get those clothes off and join us," Rita commanded.

All I could do was shake my head in what would be futile resistance.

Sensing my apprehension, Rita got out of the pool, in all her glory, and walked directly toward me.

In a whispered voice, she said, "There is nothing to be afraid of here. You've just got to relax a little." She reached up and began to unbutton my blouse. My arms were instantly turned to lead. I couldn't move. "Just relax. Let it flow. I'll help," she added as she continued to undress me.

I couldn't look at her. My eyes were drawn to the two men who were now standing by the edge of the pool. Their anatomy was more relaxed, or I suppose the correct word was flaccid.

My heart was pounding so hard as I felt Rita's hands move expertly over my body. It did not take her long to accomplish her task. I was still frozen. I wanted to cover my body from the attentive eyes of my guests. Rita took one step back, and then surveyed my entire body.

Both of her hands moved, to gently touch the roundness of my breasts. "Now, these are some nice tits," Rita observed with almost total detachment. "I didn't remember you being so well blessed." She instantly changed the subject. Taking my hand, she pulled me forward. "Come on, let's go swimming."

As we moved, I watched with amazement, the instantaneous return of the erect state of the two men. I was more embarrassed for them than I was for myself, and yet there was not the slight hint of embarrassment in either man.

"Aren't those pretty dicks?"

"Rita!" I protested.

Her laugh was infectious. "It's OK. We should be appreciative, and they're used to my openness."

For the first time, I became aware of Bill's voice. "She's right, Ashley. Rita has taught us not to be ashamed of our bodies, and we try not to be self-conscious."

The urge to move quickly to the limited protection of the water hit me like a bolt of lightning. I ran, diving into the water. The cool water was a bit of a shock to my flushed body, but it felt good. The swim was relaxing, as I got to know the two men more and saw another facet to Rita's character. Although we were four naked people in a backyard pool, it did not take long for me to realize the diminishment of most of the pressure I had been feeling. I sensed the two men knew more of my situation than I was aware. Eventually, I felt control returning to an extent that I would decide what would and would not happen.

Ever so slightly, Rita began to guide the conversation toward the carnal topics and the fledgling elements of trust were beginning to grow. Laughter sparkled among our words as our attention shifted toward the lighter and more physical side of life. Warmth began to return to my body and I was feeling a new appreciation for my best friend.

Rita eventually tugged my arm. "Come on, Ashley, I want you to enjoy a new experience. These two lovely gentlemen can give the most divine massage. They learned the technique from their mother."

I did not resist her guidance and looked forward to the occasion with an element of anticipation and curiosity. "Sounds fine to me. I have always enjoyed being pampered."

With a rather raucous laugh, Rita said, "Then, you will love this."

"Rita, you always overstate things. It's not that good," Bill responded.

"We shall see," she answered with a slight, but knowing smile.

There was a certain casualness and comfort standing with three other nude people, one a close friend and the other two newly introduced men. The appeasement of my self-consciousness came in the form of my impression regarding their attitude. To the best of my ability, I was not able to detect any unusual or expected attention from the two men. It was as if I were wearing a large, matronly, one piece swimsuit with a broad skirt over the pelvic region. There were feelings of freedom in the movements and words of this particular afternoon. Carl and I had only gone skinny dippin' a few times, and yet here I was feeling this was perfectly natural with the warm air against all my skin.

Rita motioned toward the padded lounge chair on the patio deck. I took the cue laying face down with my arms beside my torso. The two men began their heralded technique slowly and from each end of my body. Strong fingers kneaded my scalp while others pressed, squeezed and stroked the soles of my feet. The sensation was incredible. The combination with the sensual rays of the Sun added to the pleasures of their touch.

By the time Bill and John worked their way up my legs and down my back toward my buttocks, I really did not care what they wanted to do as long as they kept blending my flesh. Their movements, the pressure, the smoothness of their touch were like molten irons melting my body beneath them. From somewhere, a pair of hands gently spread my legs giving one of the men access to the crevice between. The light touch of fingers flirted with tingling hairs within.

Almost as an intrusion, hands moved indicating the desire of their owners for me to roll over. My eyes remained closed as my body seemed to float to a face up, recumbent position. The process began again from both ends of my now floating and reverberating body. There were no words as the magic hands worked their way across my body. I never was directly aware of the third set of hands adding to the sensations of touch although the mass of hands and fingers seemed to be everywhere.

The direction of this wonderful interlude changed ever so subtly and signaled the approach of the next act as first one, and then another hand caressed the soft curves of my breasts. Fingers soon enveloped my erect nipples with pulsating squeezes and twist that sent shots of electricity to my groin. I wanted to speak, to say, slow down, but my mouth would only open without even a groan emanating. At almost the same time, my legs were drawn apart once again, this time exposing the most private and now throbbing organs to the sun, the unseen eyes of others and the fingers, the magic touching fingers. The ache within me was becoming unbearable. The pressure in every portion of my veins was building with every thump of my heart. Fingers began to probe the hair, the folds of soft, wet, pink flesh for the now swollen target of their attention.

All resistance, propriety, and self-consciousness were gone leaving only a hungry yearning desire for satisfaction. I wanted to feel the explosion I could feel build deep within me. I knew the pinnacle could not be far when I felt the sensuous flickering of a tongue join the now penetrating fingers at the junction of my legs. My body must have broadcast clearly what was happening within.

The soft, cadence of a female voice blended with the excruciatingly pleasurable sensations rocketing through me. "Yes, yes. Let it go. Yes, yes. Keep it comin'. Yes, yes."

Somehow I could hear Rita's screams intertwined with my own as the floodgate of hot molten liquid erupted from deep within me, and rolled back and forth through every nerve, muscle and fiber of my convulsing body. One peak after another hit me with full force as my body continued to respond to the incessant stimulation of my source organs. The pleasure was beyond my comprehension. I had never felt anything as powerful, pervasive and dominating as the journey just concluded. With a speed that was staggering by itself, the pleasure crossed the line to pain as I raised my arms with fingers spread as widely as they would go. The signal was understood. I still had not opened my eyes.

Just as the physical sensations began to subside, I felt the warm breath, and then the soft, whispered words from Rita. "Do you want to be fucked?"

The vernacular word shot into me like a flaming arrow at high velocity. I could hear my own gasp for air. Her head did not move as I continued to feel her presence. She was waiting for an answer. My head moved contrary to what my brain was saying. The result was swift as I felt easy, full penetration of one of the men. No words were past and I could not open my eyes. The stroking was slow, deep and deliberate.

The hands of whom must be Rita stroked my hair and face as the union of my pelvis grew with intensity. Soon, I felt my head cradled between her breasts as her hands moved down my neck and shoulders to my waiting breasts. Both hands kneaded the soft and pliant flesh with a satisfying and complementary caress. The unseen physical reality all around me produced an unexpected and surprising response from me. The rhythm of the motion between my legs was increasing as the anticipated conclusion rumbled toward me. The urge to feel her took control.

With both hands, I reached up to cup the soft, curvaceous flesh on either side of my head pressing her breasts lightly against me. The change did not stop her caress. I found my fingers duplicating the actions of hers and continued through the pounding climax erupting within me. As I let the energy begin to subside, I was jolted by the reality the two men were switching places. My sense of propriety jumped to the fore, as another ready and expectant male entered me. I had never had two men in the same week let alone the same moment in time. There was a frantic pounding set of strange, foreign feelings, thoughts and sensations coursing through my body. The reaction was verging on revulsion, but could not overcome the physical blending of four bodies.

Before I really knew what was happening, it was over. All that remained was the warm caress of the sun's rays. I did not open my eyes for quite some time. A span of time passed without a clue as to the dimension of the interval. It was a faint, squeaking sound that enticed me to open my eyes for the first time.

John and Bill were spread eagle on the decking totally naked and passive. I shifted my body slightly to see what was behind me. My eyes were greeted with an intriguing image of Rita lying on her back with knees raised and right hand feverishly working the patch of hair between her legs. Her moment of self-satisfaction was signaled with the spasmodic gasps of air and the shaking of her entire body. As the convulsion subsided, Rita lowered her knees to duplicate the position of the two men. I took the cue, lapsing into a welcome slumber.

—

Lena

—

The transition from the crispness and fragrance of the mountains was just as sharp as the descent off the rim of the high plateau. Along with the changes in temperature, vegetation and scenery, the traffic on the remote Arizona highway thinned out substantially. The fresh air blowing past us on the big Harley Davidson always brought a more intimate contact with the countryside flowing along either side of the motorcycle.

The welcome warmth was also making our leathers excessive. A short stop provided the remedy to the temperature dilemma. Jack was left wearing Levi's and a T-shirt with some truck stop logo like "If you want to juice your goose, don't miss the Body Stop." The warm sun inspired my choice of a bikini.

"Damn, this country is great," was about all I could think of to say over the dull roar of the wind past our heads.

"Yep and it looks like we have the place to ourselves."

The road was smooth and wide making the ride through the open terrain easy and yet boring. The seductive rays of the sun soon began to work their insidious magic. The tingling sensations that began to draw my mind away from the scenery passing by us were the magnetic attraction of sensual pleasure. My thoughts drifted among the sensations. The urge for more was irresistible.

As I rode along behind Jack, I wanted to feel the warmth of the sun's rays across my chest. The top disappeared as I leaned back against the sissy bar. Closing my eyes, I let the wind and sun work their sorcery on the growing sensitivity of my skin and sense of feel. The wind was like a band of magic fingers pulling at the softness of my breasts while the sun produced a heat that was different, very different from just being hot. A light touch to the wellspring of female sexuality confirmed the level of excitation I was experiencing. These feelings were just too good.

An overpowering hunger began to take possession of my mind. An urge that could not be denied. The vibration of the Harley under me would provide the relief I had to have, I just knew it.

Leaning forward, I rotated my hips to bring my swollen sex button in contact with the seat. The stimulation was instantaneous. The shots of electricity began to emanate throughout my body from the source in my groin. A little further rotation put more pressure on the right spot and brought my chest and head against Jack's back.

What the hell, I said to myself, I'll give him a little excitement too while I'm taking care of mine.

Pulling his T-shirt up did not produce a reaction. When I resumed my position and he could feel the flesh of my breasts and the points of my nipples against his skin. He jerked his head around in an attempt to establish what was happening, causing the bike to wobble somewhat on the road. The smile in my eyes and the broad band of teeth between my lips established my state of mind.

He began to slow the bike figuring, I'm sure, he needed to take care of business.

"No," I shouted to him. "Keep going. You've got to keep going."

Jack did as I wished, returning to the task of driving. He had always been very accommodating especially with things sexual.

The fulfillment of my desires did not take long. In fact, it did not even allow time for a fantasy to take shape and grow. The hot ripples of pleasure rolled through my body like waves upon a desert beach. The climax was long, high, deep and very satisfying, but the remnants of the original urge were still recognizable within me.

I pressed my hips to the seat again while my head and chest remained on Jack's back. I squeezed him once to let him know I had not forgotten him.

Instinctively, my hips began a strange motion like I was trying to rub a stain off my crotch. The build-up was quick and precise. This was far too easy, far too gratifying, to be possible. The thought occurred to me that I must be dreaming. I had to be. This was just too great.

The surges of another orgasm jerked my body, again. Although the peak was not quite as great, it was satisfying nonetheless. As the waves ebbed, the desire to try for another immediately took control.

This time I had to push harder, rub harder, to achieve the effect needed. I could feel the rivulets of perspiration flowing down my face and chest. The wetness of my groin made the contact point almost slippery. There was also a recognition finally that something was missing, a distant emptiness that needed to be filled. The seduction of the stimulation was still too great to attempt satisfaction of the lesser desire.

The next one came with a mixture of pain like the poor little organ was swollen so much it was about to rupture. The release also brought the telltale flags of fatigue. I had had enough. I was done.

Collapsing against Jack seemed to be the appropriate thing to do and enabled me to recover some of the strength I lost in my exertion.

A pickup passed us in the opposite direction. I looked over my shoulder to watch to shape diminish in size as it retreated from us. A man and a woman were its occupants, and there were no signs they had the slightest clue what had just happened on this hot stretch of highway.

As my energy began to return, the mischievous nature of my inner character began to cavort with a sense of reimbursement. Retrieving an ample sample of the fluid consequence of my pleasure, I rubbed it gently on the patch of skin beneath his nose as my other hand reached around to establish the product of his arousal. I could feel his smile as I pressed against him. Jack had always like the smell of my juices, and I knew the affect it would have. I was not disappointed. This time however I wanted to do something different, something more toward the edge.

As I considered options, Jack allowed the bike to slow in preparation for a departure from the roadway. The answer I needed did not take long too arrive.

"Keep going, Jack."

This time there was a sense of confusion and frustration identifiable within his body and etched across his face.

"Trust me."

Once again, Jack did as he was asked. The buttons of his fly were easy. Extrication of the organ of his pleasure was also rather effortless especially as he moved his hips to assist. I moved to him, so as much of my torso was connected to him as the stroking commenced, slow, soft and deliberate. The response of his entire body was unmistakable. He was so hard, the thin skin covering the rigid organ could hardly move.

Using the cues of his response, the rhythm increased as I moved my body in concert with his. Holding him in this state brought a different sort of pleasure to my consciousness.

Over his shoulder, I saw another automobile approaching. I increased the pace of my stroking. A slight hesitation indicated Jack's question. Was he going to pull off to avoid detection, or was he going to give in to the carnal forces of nature? The response was clear as the bike maintained its course and speed.

The intruders were an elderly couple in a late model, light colored Buick. Both sets of eyes were looking at us. I released my grip on him exposing his erection and rose up turning toward them showing my chest. Both faces were riveted on us as they passed. I was laughing hard as I maintained contact with the woman's eyes in the rear window of the car passing behind us. I could imagine the shock of their recognition and knew we would be the topic of discussion for some time to come.

Returning to my previous task, some of his stiffness had gone, but it did not take long to recover. I stroked him with a combination of firmness and gentleness to achieve the objective. His mental involvement in the prior events must have been great because the telltale convulsions of his impending eruption arrived quickly. I leaned over just in time to be rewarded with the ejection of a solid stream of milky white source of life. The winds instantly took the fluid back into his chest without the slightest reaction from Jack. The emanation continued for a brief moment to a much lesser degree. I moved my hand, now, as if I were milking him to extract every last drop of the life giving liquid.

I held him still as his body began to return to normal. Before the transition was complete, I retrieved my bikini top from the saddlebag beneath my right thigh and used the inside of both patches of cloth to wipe up the product of his fulfillment.

Returning our attire to its original state was a bit awkward on a moving motorcycle. Jack pulled over to the side of the road where I buttoned him up as he replaced his T-shirt. He cupped both my breasts gently in his strong hands.

"That was a mind blower," he said. "Thank you."

"You're welcome."

"God, I love you."

Barbara

—

The turmoil of this hectic Saturday was drawing to a close. The only real event left on the agenda was supper. Molly was having Jason join us for the evening. With only two months left of their high school years, they seemed to be spending more and more time together. There was a mature love between them that often creates a bond for life. There was no reason why that would not be the case with my only daughter, my only child.

The constant rain and the still chilly temperatures of the early spring meant they would probably stay in tonight. Thoughts of games, or videos, or something came to me as I finished preparation of the meal. Baked chicken, linguini pasta and green beans were about as simple as any meal could get, but it would have to do.

Maybe videos, I thought, they usually bring back new videos on nights like this. Of course, it won't matter much, if they do not get here soon. Supper's just about ready.

As if on cue, Molly walked through the kitchen door with Jason in tow behind her. Like two large dogs, they shook and brushed the rain off their jackets. Jason dropped the Blockbuster video cases on the counter. As expected, they stopped to pick up two videos. Molly tried to fluff out her darkened, wet, blond hair, while Jason pulled his hair back as if he was squeezing the water out.

"Hi, Mom."

"Hi, Mrs. Boyston."

"Molly. Jason, nice to see you again."

"You saw me only a few hours ago at the mall," Jason added, as if he thought I had forgotten about seeing them downtown.

"Well, yes," I said playing the part. "I guess I did see you a few hours ago, but it's still nice to see you."

"Thanks."

As the jackets were hung up on the coat pegs beside the door, I could not help but admire the two beautiful specimens that stood before me fawning over each other. Jason was a little more than six feet and well built, mature in body while Molly had the curves of a well-proportioned young woman and was not particularly self-conscious about showing her anatomical assets. They were two beautiful young adults.

"You're welcome."

Molly interjected, "What's for supper, Mom."

"Whatever it is, I made it just in time."

"And . . ."

"And, we're having chicken."

"It smells great," Jason chimed in.

Molly finished setting the kitchen table for the three of us. Jason made a feeble effort to help. He did pass the plates to me, and then returned them to the table as I served up each meal from the pans on the stove.

It did not take long for the conversation to develop after the first few bites of food were swallowed.

"What did you guys do today?" I asked.

"We were down at the mall just messin' around most of the day, although we did go to the movies after we saw you," said Molly.

"What did you see?"

"Sommersby. You know the Jodie Foster, Richard Gere, movie."

Jason was moving more food around his plate than he was eating. He seemed to be pre-occupied with his thoughts.

"What did you think?"

"I thought it was pretty good. Anything that can bring a tear to Jason's eye has got to be good."

"Did you cry, Jason?"

"Oh, I just got a little moist," he answered.

"Moist, hell, they were coming down your cheeks."

"Oh, Molly," Jason protested.

"I thought it was pretty good. I love the line where she's practically gritting her teeth, and she says, '. . . because I never loved him as much as I love you.'"

Molly and Jason looked at each other, as if they were in another time dimension and had not heard a word of my observation.

Then, like a flipped switch, Molly turned to me. "Speaking of moist, Mom, have you ever done it when you weren't wet?"

"Jesus, Molly!" Jason protested again.

She held up her hand to him. "It's OK, Jason. My Mom and I talk about sex all the time."

My nearly adult daughter was precisely correct. Since I knew she had been intimate with Jason, probably the latest being today, I saw no reason to hold back my answers. "Yes." I wanted to let her control the pace and direction of the conversation.

"Well," she paused glancing over at Jason who could only look at his plate and stir his food more, "why does that happen?"

"It's a good sign your body's not ready for intercourse."

"See, Jason," she said, flashing a look at her boyfriend, then returned to me. "What do you do, if you want to do it anyway?"

"You work a little more on the preparation, you know . . . kissing and touching. And, if you're really in a hurry, you can always use a vaginal lubricant, or saliva, if you're desperate."

Both of them seemed to freeze in place. Molly stared directly at me. Their minds were in high gear considering their own independent thoughts.

"You mean, like spit?" Molly asked incredulously.

"No, Molly, I mean simply a little saliva."

"Like eating out?"

Jason was getting more uncomfortable by each word.

"That's one way that usually works pretty well, or you can just wet your fingers to moisten the lips of your vagina."

Jason continued to fidget in his chair, not really looking at anything.

"It's OK, Jason. Molly and I have always been very open. I think it's important for kids to have the most accurate knowledge they can, so they don't get in trouble." The words seemed to help a little. "Don't you talk to your parents about sex?"

"No, way," he answered, still looking at his plate.

"How do you learn about sex?"

"In school, or from the guys."

"Well, Jason, as I've told Molly, if you ever have any questions about sex, I'll do my best to answer them." I knew I was taking a chance involving someone else's child with topics of intimacy, but it was my lifelong commitment to my child. I needed to give more to her than my parents gave to me.

"Mom, Jason doesn't think masturbation is normal."

"Jesus Christ, Molly!" Jason exclaimed with his eyes locked on her and full of fire.

"Well, you don't."

"Molly, stop."

"Jason, it's OK. It's nothing to be embarrassed about," I said.

"Tell him, Mom."

"Only if he wants to listen."

"He wants to listen, don't you, Jason."

"Molly!"

"Oh, Jason. We've talked about this. My Mom is pretty cool."

The young man was clearly uncomfortable, but he did not respond to Molly's statement. Only a slight nod of his head accompanied the continued rearranging of the remaining food on his plate. With Jason's ever so slight acknowledgement, I decided to make a try at answering Molly's request.

"Masturbation is a normal and natural part of sexual growth and sexual health."

"See," Molly said with a friendly poke to his ribs.

"It's part of learning what brings you pleasure, and to a certain extent, I believe it makes you a better lover."

"See, Jason. I told you." There was little detectable response from her boyfriend. "Come on, Jason, listen to her."

"I am," he answered with some irritation, but more discomfort.

"Maybe you should show him how."

"God, damn it, Molly! You've gone too far."

"No, really. She showed me."

The revelation instantly changed Jason's mood and froze him in position. You could almost see his brain running in overdrive. "You're kiddin'?"

"Nope. She said it's part of growing up and being well educated about our bodies."

Molly was doing pretty good, so I simply nodded my agreement.

"You're kiddin'?" Jason repeated.

Molly shook her head. "Tell him, Mom."

Jason's eyes finally rose to mine. He was asking me to continue although he could not form any words. Alarms and thoughts of caution raced through my consciousness. I was not particularly confident I should proceed. I was reasonably certain I could control the discussion.

"It's part of being a healthy sexual partner, both people should know how to bring pleasure to themselves, how to manually stimulate their partner and how to communicate sexually with your partner."

"Why?" Jason asked with the first ray of curiosity.

"You've heard the phrase, only you can make yourself happy."

Jason nodded his head.

"There's no difference physically."

"People have always said masturbation is bad. You know, like it says in the Bible, cast not your seed upon the ground."

"I'm not going to get into a religious discussion, Jason. I can only say masturbation is usually the first step of sexual awakening and a normal part of sexual growth."

"Mom taught me," Molly said proudly apparently ignoring my statement.

Instincts gave me a chill of what might come.

"Isn't that incest, or at least, child molestation?"

My instincts were unfortunately correct. I took a deep breath to dissipate the adrenaline. "No, Jason, it isn't incest, and I have not molested my daughter. I have simply tried to teach her about life. It's no different than teaching her to walk, brushing her hair, or washing the dishes."

"Maybe so, but that's not what my parents taught me."

"Let's change the subject," I said.

"Oh, Mom, he's just talkin'. Come on, Jason, don't you want to learn the right way."

A flush of embarrassment brought a pinkish hue to his face. "I don't know."

"Molly, it is not my responsibility to teach other people including your boyfriend about sex."

"Come on, Mom. He wants to know."

"I don't think so."

"Jason, don't you want to know."

"I guess so."

"Jason, despite what Molly says, if you are uncomfortable with this topic, I'd prefer to stop. The only value is your desire to question and learn."

"I don't know. I'm curious, but something tells me I shouldn't."

"It's OK," Molly added with a low, soft voice. "Both my Mother and I are comfortable with it, so it's up to you. Besides I'd like to learn how to do you better than I do."

The image of my daughter stroking a man's penis brought a pronounced tightness to my throat and a twist to my stomach. This was just something I had to accept.

"I can't," was all Jason could say.

"Would it help if my Mom and I took our clothes off?"

Now, I was becoming uncomfortable. I wasn't really sure what Molly had in mind, or how Jason might react. The problem was not Molly since neither of us was particularly self-conscious around each other.

An obvious flush washed across Jason's face. "No."

His sense of embarrassment was quite clear. It was time to change the subject. "How about some ice cream?"

"Oh, Mom."

"Sure," Jason responded with an opportunity for relief.

"OK," Molly acquiesced.

As I rose to check the refrigerator for some ice cream, both Molly and Jason collected up the dishes. Without words, they rinsed the dishes and loaded the dishwasher.

After making the suggestion to break the tension, the freezer did not yield the desired ice cream.

"Well, maybe I was a little too quick," I said. "We're out of ice cream."

"You want us to go get some Mom?"

"No, that's OK. I'll go get it. I think I need some fresh air anyway. What kind do you guys want?"

"Chocolate chip," Molly answered.

"That's good," Jason concurred.

"I'll be back in about thirty minutes." Grabbing my coat and the car keys, I was out the door.

Fortunately, the rain had stopped, but only recently since the ground was still quite wet. The dampness in the air made the cool temperature more striking.

The drive to the grocery store was peaceful with the invigorating chill of the air blowing through the open windows. Why did it take me until the Safeway parking lot to realize the time? The store was closed. The nearest convenience store, open 24 hours a day, was about ten minutes away.

Amid the distracting conflicts of city driving, my thoughts most often returned to the conversation recently concluded. Seldom was I not impressed with the candor, openness and pure inquisitiveness of my daughter.

As most parents vow, I was determined not to make the same mistakes my parents made with me. In the household of my youth, there was no discussion of sex, sexual topics or even anatomy. I, like most women my age, could have easily been considered naive and poorly educated in matters of human sexuality. I learned only through often painful experimentation. I did not want my daughter to go through the same emotional trauma.

I enjoyed the freedom of discussion and expression our relationship possessed. My goal had been to provide a good education on topics not covered in school. For the most part, I believe we accomplished that objective. The puritanical resistance of Molly's Jason was overtly contrary to the openness between my daughter and me, but unwelcome interference was probably not the best thing to do. In time, he might let his desire for guidance express itself, but he would have to control that step.

The Circle K was open as they always were. Fortunately, for us, they had a gallon of chocolate chip ice cream although it was expensive in comparison to other stores.

The drive home was less distracting with the diminished density of automobiles running around on the little errands of life. As I pulled into the driveway, the car clock indicated I had been gone for nearly forty-five minutes.

Jason's car was still parked along the curb, so I knew they had not given up on me entirely.

Quiet filled the house. The kitchen was spotless. The living room TV was cold. Thoughts of the bedroom popped into my consciousness.

"Molly," I called out to provide a little warning. No answer. Several more calls yielded the same result. The door to Molly's room was open, the light was on, but neither of them were there. Several more calls and still no answer.

They must have gone out for a walk, I told myself, but it was a less than perfect night for outside activity. However, lovers had a universal tendency to ignore almost everything around them.

After putting the ice cream in the freezer for future use, I decided I might as well go to bed and read until I fell asleep, the usual nighttime activity for me. With a quiet house, sleep would not be far away.

As I switched on my bedroom light, I was greeted by a discernible gasp, and the graphic image of Molly and Jason in a traditional coupled position. Jason was raised up with both arms extended. Both faces were turned toward me, and then all three of us froze rock solid. Seeing my daughter completely naked with Jason between her legs provided a large shot of adrenaline. My heart was pounding as I quickly considered what I should do. Both of them were waiting for a sign on which way I was going to go.

Showing Molly how to masturbate and even watching her develop as a practitioner, or showing her how to use a condom, or talking to her about the sensations of intercourse were nothing compared to the physical evidence on the sheets of my bed. I wanted to scream, but I knew I could not. I wanted to leave, but my feet would not move.

"Go ahead," I said. The phrase sounded so dumb, but for some reason I was either scared to move, or fascinated with the sight. "Don't mind me."

"Mom, please."

We remained frozen in place. Then, ever so slightly, Jason's buttocks began to move as the frequency of their union resumed slowly. The motion of life seemed to dilute the tension of the moment. The two young ones slowly withdrew into themselves.

The two people on my bed changed rapidly. They were no longer daughter and boyfriend. They were a young, attractive, heterosexual couple joined in an exquisite display of pleasure. The fascination with the scene absorbed the last vestiges of my inhibition and sense of propriety.

An enormous magnet of desire began to suck me into the vortex. "Maybe I could join you," I said in a soft, tentative voice without really thinking about what I was actually saying.

Jason continued his effort virtually oblivious to my presence while Molly looked at me with an expression of confusion. I chose to act upon my suggestion since I had received no objection. As I began to unbutton my blouse, a slight smile rose upon Molly's face, and she returned her concentration to her lover.

As time disappeared, I was standing in my bedroom stark naked with my clothes scattered about the floor and dresser, watching my daughter and her boyfriend intertwined and deeply engrossed in their act. I moved slowly toward them without knowing exactly what I was going to do. A carnal need began to take sole control of my body and mind. I could smell the rich, earthy fragrance of sex. I needed to feel a man within me. I wanted what Jason was giving to Molly, and I wondered for just a moment if Molly would share her lover. Desire forced the answer to the question.

They continued, locked together, as I moved closer to them on the bed. The faint moans mixed with their breathing added to my desire. I could feel the wetness between my legs as a clear sign of what I was about to do.

I touched his back, wet with perspiration. My hand drifted down his lean body to the pulsating flesh of his firm buttocks. I had never been this close to two people fucking before. I had seen or watched other couples, but I had never been close enough to touch their bodies.

The sounds, the smell, the sight, the feel of their fucking approached the limits of my ability to absorb. I moved my hand up Molly's torso also wet with her own exertion. My hand moved smoothly to the soft curves of her breast. The feel was different than when I last checked a suspected lump in her youthful breast. This was the first time I had ever touched her not as a parent. Her erect nipple rolled easily between my fingers, and I could feel her body respond to the new sensation. I needed more. I needed to feel Jason. I needed what Molly was getting.

Then, with total disbelief, I felt the words come from my groin. "Would you share him?" I asked, incredibly looking directly into Molly's eyes.

Shock hit me as she smiled and nodded her head. My God, what was I thinking of, or more surprisingly, what was she thinking of. Jason glanced over at me, and then, apparently on some supernatural override, he withdrew from Molly. His large, hard to the point of exploding, penis was shiny with Molly's fluid. On all fours, I turned my buttocks toward him providing a clear sign of what I wanted.

At first, I felt his left hand touch my left hip. Then, I felt him carefully find his target and push into me.

"Oh, my God," I groaned as he filled me up with his stiff flesh. It was a feeling I had not felt in many months. It was worlds apart from the inanimate hardness of my dildo.

He began to move, stroking into me. I could feel him in my throat. I pressed back against him trying to take in more of him. Before I realized what was happening, I felt warm, soft, wet lips engulfing my left nipple. Opening my eyes, I met the eyes of my daughter lying under me suckling at my breast. Her eyes smiled as she reached for my right breast to fondle it gently, and then squeeze my nipple as I had shown her.

Closing my eyes, I returned to the overwhelming world of my carnal sensations, adding my own stroking to his. It was more than mind could handle. In an instant, I felt the distinctive warmth, the tingling sensation, of the approaching waves of my climax.

I could hear my scream although I could not feel nor control it as the peak hit me.

This orgasm was considerably different from any I had ever experienced. It was as if an electric bomb went off in my groin shooting lightning bolts to every extremity of my body. The tremors of the pleasurable shock continued for some time, probably seconds, although it felt like hours.

Slowly, my consciousness returned to what was happening outside my body. Molly was still intently at my breast while I became aware of the choppy breathing and increasing frequency of Jason's stroking. His orgasm was approaching. I thought for a moment that Molly deserved his orgasm, to feel him erupt within her, but the situation seemed so right. I decided to let him go.

Jason made no sound as the unmistakable convulsions of his climax took possession of his body. The swelling of his penis, the erratic rhythm of his thrusting and the gripping of his hands on my hips brought me a much smaller, but still pleasurable peak, like a mini-orgasm. It felt good to feel his conclusion and my additional climax that came with it.

Sitting facing each other, I felt we had not completed the session. "We need to take care of Molly, now, Jason."

"It's OK, Mom. It was fun just doing what we did."

"We should still finish you."

"Sure," Jason added.

Both of them looked at me for direction. "Lay back," I said to Molly. Then, I looked at Jason. "Why don't you lick her off."

"That's never worked for me," Molly said.

"That's OK, sweetheart. I'll give Jason a little coaching, which should help. The only thing you need to do is get lost within the sensations. Concentrate on your feelings."

Nodding her head, Molly lay back on a pillow, and raised and spread her knees. Jason needed little encouragement other than a smile from me to proceed with his task. I watched him for a moment and quickly recognized his lack of expertise. He was licking her like an ice cream cone.

"Jason, put your arm around her, here. Use your fingers to spread her lips and expose her clitoris." I guided him gently. Her clit was quite swollen and large. She needed to get off, and it probably would not be difficult. "Insert a finger or two into her and stroke her gently while you flick your tongue across her clitoris." He followed instructions precisely. The effect was quite obvious, and he could feel her response. "Occasionally, suck on it like a nipple." Again, he did what he was told.

Jason was a rapid learner and quickly became absorbed in his activity. Molly was responding well to the stimulation. She was thrusting her hips toward him. Her arms were crossed over her face. Her breasts swayed with each thrust and breath. She was a beautiful young woman and still had the tightness that had left me at about the time of her birth.

The soft movement of her breasts and the large, erect nipples attracted me to them. I wanted to caress her, to feel the round curves and the hardness of her nipples. This time, thoughts of intrusion, prohibited me from fulfilling my own urge.

I sat quietly and very still so as not to disturb either of them. Jason was working her well with his newly acquired techniques. The result did not take long to achieve.

Molly's back arched up like a bridge. Her breasts began to jiggle with the heaving of her chest, and she drew her knees out wider.

"Ohhhhh . . ." was about the only discernible word among the grunts and groans of her orgasm. She seemed to experience several peaks before her body began to relax. Molly reached down and held Jason's head away from her now hypersensitive clitoris.

Molly finally uncovered her face and opened her eyes. "My God, was that incredible or what."

"They certainly are better with a good partner, aren't they?"

"They sure are," she answered.

Jason stayed between her legs gently touching her, obviously feeling the texture of her cum.

"Whatever you told him," she continued looking into my eyes, "you sure taught him well. I've never felt anything like it."

"What did you think, Jason?"

"It felt really good to give her pleasure . . . to feel her orgasm."

"It's the intimacy of great sex."

Molly dropped her knees flat on the bed leaving Jason with his face still close to her groin. He was still enjoying the product of his work and her pleasure.

An awkward feeling came to me, and I began to move from the bed.

"Wait, Mom. Since we're all here naked, would you show me how to masturbate Jason?"

There was no resistance from Jason this time.

"First, masturbation is self-stimulation. When you do it to him, it's called manual stimulation."

"OK, whatever. Will you show me?"

I looked to Jason who was now sitting up. He nodded his head in agreement. By the time I reached for him, he was nearly erect again, the distinguishing character of his youth.

As I touched him, he became harder to my touch. "You must hold him firmly, but not too tight. You want to feel his skin move over the shaft. Short strokes, not too big and not too small. Try not to rub the head directly. Let his response control how fast you stroke him. Start out slowly and feel his response."

Jason lay back with his head almost off the bed. As I continued to stroke him, he spread his legs.

"Here, Molly, you take over."

She moved between his legs and gripped him with her right hand.

"That looks a little too tight. Loosen up a little. Now, stroke him smoothly. Feel the skin move over his shaft. Try not to let the skin get taught on either end of a stroke. That's it. Maybe a little faster at this stage. That's good."

Molly's motion was smooth and firm but not abrupt. Jason was clearly enjoying the treatment.

"Now, you can add pleasure by fondling his testicles very gently." She moved her left hand to his scrotum. "No, don't pull 'em. Here," I said reaching to replace her, "gently stroke them from the base." She took over. "That's it."

"Oh, jeez," was confirmation from Jason what my experience told me was true.

"Now, if you really want to bring him off quickly and increase the height of his peak . . . ," I said not finishing the sentence. I did not want to distract Jason with my words. Molly watched me as she continued to stroke him. I wet my finger with saliva and put it between his legs under his testicles. I easily found my target. His sphincter responded to my touch. With the wetness, I could slide my finger over the tight, smooth skin. Finding the center, I began to press into him. The result was so predictable.

Jason let out a loud, "Ah-h-h-h-h . . . ," as a large stream of white semen erupted from his penis landing on his stomach. Then, too, as Molly had done earlier, he reacted to the pleasure rapidly becoming pain as he doubled up and grabbed Molly's hand to stop the stroking. With that task complete, Jason collapsed back to the bed.

"Have you ever tasted cum?" I asked Molly.

"No."

"Try it. It has a musty, salty sort of taste."

Molly took him into her mouth as I licked some of the semen from his stomach. Jason tasted like the other men I had experienced in my life.

"Men seem to enjoy it when you swallow their cum. And, once you develop a taste for the stuff, it seems to add to the intimacy of the moment just as men seem to enjoy the taste of your cum."

By the time I finished my little finale lesson, Molly had licked him clean.

"Well, kids," I said with laughter in my voice, "I think this concludes Sex 401."

———

Carl

—

The game had been a particularly difficult one. In fact, I'd say it was the most mentally and physically demanding basketball game in my eight-year, professional career. Four years of high school ball followed by four more years of college ball at Duke University were never as tough as tonight's game. My joints hurt and several anatomical locations exhibited the initial signs of good bruises, left thigh, right ribs and shoulder. For being a non-contact sport, basketball sure had a lot of bumps, bruises and cuts. Although I never thought of myself as old, the recovery time from games like tonight's game was getting longer every year.

"You goin' with us, Carl?" asked our rookie guard, John Henry.

"I don't think so."

"Oh, come on, old man. This is Phoenix and the ladies are crazy. The Lion's Heart is a hoppin' place."

"Yeah, I know it's been that way for as long as I know, but not tonight."

"You tellin' me you can't handle naked women and free sex?"

"Nope, not tonight."

"I don't believe it," John said, shaking his head in disbelief.

The team bus pulled up to the lobby entrance of the sprawling luxury resort hotel. A throng of fans were predictably waiting for the team's arrival. Most were women, although some would more properly be classified as, girls. There were also an appropriate number of men and boys. The shouts were typical as the team filed off the bus and into the lobby. Also, as was usually the case in every city throughout the season, fans wanted autographs, just a handshake or some other touch, and then some wanted quite a bit more.

Trying to get through the lobby even with the help of the hotel security personnel usually took a few minutes. Tonight, it was even worse. Then again, this sort of thing usually happened after a particularly tough game near the end of the season.

All of us stopped to sign autographs on game programs, scraps of paper, T-shirt and such. John, as was usually the case, happen to run into a woman who wanted her bra signed which he so diligently obliged. My patience with the fans was a little short on this particular night. Every muscle in my body was tired, most of my joints hurt and the pain was still making its presence known. After a few autographs, I made for the line of security guards protecting the elevators. There seemed to be more air, more oxygen on the other side of the line.

The rest of the team including the coaches was still signing autographs as I pushed the elevator up arrow. The fact that I was the only player or coach not staying to fulfill his obligations to the folks who paid the bills did not bother me in the slightest on this evening. I just wanted to call Judy, maybe watch a little TV and get a good night's sleep.

"Hey Carl," shouted John from across the room with an appropriate pause to insure he had my attention. "You buggin' out?" came the final question as the doors to the elevator opened.

I only raised my hand in a faint wave as I entered the elevator. The doors closed. I pushed number 12 which lighted appropriately, and then leaned against the sidewall. No sooner had the elevator started to move, it stopped. The floor indicator numbers above the door showed, 2.

The doors opened. A young, attractive woman was waiting for the elevator. Soft, curly blond hair cut to her shoulder, and her lightly tanned skin complemented her soft blue eyes. She was more on the young side than the woman side, but that did not detract from her delightful appearance. She was dressed in a short red, mini-skirt cut closer to her hips than her knees and a loose white blouse, unbuttoned and simply tied above her stomach. Her smile seemed innocent enough and did not match her provocative clothing. She stepped into the elevator, looked at the buttons and pushed, 14.

As the elevator started to move, her smooth, very feminine voice simply said, "Hi."

I realized I was staring at her, which was probably making her uncomfortable. I nodded my head and returned her greeting.

"Good game, tonight," she said.

"Thanks."

"Looks like you guys are going to the play-offs."

"Hope so," was all I could say, as I tried not to look at her. I wanted to look at her and just absorb her beauty, but I knew I could not.

The numbers slowly moved up to 12. The doors opened. As I walked out, I glanced over to her and said, "Good night."

All I received in return was a discreet smile and those blue eyes, no words. I thought the lack of an acknowledgment was a little strange since she had no problem talking on the elevator, but I did not really care. My room, 1216, was half way down the only hall. I slid the little numbered card in the slot, the green light and a click confirmed the unlocking, and I'm in the door. Without even turning the light on, I dropped my game bag on the closest bed, and walked over to the window. With the drapes pulled back just as I left them earlier in the day, the lights of the city filled the room.

The telephone on the round table was good enough. I punched the buttons for home as I looked out on the abundance of lights in a variety of colors that occupied the majority of the Valley of the Sun.

"Hello," came the familiar warm voice.

"Hi-ya, Jude."

"Good game tonight, Carl. I watched you on ESPN."

"I didn't realize they were going to televise the game. Great. I'm glad you got to watch."

"You must be sore," Judy added, knowing the truth after so many other games.

"Yeah. I just wanted to call you, maybe watch a little tube and go to bed."

"You're not going out with the guys?"

"Naw. Too tired."

As I turned back around away from the window, I was startled to see the young blond standing in my room with the door closed and a much broader smile with lots of white teeth adding to her beauty.

"Are you OK?" asked Judy.

I must have sucked in a gulp of air. What was I going to say to her? There was no way I could tell her there was a strange white woman standing in my room. The 1000 miles would never make the truth come out right. I stood there virtually paralyzed as my mind raced through what few options I had.

"Carl, are you OK?" Judy asked again with a more concerned tone.

"Yeah, sure, I'm OK."

"What's happened?"

"Nothing, hon," I answered still without knowing what I was going to do, or say. If I put the phone down and threw the woman out, Judy would hear the commotion. If I told her I would call her right back, she would know something had happened. I waved my hand toward to door gesturing for her to leave. She did the opposite.

"Are you sure?" asked Judy not quite believing my response.

The young woman continued to move toward me. She raised a single finger to her lips, the universal sign for quiet.

"Sure, I'm sure."

"You don't sound the same."

Judy was probably right. There was no way this was OK. It was one thing to realize carnal pleasure with a ready, willing and able groupie in the privacy of your hotel room or limousine. It was something all together different to take the same liberties while you're talking to the woman you love. I had the only reason I could think of. "I'm just tired, Judy," I said. My mind raced through options for ending this conversation without offending Judy.

The woman stopped about halfway to me as Judy changed the subject apparently satisfied with my response. Judy was talking about a problem with an employee at her office when the beautiful blond woman pulled open her blouse exposing a pair of phenomenal breasts. Smooth, round and firm with a very small rosette and a large, erect nipple situated in the perfect location atop each mound of flesh. She just stood there holding her blouse open and smiling. Then, with a short glance down at her prize anatomical parts, she looked back at me, shook her chest to show they moved, and gestured with her eyes and head essentially asking me if I wanted to touch them, suck on them or something.

"That's not good," I said to Judy, as she continued her narration. I shook my head and waved to the woman like I was trying to shoo a fly. The only response I got was another step toward me and another shake of her breasts.

Judy was back to asking questions about what she should do. I was having a hard time concentrating on the topic. She was obviously quite troubled and had been waiting to talk to me about what action she should take. I could not cut her off. I closed my eyes momentarily in an effort to focus on what Judy was saying and eliminate the woman in my room. I'll just ignore the bold woman and deal with her once I'm off the phone.

Before I could say another word, the woman grabbed my free hand. I pulled it away. She grabbed it, again. For some basic reason, I let her pull my hand to her left breast. Almost instinctively, I squeezed her breast ever so gently. It was so soft and smooth, and somewhat cool to the touch. Her nipple was quite hard in comparison to the rest of her breast. Just the curves of her breast were seductive. She was no longer holding my hand to her, and yet, I could not remove my hand from what was probably the most perfect tit I had ever seen or felt. The woman's hands touched the inside of my thighs. The silk-like material of my sports pants allowed me to feel the delicate touch of her fingers. I tried to pull away, but not a muscle would respond. It was like my body had just revolted at a command from the brain it disagreed with. By the time, her hands reached their target, I was so hard it hurt. She sucked in a breath of air through pursed lips like the reverse of a shhh, as she felt my reaction. The process was not difficult since I was not wearing anything under the thin pants.

I could only close my eyes again and try to concentrate on Judy. Feeling no physical resistance, the woman took the inevitable next step exposing the object of her desire. I tried desperately to listen and respond to Judy. The task was nearly impossible, as I felt the distinctive sensations of being sucked into the wet, warmth of the young woman's mouth.

Slowly, ever so slowly, the woman went to work on me. This was obviously not the first time she had performed fellatio. She had been instructed well earlier in her life and she had practiced with enthusiasm, no doubt. With each stroke of her head and the stroke of her hands on my testicles, I was falling faster and faster into the crevasse of sexual seduction. I was losing control of conscious thought as every spark of all of my senses and every ounce of my strength were being drawn into her mouth.

Almost at the point of total disappearance, I heard Judy very faintly say, "You're obviously not paying attention."

"Sure," was all I could say and that was somewhat slurred.

"Look, I know you're tired. Get some sleep and call me in the morning before you guys go to the airport."

"OK."

"Good night, Carl. Sweet dreams," she said although she could not know. "I love you."

Only one more sentence and I could be home free. "I love you, Judy." Mercifully, I heard the line open tone. I dropped the phone and heard an "Ahhhh" come from deep in my gut. I put my hands on the side of her head with the intent of pushing her off me, but there was not one sliver of strength in my arms. I could only feel her head moving expertly on me. I was passed the point of any possible resistance. She had me. There was part of me that did not want her to stop. I wanted her to continue to the ultimate conclusion.

Then, just as I felt the characteristic building of the wave, she stopped as if she could sense my approaching climax.

"Lay on the bed," she said as she tried to move my hips toward the bed.

"No. Finish me off, now, this way."

"I want you to come in my pussy."

How could a man resist a request like that? My thoughts melted, as she moved me to the bed. As I started to lay back, she had pulled my pants completely down. She took my shoes off with my pants, and then unzipped my jacket exposing my bare chest.

Like a butcher appraising a chunk of meat before he cut it, she stroked my shaft a few times. With great effort, I raised my head from the bed to see what she was going to do.

"Just lay back and relax. I'm going to take care of everything."

With that said, I lay back. In a few moments, I felt her roll a very thin condom over my penis. The way this woman moved made me think she was a professional. It didn't matter. I opened my eyes to see her standing over me. Looking into my eyes, she pulled her skirt the remaining distance over her hips. She had a light brown, well-trimmed patch of hair at the juncture of her beautiful white legs. The pink of her swollen clitoris protruded prominently from the lips of her vagina.

Squatting down, placing one hand on my chest, she used her other hand to guide me into the warm, slippery depths of her body. I heard her groan, as she took me in as far as she could. With both hands on my chest, she began to move her hips. Several times, after a few strokes, she adjusted the position of her feet and hands as she worked for the optimum position. I could feel the contractions of her vaginal muscles as her hips moved. Oh God, did this feel good, so good it was almost unbearable. She moved her body, every muscle, in a way that made the condom disappear. Having experienced my share of women, I felt like a novice under this woman. I had never felt anything like it.

I opened my eyes several times just to watch her work on me. Her breasts moved in rhythm with her hips. The contrast of my black skin rhythmically disappearing into her soft white body was extremely powerful to my senses. This was like I had gone to heaven.

Once again, as I began to feel the wave of my impending orgasm build, she stopped. This time she lowered her knees to the bed leaving me still inside her. Her breathing was hard. Her breasts jiggled with each deep breath. Her body shimmered with the sweat of her labor, capturing the lights of the city coming through the window.

"I can't take you in completely. You're a little too big for me," she said. The statement was true for all women, some dealing with it better than others. "I want to feel all of you." That could only mean one thing, which was also the usual response. "Would you mind if I took you in my ass?"

Essentially on reflex, I started to get up expecting her to get off me and present her ass to me. I decided I would perform as requested from behind her. Judging from her performance so far, fucking her in the ass would probably feel no different than her pussy except there would be no cervix to run into.

"No, just lay back. I'll do this. I just wanted to know you wouldn't be offended.

"Oh God," was all I could say. This was too good to be true. I had never known nor heard of a woman taking a man this way. I put my hands over my face almost in embarrassment. She was doing all the work, and I was getting all the pleasure.

She rose off me, checked the condom with a couple of strokes of her fingers and then, she held me in position. Slowly, she pressed down on me. The distinctive tightness of her anus provided a different sensation. She took her time allowing her muscles to relax and the new orifice to open to me. She groaned loudly as she lowered herself completely down on me. The heat of her buttocks against my skin was incredible. She didn't move for a few moments as she let her body adjust. It was hot inside her. As she waited, I looked at her. Her eyes were closed and her head lowered as she mentally worked with her body. The soft white V of her thighs laying against me led my eyes to the soft brown hair and the rich pink flesh of her still swollen clitoris. I could now see the deep pink folds surrounding her vaginal opening. The pink flesh of her genitalia was immensely seductive all by itself. I reached to gather some of her wetness and run my finger over the curves of her clitoris. An audible purr came from deep within her, and her hips moved ever so slightly to my touch.

"No," she said as she moved my hand away. "I want you."

I did as I was requested. She began to move her hips slowly over me. She used the entire length. She went from all the way down to nearly coming out on each stroke. It was a little distracting at first, but I quickly developed confidence in her ability. In short order, she raised her knees and began moving her hips with the same rhythm she did using her vagina.

I watched her for several strokes. The blackness of my shaft covered by the thin, off-white sheath of the condom disappearing completely into the depths of her body occupied my consciousness completely. This woman was absolutely incredible. The visual scene was more than my senses could stand. I closed my eyes and returned my head to the bed.

The wave began to build again. I could feel the drips of her sweat on my skin as all my thoughts, feelings, sensations and life were being drawn to my groin. The growing wave was sucking everything out of me to feed its growth. I felt my body begin to twitch. This time she kept going increasing her pace as my climax approached. I knew she could feel what was happening with her body and she was intent on having me this time.

"Oh Jesus, my God," I said, as the orgasm came quickly. The pain of pleasure was so intense I almost doubled up. My body shook almost violently as the peak hit, subsided slightly and hit again. She kept moving on me like she was trying to suck every drop of life from me. In all, I felt three or four distinct peaks. I grabbed her hips as the pleasure crossed the thin line to pain. I fell back to the bed as my body gasped for air to recover.

Her body collapsed on mine. I felt the softness of her wet breasts against my chest. Neither one moved a muscle for the longest time. It may have been hours for all I know. I don't know whether I fell asleep or the time span was only a few seconds. There was no connection with reality.

The return to life came when she eventually began to move to break the connection between us. Gradually, she moved off of me. Her eyes were locked to mine as she stood, and stretched her arms and legs. She worked each joint of her body with her white blouse still open and her red skirt in a tight band around her waist. Satisfied all her parts still functioned properly although probably a little sore and fatigued, she pulled her skirt down. I felt a sense of loss as the beautiful, brown triangle disappeared. She, then, covered her breasts and ran her fingers through her hair to fluff it out.

"Thank you, Carl," she said.

I was flabbergasted. Here, she had done all the work, and I had the most powerful, incredible orgasm I had ever had. It was the first time in my entire sexual life that a woman had done all the work other than just a blowjob or handjob.

"You're absolutely incredible."

"Thank you. I hope you enjoyed it."

"I did, but please don't leave."

"I must. I have interfered with your night too much already. I got what I wanted."

"After an orgasm like that, I owe you one. I don't know how I can give you an orgasm like you gave me, but I'd like to try."

"No, that's not necessary."

"I insist."

"No. I got all I wanted and needed."

"Oh come on. Everyone needs an orgasm."

"Yeah, maybe so, but I'll take care of myself later."

"I need your orgasm," I said, wondering even if she gave me hers whether it would be real. "This doesn't feel right, you doing all the work and me getting all the pleasure."

"My pleasure was feeling you inside me, feeling your orgasm fill me up. I don't need an orgasm right now."

"Oh come on. I'm sure you must. Everyone needs a release after sex like that."

She paused to consider my request. "This was simply to bring you pleasure. That was my reward."

"It would bring me more pleasure, more complete pleasure, to feel your orgasm."

Again, she thought about my request. "OK. I tell you what. This was for you. So, I'll give you my orgasm, but I want you to just watch."

"I want to do something for you. They say I can eat some mean pussy. Let me give it a go. Let me get you off."

"No. I don't want you to do anything. You'll watch me, or I leave right now."

"Alright. I'll take it anyway I can get it."

With a nod of her head, she moved to the other bed, pulled her skirt up again and sat on the edge of the bed facing me. Closing her eyes, she spread her knees apart forming a diamond with her legs and exposing her still swollen clitoris. The wetness clearly visible on her thighs was the remnants of my ejaculation she had not tried to wipe away.

"Open your blouse."

She complied without hesitation and without opening her eyes. The rosettes of her breasts were larger with her relaxed nipples barely perceptible. Her right hand moved to her groin. Her middle finger disappeared into her vagina to gather some of the slippery fluid to help her fingers slide over her flesh. She moved her middle two fingers in a slow circular motion over her swollen clitoris. Every few minutes she would run her fingers into her vagina for more fluid. A couple of time she wet her fingers in her mouth. The whole time her eyes remained closed. It looked like she had mentally removed herself from my room to the privacy of her thoughts. I felt distant, and yet very much a part of the scene. The muscles of her thighs flexed randomly at first, and then they began to move with the rhythm of her body. By the time my attention returned to her chest, her nipples were erect and heaving with the stimulation of her approaching climax.

Watching her masturbate was like the flame to the moth. I wanted to get closer, to touch her, to be physically part of her pleasure. As much as I wanted to participate, I knew I couldn't after what she had done for me.

Her hand was moving at a feverish pace when her head arched back and a strange, almost primal, sound rose from deep inside her. Every muscle in her body was convulsing. Her body continued to shake as she brought several quick additional peaks. She allowed her body to collapse onto the bed. The scene was absolutely amazing. Here was a beautiful young woman whose name I still didn't know laying on the adjacent bed with her white blouse completely open and her red skirt in a tight band around her waist. Her knees were still spread wide. The wetness of her orgasm reflecting the light off her genitalia, and her chest heaved as she struggled for air to recover her strength.

My mystery woman slowly stood. There was a sense of pride to her stance as she rearranged her clothing.

"That was fantastic," I said finally.

"I hope you enjoyed it."

"Without a doubt."

"Good. Now, I really must be going."

"Why don't you stay?"

"Maybe another time."

"Oh come on. There so much more we could do."

"Probably so, but not this time."

I paused to think of the next line of reasoning I could use. "What's your name and number?"

"My name is Emily."

"Emily what."

"That's enough for now."

"How do I get ahold of you. I'd like to see you again."

"I won't have any problem finding you."

"I suppose not."

"Every one knows Carl Jefferies. You're a basketball legend, and you're still playing."

"I don't know anything about that."

"Oh sure you do, Carl. Don't be so modest," she said. "Now, I must be going."

My mind raced through the options I had to try to keep her here. I didn't want her to go. "Well, if you've got to go, then can I have a hug and a kiss?"

"Sure."

She walked toward me like a cat about to pounce on a mouse. I bent my knees to be on her level. I felt the warmth of her body embrace me, and it was not until that moment that I realized I was stark naked. Her lips were soft and full. Emily used her tongue like a painter uses brushes. I could feel her chest against mine as my knees spread on either side of her. I could not resist the attraction of her breast. I reached up to lightly caress the round curve of her breast.

Emily slowly drew away from me. "Really, I must go."

I did not answer her, but simply stood up to my full height. She was tall for a woman although she was a little than a foot shorter than me. I stood there, stark naked, like a stone statue, as Emily with no last name walked out the door. I was alone with only the light from the city streaming into the room.

Just as quickly as Emily had entered, and then left my room, my thoughts jumped to Judy. A sense of disgust overcame the carnal pleasure I had so recently enjoyed. Instinctively, my fingers began to punch the familiar numbers.

"Hello," came the voice of my wife across the distance.

"I love you, Judy."

"Carl, I love you," she answered. "I thought you were going to sleep."

"I was. I just needed to tell you that I love you and miss you."

"Great. Now, go to bed."

"Good night, Judy.

"Good night, Carl."

———

Peter
—

This particular Saturday afternoon was certainly more boring than usual. Being in between basketball and baseball seasons along with the overcast, gloomy and rather chilly weather presented a narrow set of choices. About the only thing my buddy Mike and I could figure out brought us to watching "High Plains Drifter" with Clint Eastwood, again. We both recognized the movie as a classic and never tired of watching it. My only concern as the urge rose was no different this time either . . . were we going to wear out the tape?

The slight distraction of my Mom asking us if we wanted a bowl of popcorn had not bothered us. We were both thankful to have the munchies.

The clash between good and evil was always so clear although, and that was the neat part, the drifter never seemed like a preacher, nor a particularly good person. He did good things for the others, but there was something dark about the character. Clint did really well with the preacher.

Mike and I liked mostly the same things. "High Plains Drifter", of course, but we also like sports, we liked girls without question, and we liked cheeseburgers with lettuce, tomato and onions and lots of ketchup. We've been hanging around with each other since we were seven, that's when his family moved into the neighborhood. Now, with one year of high school to go, we seemed to quite often gravitate to the topic of college. Neither one of us really knew what it was we wanted, nor where we wanted to go to school. USC or UCLA were the most likely choices simply because they were local universities. Both of us bounced back and forth with the top choice depending on which school was winning in sports at the moment. We were not that worried about it since we both agreed either school would suit our needs...lots of beautiful girls. Attractive females with bodacious, unbridled and prevalent ta-ta's were about the only thing we were really concerned about.

Somewhere in the distance, the telephone rang. It was probably for either Mike or me, but we were busy. I knew my Mom would get it.

"Pete, telephone," came the summons from my mother.

"Whoever it is, tell 'em I'll call back. I'm busy." That felt better. There was only about 15 minutes left in the greatest movie ever made and I was not about to be interrupted.

"Pete, it's John. He says it's important."

A quick glance at Mike with apologies on my face, I asked, "Pause it, would you, Mike?"

"Oh, come on, Pete. It's just about over. Johnny can wait."

"He says it's important."

"Everything's important to him."

"Come on, Mike. Just pause it."

"OK. OK," he answered with some irritation.

The smells of Mom's spaghetti sauce simmering filled the kitchen. She held the phone out to me with the expression of an annoyed receptionist. "Yeah, John. This had better be good. I was near the end of 'High Plains Drifter'."

"Well, I think it's good."

"What already?"

"My Mom wants to do another circle."

A flood of thoughts, images and sensations instantly filled my head. Four or five of us had only done the circle twice before. I could feel my heart racing to pump the hot blood around. I looked quickly at my mother to see if see was watching or listening to me. She seemed thoroughly involved in cutting vegetables for tonight's salad.

"Mike's over here," I answered with a tone asking a question more than making a statement.

"You know the rules."

"Ask your Mom if he can come too."

"No, Pete. You know the rules."

A quick look at my Mom, again. The attraction was simply too great. "All right. I'll be right over."

"Great," he said, as the handset was halfway back to the cradle.

"I'm going over to Johnny's."

"Oh good. Say hi, to Missus Browner."

The images in my brain were well beyond the normal greetings between neighbors. "Sure, Mom."

"Tell her, we need to have coffee sometime when she's free."

"Sure thing."

"You need to be back by six."

"No problem."

Mike waited patiently with the remote in hand. With a glance to confirm my return, he restarted the movie.

"I've got to go over to John's."

"No way. We have to finish this."

"I can't."

"Well, then, I guess I'll go with you."

The awkwardness of the situation almost overpowered the other images still firmly occupying my thoughts. "You can't, Mike. Sorry. Why don't you stay and finish the movie. I'll call you later."

"Man. What a pal? Hope it's worth it, dumpin' your friends."

I wanted to say, yeah, it is really worth it, but I knew I could not. "Don't give me that crap, Mike. I will only be an hour or so."

"Yeah, sure."

He obviously accepted my suggestion to finish the movie, so I quietly left the house. The short walk, five houses down the street, was like two similar walks. My heart pounded away in my chest. The anticipation was excruciating. I suspected this was actually going to be the fourth time. My body certainly told me so. I could feel it in my chest, my stomach and my groin. My thoughts overdriving with images of the past events and imaginings of what this event would bring. The three previous occasions were similar, and yet each was uniquely different.

Missus Browner was quite young for a mother of a 17-year-old, according to my Mother who was ten years older than her. She had always been very nice to us as we grew up. The fact that she was also a very beautiful woman made her pleasantries even more enjoyable. John was a very lucky boy, but of course, we all knew that anyway. Then, life changed for all of us a few years ago when Mister Browner was killed in a traffic accident. Things really changed.

The doorbell rang inside the house. My heart practically leapt out of my chest when Missus Browner answered the door. The plaid, flannel shirt covered and yet seemed to accentuate her chest. The faded Levis added to the shape of her hips and legs.

"Hi, Petey," she said with her sweet, warm voice opening the door for me to enter.

"Hi, Missus Browner. How are you?"

"Oh, pretty good, but I'm going to be much better."

The lightness of her words and the pat on my shoulders added to the pressure within me. The thought of my Mother's request passed through my mind like a flash of lightning, but did not match the other thoughts boiling away. The moment passed.

"You're the last one. Are you ready for some fun?"

"Yes, ma'am."

"Good. The others are in the basement. Why don't you go on down? I'll be down shortly."

The lights were on, although numerous candles were lit and spread around the room. It had all the signs. This was the way all three previous events had been set up. The other guys, John, Bill, James and George stood together in a small clump although John was the only one who could stand still.

"Hi'ya, Pete," several of the guys said.

"Hi, guys."

The additional footsteps coming down the stairs stopped any further discussions we might have had.

"All right guys, you know the rules. Are you ready to play?"

Different words were used by each of us, but all meant the same thing. Almost by instinct, we moved to form a circle as she turned out the overhead lights and bathed the room in the warm glow of the candles.

As Missus Browner moved to the center, we began slowly at first. Clothes were discarded on the floor behind us. The process did not take long. Three of us had full erections with the other two not far behind. Satisfied with the state of things, Missus Browner began taking off her clothes. We were not allowed to touch ourselves until she was totally naked and properly positioned.

The urge to relieve the pain was strong as it always was.

First, her jeans. The soft, white, T-back panties accentuated the smooth curves of her buttocks. Oh, the pain. Then, the buttons of her shirt slowly and carefully undone as she turned to look at each of us, first in the eyes, then directly at our manhood. We were all now fully erect with no help except the stimulation of her disrobing and the anticipation of the sights to be seen. Oh, the pain. The shirt was soon gone leaving the complementary bra restraining her ample bosom. Oh, my God, the pain. Her hand reached for the clasp the joined the two round cups. Her nipples were full and hard, protruding from the soft material of the bra. Oh, the pain. The urge to stop the pain was intense and verging on unbearable. I was positioned this time to be the first to see the absolutely gorgeous breasts, so round and full, with the reddish-brown around her nipples all scrunched down to raise her nipples so high and prominent. They were beautiful, but my God, the pain the sight caused. It couldn't get any worse. So, delicately and smoothly, she removed the skimpy panties. Her breasts moved freely and gently as she positioned the large turntable and then placed herself on it with her legs crossed but open. The pink flesh between her legs and among the soft brown hair was so obvious and attractive.

"You may begin, boys," she commanded, as if she were alone talking to herself.

The command needed no second stating. I was oblivious to anything other than the incredible scene turning slowly in front of me and the feelings in my right hand. Satisfied with progress, Missus Browner, as she had done on only one other occasion, began stroking her now swollen and protruding clitoris. The stroking soon turned to a rapid rubbing. She had trouble keeping her eyes open to watch us as she became more and more absorbed in her own masturbation. The image of a beautiful, grown woman sitting Indian style on a rotating turntable with her right hand nearly a blur between her legs, and her left hand caressing her breasts and squeezing her nipples made the pain in my groin far worse. My hand ached and the muscle in my arm burned from the feverish exertion.

Relief came in nearly an instant as the peak shot into the stratosphere. My legs wobbled as the ejaculation continued. The violence of the orgasm pulled the plug on all my strength as it drained from my body. I fought to remain standing.

Gradually, the female voice began to grow back into my consciousness. Missus Browner was regaling in the results of our efforts. I missed the others, but apparently I was the third to get off. James and Bill were still hacking, focused completely on the beautiful woman at the center of the circle. John and George stood, or rather slumped, as I'm sure I was and took in the scene.

In a few moments that seemed like forever, Bill groaned and a strong burst of white, sticky fluid shot across the distance to hit Missus Browner in the chest between her breasts and continue to the back of her left shoulders.

"That's it, Billy. Let it all go. Give it all to me. That's it," she kept saying as if she was coaxing him to finish a long race. Just as Bill's event began to ebb, James finally reached his ending with not quite the same result as his landed on her legs and the floor between them. Missus Browner gave him the same urgings, though.

She stopped her own stimulation apparently without a conclusion. "Very good, boys. I got some from all of you, but it wasn't enough to get me off this time. I need more." She stopped the turntable, moved off it to sit beside it, and pushed it away from her. "I need to feel someone inside me."

We all looked at each other. Only John was smiling, as if he knew what was coming.

"The first one to get it up can have a go fucking me."

I could not believe what I heard. The very object of my masturbatory fantasies so near and I could not take her offer. I took John's lead and began the efforts of resurrection.

The expressions on everyone's face, except John, were identical. Missus Browner lay down with her knees raised and spread apart and her genitals pointed directly at James. All five of us were pursuing the same goal. She watched each of us, by now gathered together, gauging progress. Nothing was said. My eyes were riveted on the pink folds of flesh between her legs glistening with wetness.

I had dreamed of this experience. Dreamed it, fantasized about it in so many ways, and here it was. She waited for me.

"It looks like we have a winner."

It was not to be.

"Come here, baby. Come make love to momma. That's my boy," she said to her son who was also clearly the winner.

James and Bill stopped their efforts while George and I continued. We watched with curiosity and fascination as John slid effortlessly into his mother. There was something absolutely beautiful about watching the two bodies move together, something very attractive, very seductive.

John's arms remained straight keeping his torso above his mother's. Beads of sweat began to rise on John's body reflecting the light like little jewels. I could see just enough of their point of union. My attention shifted quickly between the shininess of the rigid shaft rhythmically disappearing into the folds of pink flesh and the jiggle of her breast with each thrust.

The thought of witnessing something illegal was the farthest from my mind. Quite the opposite was true. I was watching a gorgeous event that had the expected reaction.

Off in the distant reaches of my mind, I began to notice the pain returning, slowly but assuredly. I was not entirely sure why I continued to stroke myself other than it seemed the appropriate thing to do based on what had just happened and what was happening before me.

The beads of sweat were now rivulets down John's back. His rhythm took on a new urgency that was even more pronounced by the soft, white, smooth legs wrapped around him and urging him onward. Then, in the silence of his own mind, the convulsions of his climax signaled an end to his ecstasy.

John collapsed to his mother's chest. She embraced him and stroked his head. Words passed between them although too low to be audible to the rest of us.

As they lay there motionless, I glanced over to the other three. George slowly stroked his fully charged organ, or rather caressed it. Bill stood like a statue, mesmerized by the scene, without any signs of physical response. James apparently regained partial arousal without manual stimulation.

"I'm not quite finished," Missus Browner said, as John removed himself from between her legs. "Who wants to be next?"

Before I could move a muscle, George was descending to the beckoning cradle of the woman. A brief glimpse at the site of my interest, before George took his position, revealed elements of the white residue that was the product of the coupling of mother and son.

Although there was no assurance of further couplings, the prospect became quite irresistible. My body did not need much additional stimulation. I was fully ready if the opportunity should arise. Bill and James had now taken up active efforts for probably much the same reasons I had, the possibility.

I became more aware of Missus Browner's words. She was more like a coach than a lover, or at least what I imaged as a lover. The words of encouragement and release were mixed in with appreciation.

"That's it, George. Keep it coming. Yes, that's good, yes," she said, as she wrapped her legs around him as well. Her feet underneath his buttocks seemed to push him on. "Let her go. Let the rocket go. Come on now, give it to me. Give it all to me."

Missus Browner must have recognized the building signs being much closer to the action. "There you go. Oh, yes, let it all go."

George groaned almost as if he was in pain as he climaxed in short order. Without any encouragement, George decided to extricate himself. No words or other contact exchanged between them.

No one moved, each of us transfixed by the deepening reddishness of the inviting folds between her legs. A small puddle of fluid formed beneath her. George's deposit must have been large, since we could clearly see some of it flowing from within her.

"Petey, it looks like you should be next," Missus Browner said ever so seductively as she stretched her arms to me. "Come to me."

She patiently let me find the opening. I could feel a sigh within me although I could not hear one as I felt the nearly hot, slipperiness of her flesh envelop me and take me in. The thought flashed through my brain in an instant...so this is what it feels like...and then it was gone as the physical-ness of this event took over. The strokes seemed to come naturally.

"Wow," she said pressing her hands on my chest. "You're a little bigger than I expected."

Jolting thoughts of dejection, loss, disappointment, confusion and fear burst through my consciousness. What had I done wrong? What did I do to her? Why can't I change something and keep going? I pulled out without a tremendous feeling of loss.

Missus Browner quickly turned over in front of me. "Come back in, Petey. I'll just need to take you from behind."

Instinctively, I responded, "Are you sure?"

"Of course, I'm sure. Now, come on back to me. I want to feel you inside me. I want your orgasm inside me."

Feeling somewhat intimidated and not knowing exactly what to do, I edged closer to her.

"Come on now. Let's get with it," she said as she reached between her legs to grab me. "Oh, yeah, you're nice and hard, and slippery too." She guided me into her. The rest of the moves did not take long to figure out.

Placing my hands on the smoothness of her hips, I began stroking.

"Nope. That's not going to work either."

I stopped my stroking, and then began to pull out.

"No. No, Pete. Stay right there for the moment." She turned to look at John sitting on the couch. "Johnny, sweetie, would you get us the K-Y in that drawer?"

Quickly, as he was requested, John handed a white tube to his mother. "That's it." Missus Browner pulled away from me, turned slightly, squeezed some of the clear jelly substance from the tube and rubbed it all over my penis. She took some more on her fingers, squatted down to spread her legs and smeared it between her legs. "Now, that should help. Let's take you in the back door. There's plenty of room that way."

"What do you mean?"

"Just come here. I'll take care of the rest."

I moved toward her not really knowing what was going to happen. I thought I might know, but that would be ridiculous. She touched me gently, guiding me to the spot she wanted.

"Now, you hold still and let me push on to you. OK?"

"Yes, ma'am."

She made sure of the placement, and then slowly pushed back. I felt the flesh relax against the pressure. My God, she's taking me into a different place. A million strange and new thoughts boiled within me without many answers. I felt her buttocks press against me and yet I did not move. She chose to move on me for a short time.

"OK, you can do it now. I'm OK," she said softly, but with firmness.

Instinctively, I began to stroke slowly as I felt her muscles continue to relax. It was warm, almost hot inside her. It did not feel like her vagina, but it was similar, and felt very good to me. I felt her move, twisting her torso to look over her shoulder. Thinking she was going to give me some instruction, I stopped.

"It's OK, Petey. Keep going. Johnny, sweetie, would you be a dear and come take care of mommie's breasts."

"Sure," was all I heard as I continued to stroke with the hint from her hips.

John lay down on his back moving underneath her, taking the nipple of her left breast into his mouth. He had to be sucking on it. Eventually, he reached up with both hands to knead the flesh of her ample breasts.

"That's it, honey. You keep going," she said to John, as she shifted one breast and then the other over his face.

The sensations of relief grew from my groin expanding into the rest of me. The pace of my stroking increased with the growing sensations. Her hips responded to my rhythm as she rocked back and forth against me. The telltale signs of the approaching peak were undeniable, but not particularly welcome. I wanted to continue, but there was no resistance to the approaching climax.

She must have felt the changes. "That's a boy, Petey. You give it to me. Give me your best shot right square in the ass. Come on, now."

At that point, all resistance ended with the eruption thrust deep within her.

"Oh, yes. That's so good." As the convulsions began to subside, she wiggled a little probably more to feel the changes than anything else. "Good one," she said. "Now, pull out slowly so I can adjust."

I did as I was told. In fact, I held fairly still and she pulled off me. Once disconnected, she rose to a kneeling position. Johnny still lay before her.

"Now, that was different. I hope you enjoyed it," Missus Browner said to me. She looked around to the remaining two who were both ready. "All right. It appears I have two more takers," she said with a chuckle. "Who's next?"

Bill hesitated just a moment. James jumped to the saddle. John decided to remain at his mother's breast. I absorbed the scene with total fascination. A thought occurred to me more than once. What on earth was going to happen next? James' conclusion came quickly with a great deal of announcement.

Without many missed strokes, Bill took his turn enjoying the pleasures of the older woman and mother of our friend.

The immediate world began to blur smearing reality with fantasy. This afternoon had to be the most important day in my education of life. Time would undoubtedly tell the story, but this was certainly a day I would not soon forget.

—

Roger

—

Here I am with my level of desperation finally driving me to seek professional medical assistance. The personal disappointment coupled with my pride simply would not tolerate the continuing abuse to my ego. The feelings, desires and needs were still strong and alive. It was the passage of time and the corrosive deterioration of the growing frequency of failures. The attraction and availability of females were never the problem. In fact, if anything was true, it may have even been the abundance of willing partners. Opportunity was about as much as I could ask. But, opportunity is not the only ingredient for a satisfying, or even gratifying, relationship.

The thought remained with me . . . the death of my wife, partner, friend and lover three years ago left me without the social skills and confidence for modern intimate relations. There was still a twinge of resentment over the loss of my best friend. The conflict between my ego which would not let me ask for help, my desire which put my ego at risk with every date, and my logic which told me I could not fix this by myself, tore at my soul more each day. Celibacy was simply not acceptable.

So, today was the magic day. I passed all the intervening hurdles. What kind of doctor? Should it be a man or a woman? How do I describe my problem? As always, the Yellow Pages provided the information. Only after at least five aborted attempts to contact the doctor due to my lack of courage, did I finally let the telephone ring.

I made it all the way to . . ."What's the problem?". . . one time. I scratched that doctor off my candidate list. Anyone who worked for a sex therapist and thought they needed to ask, what's the problem, could not be particularly empathetic. Finally, I found the right one. It just felt right. Doctor Joanna Klein, MD, PhD, et cetera, et cetera. Her nurse, or receptionist, or assistant, seemed quite discreet, gentle and kind. Today was the day.

The office was subtle and more like a botanical garden than a doctor's office. Only a couple of chairs were in the reception room and virtually no magazines. They do not expect you to wait long, nor stare at others with similar afflictions.

"Good morning. You must be Roger?" the young, delightfully attractive woman asked.

"Yes, I am," I answered with some trepidation.

"Would you come with me, please?" she said leading me down a hall way and into a rather large examination room. "Would you mind?" she asked motioning toward a chair and desk. "Would you please complete this questionnaire and push this button when you are finished? The doctor will be in shortly."

The questions were the usual spectrum of health and personal queries, and then came the questions meant to illuminate the reasons I was in the office.

The form was completed and reviewed before I pushed the notification buzzer. I wondered . . . . What the doctor would look like? How would she handle my case? Would I feel any more embarrassed than I already did? The questions kept coming at me with no answers.

The door opened. A woman, about my age with a long white coat completely unbuttoned with a simple, light blue skirt and white blouse underneath entered the room with the younger assistant I had seen earlier. The older woman had to be the doctor.

"Good morning, Mister Jameson. I'm Joanna Klein," she said, extending her right hand.

Her hand was warm and soft, yet surprisingly strong. "Nice to meet you."

Doctor Klein sat down in a chair opposite me. Motioning behind her toward the younger woman, she added, "This is Mary Robeson, my colleague. She's also in an apprenticeship program in this field of medicine. She will be observing and assisting as long as you have no objection."

I did not see any reason why I should object, although the thought did occur to me that the more people who knew I was in a sex clinic the more likely my exposure. I shook my head to indicate I did not object, besides she was young and quite attractive. Doctor Klein was equally attractive for her age. Her skirt was hemmed just-above-the-knee. The elegant white, silk blouse buttoned in the front. As she had moved toward the desk, the roundness of her breasts contained in a thin lacy white brassiere was clearly illuminated through the thin blouse. It was somewhat difficult to resist looking at her chest. Joanna, in fact both women, kept their hair pulled back in a tight, well-shaped bun. Joanna was a medium brunette. Mary was a strawberry blonde.

"Pardon my directness, Roger, but I find the best way to do this is simply to jump in." She waited for a nod of consent. "If I interpret your answers on the questionnaire, you are suffering from intermittent impotence. Is that correct?"

The word sent a shiver through my entire body. "I suppose you could say that."

"Well, then, would you give me a little more detail about your history and symptoms?"

The description involved narrative on my part, as well as questions and answers. Within about fifteen minutes, it appeared she had a reasonably good picture in her own mind, even if I did not. "Would you take a seat on the examination table?" she asked motioning toward the medical examination table in the center of the room. "We always begin with a routine physical examination to establish a physiological baseline from which to work."

The exam was indeed routine including blood and urine samples for laboratory evaluation. After nearly thirty minutes of various tests, checks and questions, I was beginning to wonder if she was ever going to check the part of me I was having trouble with. Just about the time I was convincing myself a genital exam would probably wait until the results from the lab tests, she answered the concern for me.

"If you wouldn't mind, Roger, would you drop you pants and under-shorts," she paused to raise the devices everyone knew to be gynecological stirrups, "and, place your legs in these rests?"

"You're kidding?" I protested.

"All men seem to react that way, but I find it much easier to do a proper exam with genital region positioned correctly."

"Can't you do it the regular way?"

"And, what's that?" she asked patiently.

"Standing."

Patience and tolerance surrounded her answer. "As I suggested earlier, I have found this method more effective to insure a complete and proper examination. If you have misgivings about the procedure, we can certainly complete the exam standing up."

I thought for a moment, considered her words and eventually overcame my reluctance. "OK." I had never been in this position with or without a woman or any person for that matter. It was comfortable, but very awkward and a bit embarrassing. After all, with my legs spread apart, a bright light shining on my groin and an attractive woman positioned between my knees, it was certainly far from normal.

Doctor Klein, with her now gloved hands, visually examined my penis, testicles and anal area. The KY lubricant tube broadcast the next element, which added to my embarrassment.

"I need to check your rectal area and prostate, Roger. Please relax your sphincter as I enter, if you will."

She did not wait for a response. I felt her finger slide passed the con-tracting muscle and move purposefully around the interior.

"Are you comfortable?"

"It's more awkward than uncomfortable."

"Good. I'd like to check a few extra items while I'm in here. What do you feel when I do this?"

Her finger moved back and forth over a specific spot. At first, the action felt slightly uncomfortable, and then a tingling sensation began to emanate from my genitals. Soon, her movement began to feel quite good, which was also indicated in my growing response. "It feels pretty good."

"What I'm doing is massaging your prostate gland. It appears to be working quite well." She withdrew her finger gently. "Well, Roger, the preliminary indications suggest you are in excellent health. We shall wait for the lab results before making a more definitive finding. If you will allow us a week to collect up all the lab results, form an opinion and offer a program to help you. One essential element is what do you want to accomplish as far as your sexual performance is concerned?"

The matter-of-fact question brought an element of uneasiness like an unscratchable itch. I knew what I wanted to say, but not whether I should say it. Admission was recognition of being less than a man. In the end, I decided to be honest with myself as well as with the doctor. "I want to get erections normally and enjoy sex."

Doctor Joanna Klein wrote her notes on her record sheet without the slightest visible response. "First, I think we can help you. Second, I hope you recognize you are getting older. Age alone does affect sexual performance."

"I know that. I'm not asking to be twenty again. I'm just asking to get an erection, enjoy good sex, when the proper moment arises with an attractive woman."

"That should not be a problem. We shall see what we can do. Then, we'll see you a week from today, if that's all right?"

"OK. Is there anything I should do between now and next week?"

"No. We'll begin next week."

"OK, then I will see you next week."

———

The week passed agonizingly slowly. Life stagnated under the weight of anticipation, for what I hoped would be my mid-life salvation. The signs of excitement were undeniable on appointment day.

"Good morning, Roger," Doctor Joanna Klein said as she entered the room followed once again by her assistant and intern, Mary Robeson. Both women wore white lab coats buttoned up this time, which gave them a more sterile, neutral appearance.

"Good morning."

"Since it is often awkward for patients, I would suggest you can call me, Joanna or Doctor, whichever you feel more comfortable with."

"Thank you. I think I'll use Joanna, if you don't mind."

"Certainly, not." Joanna motioned to the desk. She opened an understandably thin file. "We have all the lab results. There is nothing outside the normal range. All the indications confirmed your good health. So, down to the topic at hand." She paused to flip to a new page. "Before we open the discussion regarding your treatment, I think there are a few items I'd like to make sure you are aware of. You should have every opportunity to terminate treatment. In fact, I would encourage you to terminate treatment at any time you become uncomfortable with your progress or my methods." She waited for a nod from me. "First, I am a participative therapist, meaning we will engage in certain sexual activities during your treatment. I must ensure you recognize the absence of emotional involvement, and the fact that any activity is absolutely not gratuitous. While I hope you enjoy your treatment and derive pleasure from it, the only purpose for any sexual acts is solely and specifically for your successful treatment. Does that make sense?"

My heart rate continued at a surprisingly high level. I had never considered nor dreamed I would actually have sex of any kind. Well, I had considered I would have to masturbate or something, but not intercourse. While Joanna Klein was not an exquisite model, she had her attractive attributes that made the possibility certainly intriguing. "Yes, it does."

"Good. Do you have any questions?"

"None that I could put into words?"

Her delicate, subtle laugh brought some lightness to the conversation. "Quite understandable. Now, let's proceed." Again, she paused for a response. "There are some more tests which more specifically reach for boundaries and content of your sexuality. I've constructed these tests over the years and have had reasonably good success with them as a predictive tool.

"The first is another questionnaire which should take about 30 minutes to complete. It asks some fairly explicit questions regarding your sexual experience, preferences, fantasies and knowledge. I would ask you to be as candid and forthright as you can, even though some of the questions may make you a bit uncomfortable. The second is a more physical representation."

The thought of either of them touching me, or me touching them jolted my heart once more. My imagination raced through some possibilities.

"We'll make you comfy in a private room meaning there are no one way mirrors or closed-circuit TV. We will not be observing you. You'll be stimulated by a series of still and motion pictures as well as sounds and smells. Some will be pleasurable and some will be offensive. Again, we are trying to find the boundaries and content of your sexuality. Your only response for our benefit will be through a two-position button that we will explain later. That will conclude today's visit. From here, we'll get into the program."

"OK."

"Good. Here's the questionnaire and pencil. Please take as much time as you would like. If you have any questions, please push the call button. Either Mary or I will clarify any questions. When you are complete, again press the call button and we'll move on. Any questions for now?"

"No."

Both women departed the room. I took a deep breath and began the questionnaire. The questions covered the types of subjects you would expect, gender preference, gender experience, frequency, duration, first experience, most memorable among many others. The sexual stimulants section ushered in a flurry of thoughts.

Someone probably did find colors, feet or children stimulating. The bizarre ones were really far out like excrement, pain or humiliation. The thought someone might actually like some of the gross items turned my stomach a bit. I tried to be clinical about the questions, but it was not as easy as I thought it might or should be.

The last section asked for short essay type answers dealing mostly with desires for the future and considerations of level of achievement, from unsatisfactory to desirable. Several of the questions made me stop to think about what I really did want from treatment.

The push of the call button brought only Joanna Klein this time. She made no attempt to look at the questionnaire filing it into the record folder to undoubtedly be studied later.

"If you'll follow me, we'll get you started on the next phase."

Joanna led me out of the examination room and down the short corridor to a smaller room with indirect, softer lighting. A cloth covered, recliner type chair and a coat rack were the only pieces of furniture of any kind in the room. As she had stated earlier, there were no mirrors, holes except for the projector, or other observation devices in the room. The temperature was also noticeably warmer than the examination room.

"Let me explain the process here. As I said earlier, in this sequence, you will watch, hear and smell a wide variety of items. Each element will last about five to ten seconds. The only action I'll ask you to perform is to use this switch. Push forward to hold the sequence. The computer will continue the item until you push forward on the switch again. Pull back to skip to the next item. If you do nothing, the computer will move to the next item at the appropriate time.

"The key here is to relax and enjoy those items you find pleasurable for any reason whether it is curiosity, fascination or sexual stimulation. It doesn't matter. Just enjoy.

"I'll also ask you to be completely naked and remain in the chair until the computer indicates the conclusion of the series. If you get an erection and choose to do so, you are encouraged to masturbate to climax. Please do not have any concern about your ejaculate, we'll take care of any result. You can masturbate as often as you would like. At the end as I said, I'd like you to remain in the chair. I'll return to ask you a few questions, and then you can clean up and get dressed. Is that OK?"

"I guess."

"Do you have any questions?"

"No."

"Very well, then, if you'll undress and be seated. I'll make sure you're OK, then leave you alone until the conclusion."

With only a slight hesitation from years of implicit modesty, I undressed completely while she checked the chair and the signaling switch. She motioned to the chair, which was soft, uniformly supportive and warm.

"Comfortable?"

I felt a little awkward being completely nude in front of a fully dressed woman, but other than that I was quite comfortable. "Yes."

"Here's the switch. The handgrip keeps the orientation correct. Forward to hold. Back to skip. After I shut the door, push forward to begin the program. Any questions?"

"No."

"Enjoy," Joanna said, and closed the door behind her.

I took a deep breath, swallowed hard and pushed the switch forward. The show began with a title along with the copyright disclosures recognizing Doctor Joanna Klein's ownership. The first item was a still picture of a teddy bear, then a puppy, a sheep, a flower, a woman's nipple, a coastal ocean sunset, and so on. The sounds did not begin until a motion picture scene of a mountain waterfall. The smells began with a pile of dog excrement, much to my chagrin.

The scale of stimuli was incredibly broad and increased in breadth as it continued. The first image that caused me to make an input to the switch was a young, prepubescent girl performing fellatio on a man. Anger and revulsion pulled back on the switch. My first forward push came with a sequence of a woman squatting rhythmically on a man complete with the sounds of their joining. I watched the extended scene and felt the reaction. Without hesitation,

I began stroking myself. The feeling grew quickly until the man in the scene climaxed. The woman's motion slowed and eventually she pulled away from him to a view of his semen dripping from her vagina onto him.

The next several items were far less pleasant and did not help me conclude the activity I had started. A couple items caused me to pull back on the switch. Just about the time I began to consider stopping, a motion close-up of an excited and displayed female genitalia showed the contractions of the vaginal muscles as well as the shimmering flow of her lubricating excretions. There was a primeval, carnal beauty to the image, which was pleasantly accompanied by the clearly distinctive smells of a woman and sex. The stimulation was sufficient to regain complete arousal and to conclude the activity with a strong, satisfying orgasm.

Much to my amazement the show continued through unique sights, smells and sounds. Some were ugly and distasteful. Most were pleasant, interesting and enjoyable. Only a few were stimulating. In all and incredibly, I had three orgasms during the period. The last two, while successful, were not as fulfilling as the first. The satisfaction came with the recognition of the first time in probably twenty years I had had more than one orgasm in a day and most often in a week.

As instructed, I waited for Doctor Klein to return. My groin, legs and part of the chair and floor were covered with the product of my efforts. A deep, dull ache remained as a consequence of what my body surely considered to be abuse.

Joanna Klein knocked and then entered. I sat there in all my glory. She matter-of-factly handed me a warm, damp towel that I used without suggestion. She held out a dry towel, until I was ready for it.

"It would appear you received some successful stimulation from the exercise."

"Yes, I did."

"In general, what did you think?"

"In what way?"

"Do you think the sequences hit some if not all of your sexual likes as well as dislikes.?"

"Pretty much, I'd say. There is some really beautiful stuff, and unfortunately, some really revolting items. I found my emotions jumping from one extreme to the other. In fact, I have a bit of a headache from it all."

"That is a fairly common reaction to what amounts to sensory saturation or overload. I'll give you a couple of aspirin after you're dressed. Do you have any questions?"

"What will you do with the information?"

"I will categorize your responses to the questionnaire and physical stimuli which will help us plan your treatment."

"OK."

"Please, get dressed and meet me in the examination room."

"Sure."

There was some satisfaction with the events of the morning although it was certainly not what I ultimately wanted. I had never really had any problem masturbating when the urge presented itself. It was readiness for intercourse that presented the most difficulty. Both Joanna and Mary were waiting for me.

"For the next week, I'd like you to perform a simple exercise by yourself. First, I'd like you to avoid or resist any situation where sexual contact in any form might be expected. Second, use a stimulus or situation that you find most pleasant and masturbate once and only once each night. If you wake up with an erection and the urge comes to you, by all means take advantage of the moment, but morning events should not preclude the evening exercise."

"I've not had a problem with masturbating, Joanna. My problem is intercourse."

"As you have said, Roger. These are simply exercises leading toward your objective. So, if you will indulge me, the exercises will help. OK?"

"Sure. No problem."

"Then, we'll see you next week at the same time."

———

The exercises went reasonably well although they were less enthusiastically carried out on a couple of days. I had only one morning episode. Since Joanna Klein had not told me any success criteria, I was not particularly sure what would be considered good or bad.

This week's session began as all the others had with questions. This time it was questions about the events of the week to bring her file up to date. With some embarrassment about relating the details of several masturbation sessions to another person, let alone a woman, I answered her questions although she pulled the detail she wanted from me. There was no emotion in her voice. The probing for explicit detail yielded a couple of thoughts of voyeurism or at least some quirky fascination with other people's sex lives. Her professional demeanor dispelled any concerns on my part. In a strange way, I was thankful for her attention to detail.

"You did pretty good with your assignment."

It felt odd hearing a woman congratulate me for a very private and personal activity. But, that was why I was here after all. "Thank you."

"Now, let's get started and see if we can make some progress. If you'll follow me." Joanna rose to lead him again into the corridor and another room opposite the file room.

I had to smile thinking of the experience of one week ago. The new room had a variety of furniture including a bed, several types of chairs and benches, cabinetry with a sink, refrigerator and stove, and most noticeably a large open shower area in the far corner. This room felt more like a family room, a bit unusual maybe, but not a clinic or hospital.

"I will lead you through this although I would appreciate your participation, namely feelings, emotions, thoughts or ideas during any part of your treatment."

"OK."

"All right then." Joanna motioned to a couch.

The discussion was carefully orchestrated by Joanna Klein, containing information about male physiology and the linkage between the physical, mental and emotional elements of human sexuality. She reinforced many of the elements I already knew, emphasized nuances I hadn't fully appreciated and gave me new information. The discussion was interesting as well as intellectually stimulating.

"Now, with that said, I'd like you to get undressed and lie on the table face down."

I did as she requested. My uneasiness around her was definitely decreasing. As I turned toward the table, Joanna was standing completely nude, watching me. I stood looking at her. She had a delightful figure for her age. The attractiveness had a positive effect although not complete. It took her motioning toward the table to move me. She positioned my arms and legs.

"I'm going to demonstrate some touching techniques which I would like you to practice on me."

She did not wait for any form of acknowledgement as she straddled my lower torso. The massage was absolutely delightful with no sexual elements. She talked about levels of touch, sensitive spots and pleasure zones. A gentle pull on a shoulder was a signal to turn over. She moved to one side, as I turned over.

I wanted to look at her body, but resisted the temptation. I wasn't really sure if I should or shouldn't. Joanna straddled me again.

"Roger, it is quite all right for you to look."

"I wasn't sure."

"One of the reasons I'm naked is to enhance your stimulation. In fact, I do not object if you want to touch me in any way you think appropriate.

Think of me as your lover."

"OK."

A similar process was repeated although specifically pointed at the front portion of my anatomy. The touch of her hands complimented her appearance. While her breasts did not stand up like a teenager anymore, they were full, well shaped and magnetic. I wanted to reach up to touch them, but couldn't bring myself to do it. The feel of her pubic hair brushing against my skin added to the sensations. Her efforts had the desired results. Soon, I was fully erect and hadn't actually realized it.

Before I knew it, Joanna took me inside her. She talked about the feelings, the sensations, as images for my mind to consider and focus on in preparatory sexual situations. The movement of her breasts broke down the last resistance I had.

They were soft, smooth and pliable with hard nipples in the middle of my palms. The smile on her face conveyed her acceptance. The delightful body brought incredible sensations back to my consciousness. Joanna stopped her motion.

"Roger," she said, struggling for more air, "I want you to close your eyes." A pause for breath. "Fantasize about your most pleasurable moments or situations." Again, a pause. "Let the feeling emanate from within. Let yourself go. Don't worry about me."

A nod signaled my acceptance and her continuation. The result she implicitly sought did not take long to achieve as my body convulsed in silence flooded with the ecstasy of a powerful climax. She continued slowly. I could feel her vaginal muscles gripping me, pulling every last ounce of feeling from me.

Joanna lowered herself onto me pressing her breasts against my chest. We remained joined, as she rested. There were no words for the moment. In time, her breathing subsided.

A joint shower brought its own refreshment. She emphasized the importance of thoughts and focus as she talked about the events of the morning. To my surprise, she encouraged me to wash her body, to feel the curves and textures, to enjoy the human body. Joanna was also very careful to point out the need to understand and appreciate the emotions associated with their sex. In a way, she was saying it was perfectly OK to enjoy sex just for the pleasure. The emotional involvement added significance, but was not a prerequisite to enjoyment.

———

The exercises, experiences, discussions, and instruction continued for another six weeks. After the first physical session, Mary Robeson became an ever present, but distant observer. At first, it was difficult being naked, even though Joanna was usually nude as well, in front of her. She was always fully dressed standing or sitting in the corner near the entry door. Performing sexual acts presented an even greater distraction. Joanna worked to alleviate my inhibitions.

The patience and genuine caring Joanna Klein offered added substantially to the spontaneity and enjoyment of sex. She was certainly a great lover who seemed to always fit. Her advice and coaching gave me the confidence I needed. The education also included considerable insight into the other half of sexual satisfaction - pleasing a woman.

The almost clinical discussion regarding manual stimulation, cunnilingus and positions for intercourse intended to provide the maximum, or at least adequate, clitoral stimulation. Virtually as a side note, I learned for the first time how to feel a woman's orgasm.

Using her own body as a demonstration tool, Joanna helped me bring her to orgasm, in a few instances, multiple orgasms, and then carefully described the physical phenomena present. Her body was particularly illustrative, or my appreciation of a woman's orgasmic response was particularly low.

I was now achieving spontaneous erections in a variety of sexual situations. Control of my response had also returned. I had not enjoyed sex so much nor felt so young since my early twenties. Just the feelings were invigorating.

"Today is graduation, Roger," said Doctor Joanna Klein.

"You've help me more than you can ever imagine."

"I can feel your renewed confidence. You've come a long way."

"I haven't felt so alive in many years."

"That's a common response. But, we have one last exercise for you."

My mind considered all the possibilities I could think of. We had done so many different things over the last two months. I could not imagine what it might be. "What's that?" I asked.

"Mary is in the other room waiting for you."

"I don't know if I can do this."

"Of course you can. You have all the skills you need. You can pretend she is a date, or a prostitute, or anything you want. She will follow your lead. You only need to do or ask. She will initiate her own actions as she feels your direction. Don't worry about a thing. Simply enjoy some good sex."

"Are you sure?"

"Absolutely. Have fun, Roger. Enjoy yourself. Enjoy sex as I know you can as a celebration of life."

I could muster only a nod of my head and an expression of acceptance.

Mary was waiting as Joanna had said. She was not wearing the lab coat that was her usual attire. The simple blouse and skirt made her appear younger than she had ever before. This was also the first time I had noticed a genuine smile, friendly and warm.

"It's good to see you again, Roger."

"Same here, Mary."

"I know Joanna explained all this to you, but do you have any questions?"

"No."

"Are you OK with this?"

"I guess so."

"It is a bit awkward, I'm sure, so let me break the ice," she said, as she moved toward me to give me a full kiss with feeling.

She took both my hands and moved them toward her breasts. They were soft but firm. Her nipples were fully erect beneath her blouse.

The buttons moved easily as I opened her blouse to reveal a beautiful set of young, moderate breasts asking to be touched and fondled. She responded to my touch. The skirt came off of a velvety triangle of hair perched on top of her long slim legs. The attractive woman before me conveyed her confidence, comfort and enjoyment of the situation.

Mary took her cue standing completely naked before me and began to remove my shirt and trousers. A few doubts raced through my consciousness. Mary soon released the physical proof that dispelled my doubts. The warmth of her mouth slowly pulling me in heightened my arousal. I felt good, whole, alive, young and ready. I appreciated the extra care from Joanna and now Mary. I knew I could just let go right now and be quite content with the result. There had to be more.

Gently, with a light touch to her shoulders, Mary moved to the bed. Above her without penetration or even contact, I began to kiss her soft, full lips progressing in greater circles around her face and down her neck. Some purposeful suckling at each breast enhanced my sensations and brought an obvious response of pleasure from her.

With only the slightest sign, her knees came up and apart. The soft, pink, engorged, folds of flesh cleaving the mound of light brown hair provided the only invitation I needed. The taste and smell of her were divine making the pleasure of my service all the more complete. I licked, sucked, flicked and stroked the hardened protrusion of soft, smooth flesh with great care and enjoyment. My fingers moved about the other sources of pleasure.

There was no way to determine the passage of time. The measure of my satisfaction came with the tightening muscles, the arching of her back, the staccato breathing and the muffled, contained moan from deep within Mary. The convulsions of her climax brought a rush of heat within me, and a smile to my face.

As Mary's body began to relax, her eyes opened and the come-to-me hand gesture gave me the signs I wanted. "Roger, come to me before I cool down. I want you inside me. I want to feel you move within me. Fuck me, Roger, fuck me."

The words shot jolts of electricity through every joint in my body. Her body glistened with the sweat of passion. The image, the feelings, the thoughts were so powerful I thought I would let go before I was joined with her. My heart nearly leapt out of my chest.

The hot, slippery flesh of her groin pulled me like the most powerful magnet ever devised. With as much restraint as I could muster, I extended the moment of penetration, watching myself disappear into her ever so slowly. The heat was incredible, almost unbearable. Before I was completely joined with her, I could feel the erotic muscles working to pull me deeper, to grip me tight.

The movements were slow and defined. Mary rolled her hips toward me, adding the stimulation to our union. The recognition of her own purpose came quickly to me.

I had not considered the possibility of a second peak for her. The recognition provided an alternate focus and a renewed objective. Mary moved to let me know the direction she needed, the intensity, the rhythm, and the pressure. The thought of bringing her off again gave me the energy to over-come the mounting fatigue. The ache added to my sensations.

Mary's second climax burst out before I could absorb the visible signs. As she groaned with her own rich, full pleasure, I pushed for my own. The end did not take long to reach.

My body, every extremity, became uncontrollable as my eruption con-sumed me. The pressure, weight, pain and pleasure mixed rapidly, as Mary gripped me with her arms and legs, and every muscle of her body. Her body was attached to me, suspended above the bed as if it were the only way to feel every jerk, spasm and twitch of my body in climax.

In an instant, I collapsed to the bed pushing the air from her chest. We rolled to our sides, both of us gasping for air and drenched in rivers of perspiration. We remained joined, speechless and immovable for the longest time until her leg began to tingle from lost circulation.

The joint shower added a pleasant, finesse, last touch to an incredible lovemaking session. Mary's caring and attention continued as if we were two young lovers enjoying our first encounters.

The debriefing and concluding remarks and comments from Joanna, Mary and I brought an end to the most delightful, rewarding and consummate medical treatment I had ever received.

I was cured and ready for a new, enriched life, intended to be fully enjoyed. Thank God for great sex.

—

Debbie

—

The thought of babysitting did not bring enthusiastic thoughts. Nearly a month had passed since Jimmy dumped me for that blond bimbo, Dorine, and I was not feeling any better. My friends, male and female, all tried to coax me to parties and other social events to no avail. I simply did not have any interest. I couldn't face the others. School was tough enough. And, if I saw Jimmy or Dorine, I'd probably scratch their eyes out.

I was still angry. The shock of the bastard sending his best friend to tell me he didn't want to see me anymore was the worst part. I hadn't talked to him, despite numerous attempts, since that day.

The idea of spending a weekend looking after a 13-year-old boy who was nearly as big as I was put a good knot in my stomach. But, I needed the money and Billy was a pretty good kid. I had been taking care of him somewhat regularly since he was five. We got along pretty well, and at least, I didn't have to worry about him dumping me. Mr. and Mrs. Fisher decided this was the weekend for their once or twice a year away from their only son. Their plan made me envious, a few days in the mountains skiing the fresh snow. I would much rather to be with them than Billy, but he would have to do.

The prospect became easier with the realization I would net about $100, considering the Fisher's usual generosity. Plus, the spacious, multi-story home was always an impressive place to be. The big screen TV, awesome stereo system, beautiful view and well-stocked kitchen always made the burden more bearable.

"Debbie, here's the address and telephone number of the lodge. Don't hesitate to call us if you need to," said Mrs. Fisher.

"No problem."

Mrs. Fisher leaned close to my ear and whispered, "I know he's getting bigger, but I just don't think he's ready to stay by himself." I nodded my head. "Don't take any crap off him," she added with a smile.

"Be good, Billy."

"Sure, Dad. No problem."

In a few minutes, their car had disappeared over the edge of the hill. After a quick survey of the TV Guide, we determined the lack of interesting movies or any other programming on this cold, quiet, Friday evening. The ala carte meal went quickly with only casual conversation about school, basketball and the local gossip. We watched his choice from the family video library, *Dirty Harry*, not exactly my favorite, but passingly entertaining for the consumption of time. We both opted for bedtime a little before midnight.

The room I got on occasions like this was the large, well appointed, guest room that had a spectacular view of the valley with its sprinkling of colored lights. Every time was I here when the weather was decent; I had to stare at those lights. The scene was significantly enhanced by the crystal clear night, cloudless sky and the burning brightness of stars above.

Lying in bed, I couldn't see the lights below, but the stars filled the glass cutout in the roof. The image had the usual and expected effect. I moved my right hand into my pajama bottoms and began to move the skin between my legs back and forth waiting for the desired sensation to grow. The distraction of my earthly problems made the process doubly or even triply more difficult, but with time and patience, I eventually found the feelings I wanted.

The ache in my arm provided the real sign of how hard it was this night to reach my goal. Even the orgasm was not that good, but it was better than nothing. The climax brought the release and relaxation I wanted.

The setting, the bed, and the release enable me to wake refreshed and feeling at least decent for the first time since Jimmy. I was bound and determined to not let any of the past bring down the first good morning I'd had in a long time.

For some strange reason, I felt this overwhelming urge to make a big breakfast. The potatoes were frying along with the fat strips of fresh bacon. The delightful smells wafting through the house finally brought Billy to consciousness. As I continued with my task whistling a non-descript tune, Billy appeared in his boxer under-shorts.

Several elements of the picture were different. While I had seen him many times in his shorts, this was the first in a pair of boxers. I had seen him naked many times when he was younger giving him a bath or whatever. Definition began to mark the muscles of his chest, stomach and arms. This was the first time I had seen the darkened shape underneath his rather thin undershorts. My mind instantly focused on other things although he did not seem to even consider the differences. I decided to pretend nothing was unusual or abnormal.

We both enjoyed the breakfast, which took nearly three quarters of an hour to consume, and we still didn't finish all the food. The plans for the day were discussed during the meal and proved to be quite simple. I would drive us both into town, dropping him off at the gym for several hours of basketball with his friends, while I went to the mall for social window shopping with a couple of my friends. Later in the afternoon, I'd pick him up and we'd both go a movie.

The plan was executed without a hitch. Billy enjoyed himself, as I did for the most part.

"What do you want for dinner?"

"I don't know."

"How 'bout we make sandwiches and soup?"

"That sounds OK."

"Good. Then, you get the stuff out for sandwiches while I make us some soup."

Our respective tasks proceeded along without words. The final contribution to the table brought the first words.

"Debbie, what is sex like?"

"Billy, what kind of a question is that?"

"A real one."

"That something you should ask your parents, not me."

"I have, but they won't give me an answer. They just say I'll figure it out when I'm older."

I was surprised by the reluctance of the Fisher's to answer their son's honest and natural question. My parents had always answered my questions about sex from an age when I was younger than Billy. My questions had often made one or both of my parents quite uneasy, but they answered them to the best of their ability. As a result, I had always felt very comfortable and confident about sex. It also helped me begin early. I had my first intercourse before my breasts grew. "They're right," was all I could figure out to say.

"But, that's not fair. Other kids know more than I do."

"Sometimes that's the way it is, Billy."

"Have you had sex?"

"Billy, come on. That's a bit personal."

"Well, have you?" he asked, again ignoring my protestation.

I thought for a moment about Billy, his parents, my parents and fairness. "Yes."

"What was it like?"

"At first it wasn't so much fun, because it hurt most of the time. Now, it's great. As my parents told me, sex is an essential facet of life to be enjoyed and shared with someone you love."

"Did you love Jimmy?"

"Look, Billy. I don't want to talk about Jimmy or anyone else. You got it?" The anger in my voice was more than I intended. His question was innocent enough, but the nerve was still exposed.

He made several additional attempts to penetrate the instant wall that jumped up with his question. I suppose I wanted to stew a bit since he brought me back to reality. It did not take me long to figure out I needed to get my mind off of the past. I thought about going out for a drive or something, but couldn't convince myself to deal with the cold. Instead, we watched some unimportant movie on HBO, but at least it was funny and I did laugh.

Billy respected my feelings for the remainder of the evening. We did talk about our likes and dislikes in movies from adventure to romance, from horror to comedy. I found myself enjoying the conversations with Billy. He was maturing rapidly and was becoming more interesting than just a little kid.

The end of the evening proceeded pretty much along the lines of the previous night. The scene outside was virtually identical. As I settled into the deliciously comfortable bed and before I could take up my most common nightly activity, Billy appeared in my room with only his under-shorts on and the convenience slit opening with each step.

"What's wrong, Billy?"

"Nothing. I can't sleep, and I've still got a few questions."

"Can't they wait until morning."

"How do you know if you're in love?" he asked, ignoring my question.

I considered whether I should try to answer the question. If I did, he would probably ask more. If I didn't, he might ask more anyway. "The feelings you have."

"What do you mean?"

"You feel like you want to be with that person all the time. You want to be close to him. You want to feel him."

The line of questioning continued along the philosophical path. I did not consider myself an expert by any measure, but Billy was asking questions I had asked myself a few years back. Fortunately, my parents helped me answer the inquiries of life.

Billy was a smart kid, perceptive, thoughtful, kind and generous. The conversation was actually stimulating. He made me think about many topics I hadn't really spent much time on. He also took on a different dimension.

"You're shivering."

"It's OK."

"Why don't you put on a robe, then?"

"It's OK, really."

The discussion continued, although I was certainly more aware of his condition. I like the bedroom cooler than most people. The temperature brought easy justification for burying myself under the sheets, blankets and covers. It was a big bed, king size, I thought.

"Come on, Billy, at least get under the covers. You could get frostbite dressed like that."

There was no hesitation. Several minutes passed in silence until his shivering stopped. The contemplation was quite evident on his face. In time, he rolled onto his side, propped himself up on his elbow as I lay on my back with my arms behind my head.

"What does a breast feel like?"

The question seemed serious and innocent enough, although it did make me slightly uncomfortable. I wanted to be serious in return.

"It's round and soft kind of like a plastic bag full of pudding."

The answer made him think. "Can I feel yours?"

"No," I protested.

"Why not? I won't hurt you."

"I'm sure you won't, but you only do that with a girl you love."

"I love you."

"Billy! No, you don't. You may think you do."

"I think I do."

"Maybe you do, but it's not love."

"Everything you've described about love, I feel."

I didn't know what to say to him. As I considered the possibilities, he reached over and touched my breast. I immediately pushed his hand away.

"Don't Billy."

"What would it hurt? I just want to know what it feels like."

Several more attempts produced the same response, but then I actually began to think about it. What would it hurt? He's not family. He's innocent enough. I do enjoy him, and he's just curious. The next attempt I let pass. What the hell! It would probably be the best day of his life.

Billy moved his hand softly and gently over the curves of my flattened breast. The intense curiosity froze his facial expression. Apparently, he wasn't satisfied feeling me through the cloth of my pajama top. Without asking, he carefully opened my top to expose both breasts. His hand repeated the searching touch. My nipples were now quite erect and hard partly from the temperature and to a certain extent the stimulation. He was the gentlest and most appreciative person to ever touch my breasts.

"They have little lumps in them."

"That's part of the organ that makes milk for babies."

"Can you get milk now?"

"No, only once you've had a baby."

"Does it feel good when someone touches your titties?"

"Sometimes."

"Does it feel good now?"

"Yes."

"What feels the best?"

Without thinking, I reached up to my right breast. "When you squeeze and roll the nipple between your fingers like this."

"Like this."

"A little harder." He was the perfect pupil. "That's it." I closed my eyes. The feelings were drawing me into the vortex. I could feel the ache growing in my groin. I heard myself groan with pleasure. Billy stopped probably because the sound made him think he was hurting me. "It's OK, Billy. It just feels very good." He returned to his own enjoyment of the mounds of flesh. He was learning and I was enjoying.

With his curiosity success, Billy decided to take the next step to satisfy the questions in his own mind. His hand moved down my abdomen and into my pants.

I wanted him to stop, but I didn't want him to stop. I made a rather feeble attempt to resist his inquisitiveness. His fingers touched and probed ever so gently. I could not help responding to his touching of the important spots.

All resistance, reluctance, regret and sense of propriety vanished as I quickly took off my pants. My knees moved outward instinctively passing any hesitation.

His fingers felt the swelling cylindrical finger between the folds. I could feel him consider the texture of the moistened petals of the flower and slowly enter the superheated interior. I let him move in his own direction until I could not stand the pain any more.

I softly grasped his wrist to move his hand where I wanted it. With careful direction, I showed him what I needed. He learned quickly. I had to refine his technique several times to get it precisely correct.

My mind drifted among so many images, each adding to the sensations emanating from within me. The effort did not take long to illuminate the desired objective. The rest of the climb was going to be easy with the hastily trained and nearly expert assistance. The peak came quickly and violently. It was impossible to contain my pleasure. His movement faithfully continued bringing the inevitable pain of hypersensitivity. I stopped his hand.

Without thinking or opening my eyes, I guided his fingers to the product of his efforts. "Feel that?"

"Yes."

"You did real good, Billy. That's my cum. That's what happens when a woman climaxes."

"Is that what happened?"

"Yes, it most beautifully is."

"Wow."

I had a ballooning urge for more. I reached to him this time to find what I had hoped for. He was indeed fully-grown in every way. Two feelings conveyed me to the next step. I needed the satisfaction of being filled with him, and I wanted him to have the ultimate reward for a job well done.

The hesitation or reluctance to my guidance directly reflected his lack of experience. He did not resist, he simply did not quite know what I was trying to get him to do. After getting him between my legs, I reached for him again, this time guiding him directly to where I wanted him.

"Push into me," I directed. "That's it. Feel the heat and wetness surround you. All the way in. That's it. Oh God, does that feel good. You've definitely grown up, Billy. Now, move your hips in and out." The coaching did not take long.

The instincts of eons of evolution took over. He responded to each adjustment I made to his position. The progression through the recognizable phases did not take long. Not surprisingly and to my regret, his excitement brought the inevitable conclusion.

"Oh, oh," was all he jolted out more from surprise than pleasure. It was probably his first orgasm as well as his first intercourse. His instant expansion, convulsions and final spasmodic thrusts gave me an added sense of pleasure, satisfaction and accomplishment. It felt good.

Without further words, we both drifted off into the womb of sleep.

———

Erica

—

The long summer days and warm temperatures always brought a strange alteration of the normal life process in Bolinas. The fogs, mists and rains along the Northern California coast moderated everything except for these few summer months. This particular Wednesday was becoming the exception to the exception. The warm breeze flowing through the open windows of our secluded home, overlooking the Pacific Ocean, brought to the peacefulness of the day the primal, near carnal, smell of salt air mixed with the heavy scent of pine.

Hosting the weekly gathering of long-time friends rested with me this week. The pitchers of iced tea and lemonade, complete with heavy condensation dripping down the glass curves, sat among the small triangular, light sandwiches, crackers and cheeses. The large bowl of fruit dominated the table.

As I had to do each time I was the hostess, the living room furniture was rearranged in a partial circle, so we could talk comfortably and conveniently without disrupting the view we all enjoyed. Everything was ready.

My bare feet on the wood, tile and slate slabs of our floor yielded some cooling to the warmth of the afternoon. The silky smoothness of my light, airy blouse on the bare skin of my breasts helped with the temperature. My baggy shorts kept my legs cool.

The door chimes rang, followed by a single knock announced the first arrival. "Hello," came Joan's extended deep voice. She rarely arrived other than first.

"In here," I responded.

The soft yellow mini-dress, buttoned down the front accentuated the long trim legs and the best figure of the five of us. Joan Harris always had a smiley, ebullient mood even when she was down. It was her protection mechanism.

"What's cookin'."

"Nothing much, Joan. If anything, I'm trying to avoid cooking with temperatures like these."

"Yeah, I know what you mean. You only need air conditioning five days out of the year, but you still wish you had it on those five days." We both laughed at the reality. "I think I'll kick off my shoes, too."

"It does make it seem a little cooler."

The door chimes announced another arrival. This time there was no knock. The intertwined voices of Betty Johnson and Ann Foxstone filled the rooms. The same discussion regarding the abnormal temperature and various methods of keeping cool without air conditioning occupied the minutes.

Ann wore shorts and a simple T-shirt with the Nike logo and phrase 'Just Do It" emblazoned across her ample chest for such a svelte figure. Her shoulder length, fine, light brown hair pulled back into a ponytail accentuated the delicate features of her unadorned face.

Betty, on the other hand, was our full figured friend and fairly proud of it. She knew she carried a few extra pounds, but it gave her the cleavage most women, who worried about what men thought, dreamed of. Her jet-black, short hair added intrigue to her other characteristics. Betty was the most jovial of the group who could always see the bright side to an otherwise black situation.

"Jill is late as usual," Joan announced meaning we should not hold up important discussion for one missing friend.

Everyone moved toward the living room to find a seat to settle in for our weekly afternoon gossip session. The informal, unspecified event had been a fixture in our lives with only a few exceptions for more than two years. The topics ranged the full breadth of human experience.

As was most often the case, Betty began the discussion. "Well, have I got news for the group today." She made certain she had everyone's attention. "Guess who Roger Jones is having an affair with?"

"Who's Roger Jones?" asked Ann innocently.

"Who's Roger Jones," protested Betty. "Where have you been, girl? He's that young buck of a new football coach at the high school. Haven't you been paying attention to the discussions?"

"I guess not."

"Well, anyway, he's having an affair with Susan St. John."

"No way," responded Joan.

"Yes, indeedie. It's true. I happened to see them come out of a room at the Valley Inn. I later made sure I caught up with our dear Susan to get the details." She paused for questions. There were none in anticipation of more details sure to follow. "She said she met him at one of her oldest boy's school functions. They struck a few notes in the same key, and she bedded him a few days later."

"Do tell, Betty. Details, we need details," I said.

"Seek and ye shall find. She tells me he's good, the biggest dick she's ever had, and what's more, he knows how to use it."

"My, my, one of those rare animals," commented Joan.

"Does Susan have the same point of reference as the rest of us?" I asked.

"From the sounds of it. This guy can go off two or three times in an hour AND," she emphasized, "he can hold it until she goes."

"Well, I'll be damned," said Joan. "A real rare animal indeed."

"I think we should all have a piece of that," suggested Ann.

"Yes, well, I dare say, Susan is likely to be rather protective of her little find."

"Maybe, but we should still each have some. That's a little too good to be true."

"That's not all."

"Go on, now."

"Susan says he's a near expert with the tongue as well."

"Now, we know she's making this up," replied Joan.

"Hello, everyone. Sorry I'm late," announced Jill Ranson, as she floated into the room with a most conspiratorial grin on her face.

"You sure will be when you hear the latest," said Joan.

"Maybe, but you need to ask me why I'm late."

"Susan St. John is having an affair with Roger Jones and apparently he's quite the stud," Joan blurted out. "OK, now why were you late?"

"Is he really?" asked Jill.

"So, Betty says."

"My, my, but I'm late so I'll catch up later. I'm late because I was doing my exercises."

"You don't exercise, Jill," I said.

"These are different exercises," Jill responded with a very smug look on her face, "and you won't believe it."

"Do tell."

"Last week, I received a book from a good friend of mine. She lives in England. It's by a woman named, Swift, Rachel Swift, and the title is: *Women's Pleasure*."

"Sounds interesting, I suppose."

All eyes were on Jill and no one moved. "It sure is and especially when you hear the rest of the title. 'How to Have an Orgasm as Often as You Want'."

"You're kidding?" said Betty.

"Would I kid about something like that? Anyway, you simply won't believe this. She's got a whole program laid out complete with exercises to build your self-confidence, skills, self-esteem and experience. She even outlines stuff for the guys to do to help women achieve orgasm."

"More, more."

"She starts out to familiarize yourself with your body and progresses to masturbation."

"Yeah, but we've been through all that," Betty said.

"Yes, we have, but there's more. She goes into things like masturbating in a wide variety of places, positions and moods to get your mind used to variations. The idea being you get used to feelings and learn to focus on them, and then you can do the same thing with a cock."

"So, you've been tossing off which is why you're late," said Joan.

An enormous smile blossomed across her face. "You've got it. I got off three times on the way over here with the last one standing at your front door," she said proudly as she looked at me.

"It can't be that easy," I answered.

"Sure it is. You want me to show you my new found skills?"

"Come on, Jill. You're not suggesting you masturbate here in front of us."

"Sure I am. Why not? We're all friends. I don't have anything you don't have. Plus, I want you to see what I mean."

"No."

"Oh, come on, Ann. What would it hurt? We've all been skinny dipping together. Let's see what she's learned."

Without concurrence from everyone, Jill stood up and promptly stripped completely nude. She carefully put her skirt on the chair to be neat and sat back down spreading her knees and placing her heels together. The pinkish and somewhat swollen details of her genitals plainly displayed for all of us. She seemed absolutely oblivious to our presence.

We watched with spellbound fascination as her fingers gathered the glistening moistness between her labia and spread it over the protruding bud. Her fingers and then her hand began to move with a clear purpose as she ascended into her own world. The magnetic attraction of her activity brought a noticeable wetness and ache to my groin. In my own way, I wanted to join her, but my curiosity kept me captivated. The others appeared to share my feelings including Ann. The incredible exhibition paused several times for Jill to fondle her breasts, squeeze her nipples, spread her labia like the petals of a delicate flower, and then return to her clitoris.

The entire process took probably five minutes although no one could actually tell how much time passed. The end came obviously, as Jill arched her head back and her hand became a blur. Her breasts jiggled with the heaving of her chest. Only a slight groan punctuated her response. Her movements slowed substantially to a stop before she opened her eyes and returned to us.

"See what I mean," said Jill with a soft, breathy, content voice.

"I wish I could do that," Ann said matter of factly.

"You can. You just need to become comfortable with your body and relax."

"No."

"Sure you can. Let's all try something."

I instinctively knew given the expression on her face something extraordinary was about to happen. The others sensed it as well, based on the moans.

"Let's all get naked and get comfortable with ourselves."

"Really, Jill. We're not bi like you. I'd feel so awkward," said Ann.

"This has nothing to do with my sexual preferences, Ann. It's just good, clean, healthy sexual education." She paused, and then decided to add, "for adults nonetheless."

"Sure, why not," responded Joan, as she began to take her clothes off.

Surprisingly, Betty followed suit without a word. Seeing my friends completely naked and at ease in my living room was enough to inspire me. I quickly stripped.

Ann looked at the four of us, without a stitch of clothing on, and with a variety of body types. She resigned herself to joining us. Soon, five naked women sat in a partial circle silently absorbing the sights.

"Let's take advantage of the moment to put our own bodies in perspective," suggested Jill.

"What do you mean?"

"Let's examine, feel and appreciate the details of each of our bodies. It should help us understand and appreciate our differences as well as our similarities."

"Jesus Christ, Jill. You can't be serious."

"Sure I am. Being able to have an orgasm any time you want it depends on accepting your body and learning to appreciate the features. Knowing others, helps you appreciate yours. So, come on, check me over."

With an eerie and irresistible force pulling me into the cyclone, I walked toward Jill. She looked directly into my eyes and returned to her masturbatory position. Before I knew it, Jill was caressing my breasts and purposefully raising my nipples. She took my hands and placed them on her breasts.

"Feel the shape, the softness. Feel how my nipples rise to your touch." She then took my right hand, which possessed no restraint and moved it to her genitals. "Feel the smoothness of the lips, the wetness, the softness of my pubic hair, the rigidity of my clit." As I felt her, Jill moved about my genitals, which were now fully inflamed.

Without realizing it, the others joined us. In a moment, hands drifted gently about our bodies. Jill was right. It was incredible to feel the characteristics of four other female bodies. I had never felt the details. In fact, I had never been this close to a naked female. It was fascinating.

"Now, feel your own details. Notice the differences, as well as the similarities. Isn't it amazing?"

No one answered as the personal investigations continued.

"I'm so hot," said Joan, "I need a cock."

"Do you have a dildo?" asked Jill to me quite innocently.

"My God," I protested.

"Come on, Erica. It's just a piece of plastic. It's not Jim's member."

"Go on, Erica," said Betty. "Go get it. I think we all need it, now."

Reluctantly, I did as I was requested. When I returned, I could not believe my eyes. Ann, the one of us who objected the most, was masturbating in a similar position as Jill. The other three watched carefully as we had watched Jill. Only Jill worked on herself as she watched.

"You want the dildo?" asked Jill to Ann.

A slow nod of her head provided the answer. Amazingly, without the slightest hesitation, Ann slid the flesh colored plastic penis deep into her vagina. She moved it slowly and only occasionally as she continued to work on herself. The smooth gyrations produced a seductive sexual dance. Her enjoyment of the moment was boundless.

In a few minutes, I realized that the other three were masturbating as well. No resistance remained as I felt the relief of my fingers massaging the ache between my legs.

"Oh dear God," growled Ann, startling me, and apparently the others as her body shook with the convulsions of her orgasm. The moans continued for quite some time as she enjoyed the richness of her own climax.

The sensations deep within me were unmistakable. The purposefulness of my actions blotted out the rest of the world. My senses became hypersensitive. The smell of sex saturated the air dominating the sea and pine. The sounds of four purring and groaning women mixed with my own. The build-up of the electric charge within my core foretold the approaching discharge. The course was unmistakable. The race toward the peak was inescapable. I wanted the end. I needed the release. The climax I had to have flashed in an instant from my groin jolting every muscle into an uncontrollable shaking along with the waves of heat. The sigh of relief concluded my effort and gradually returned me to the room.

Jill either finished again or stopped to watch the others. Ann and Betty were finished as well. All four of us watched Joan as she reached the pinnacle of ecstasy the rest of us enjoyed.

Before I fully regained my presence, I felt fingers touching me. I looked down to see Jill between my legs gently stroking my petals and probing my depths.

Jill looked into my eyes with her fingers still examining me. "You have the most delightful cum," she whispered.

I felt a strange closeness to her. "Thanks."

As Joan slowly regained awareness, she began to laugh modestly at first, and then uncontrollably drawing each of us into the swirl of limitless satisfaction, pleasure and camaraderie.

"What did you say the name of that book was?" Joan asked, as she gained composure.

We all laughed again. The recent activity blended with the image of five naked women sitting in the plush living room of a coastal house.

"*Women's Pleasure*," Jill finally answered which brought another round of boisterous laughter and concluded a day none of us would ever forget.

———

Frank

—

The entire day from the late train, to the unusually hostile customers, to the damn market, to the cold and rainy day, turned out to be one of the worst in memory. The thought of another two hours of train ride out of the city with a railcar full of workaholic zombies proved to be the deciding factor.

This particular evening would be different. One hour out for a good workout with weights, machines and a long run on the treadmill while he watched the CNN Headline News should eliminate most of the knots in his muscles and joints, and the nauseous sensation in his gut. Maybe a massage would take care of any residual tension after the workout. If he went the full course, Frank knew he would arrive home near midnight giving him barely five hours of available sleep time. The day's burden deserved the extra treatment.

"East Side Athletic Club, please," he said to the taxi driver.

"Sure thing, Mac," the large man answered as he jumped into the un-yielding traffic. "Ya inna hurry?"

"No, not particularly."

"Good. The street seem ta be kinda nasty tanight."

"Great. It certainly fits with the rest of my day."

"Bad one, ay?"

"That would be putting it mildly."

"I'll do what I can ta make it betta."

"That would be appreciated, thanks."

The taxi ride across town was less aggressive than was most often the case. Frank was grateful for the reduced stress and was happy to give the driver a generous tip for the effort.

The athletic club appeared to be nearly deserted on this Monday evening. Maybe things were beginning to take a correction to the good side. Frank changed into his workout clothes, which provided a slight sense of relaxation. His suit, white shirt and tie seemed more like a uniform every day. He needed the break.

Frank took a good twenty minutes to stretch and warm-up before he hit the weight room. Almost every muscle resisted the demand to stretch and loosen up. Simply limbering exercises felt nearly painful. The weight room was empty, which enabled him to quickly complete his usual free weight exercises. Fine beads of sweat began to pool and run down his torso and extremities. He began to feel better.

The machine room, as they called it, was nearly empty. An elderly woman, who appeared to be about twice his age, was the only other person using the equipment. Frank worked his way through a series of machine exercises that often reminded him of medieval torture devised by some diabolical mind. As he neared the end of the machine segment of his workout, three, wet, glistening young women who were painted in various colorful forms of skintight attire entered. They seemed to be oblivious to the fact their clothing did little more than color their skin. Every bump, curve and crease accentuated their youthful appearance.

"Looks like you're working up a good sweat," one of the lovely young women, a firm brunette, said as she took the machine next to Frank.

"You could say that," he answered. "Looks like you have as well."

She laughed a free, open, deep laugh. "I'd say this qualifies," she responded as she slid her hands up the sides of her torso like a car show model. Her hands brushed her breasts causing them to jiggle slightly drawing more of his attention. Her two friends – both blondes, one slightly darker than the other – laughed with her.

The three young women continued with their workout, social hour without much inhibition. Their voices were not particularly muffled, nor were their topics dispassionate. Frank felt like a fly on the wall, as the three joked and laughed about men of mutual acquaintance, office politics, orgasms and foreplay. Frank could not believe the words that filled the room.

The older woman must have reached her limit, as she left Frank alone with the three women. She had a disgusted look on her face and shook her head as she glanced at Frank as she exited the room.

As their words became more intimate and provocative, Frank began to sense he was being toyed with, like a small mouse batted around the room by three large cats waiting for the moment they were finished with their prey. He tried to ignore the women, but soon felt them moving closer to their prey. Frank's voyeuristic urge proved incapable of overcoming a growing sense of embarrassment. He grabbed his towel and left the room to peals of laughter.

Frank could not quite contain his frustration and maybe even a little anger. The tension in his neck and shoulders returned to the verge of pain. He wasted over an hour trying to relax, and now felt worse than when he came into the club. Maybe a hot, leaching sauna would eliminate the tension.

The multiple layered benches of the sauna's redwood interior were empty when Frank entered. The dry heat made his head throb, as he scooped several ladles of water onto the hot rocks. The steam brought a more enveloping heat making the air heavy and saturated with moisture. Frank placed a folded towel on the bench opposite the door, rolled another up as a pillow to lean against, draped yet another towel across his lower torso, and soaked yet another towel in cold water to cover his head.

Every muscle in his body began to unravel. The soothing heat and solitary occupancy leadened his eyelids. Random thoughts of the day's events, the weather, future appointments and list-loves initially filled his thoughts, but gradually dwindled as he dozed.

Frank heard the door open, but his relaxed state kept his eyes closed. He did not particularly care if anyone else shared the large sauna. There was more than one new arrival, but there was also plenty of room. No words or sounds disrupted the quiet, peacefulness of the hot room. The sound of a soft feminine moan opened his eyes. The scene caused Frank to suck in a quick breath.

The darker blonde knelt between the wide-open legs of the brunette tending to her pleasure with focused attention. The lighter blonde sat near the pair, tending to herself. The brunette's eyes opened with Frank's gasp. She smiled and winked at him. The woman squeezed her breasts and pulled on her nipples several times as she enjoyed the efforts of her friend.

The incredible scene continued for several minutes. The solo woman appeared to climax several times while the brunette enjoyed the attention, but did not seem to reach a pinnacle. Apparently satisfied with her efforts, the lighter blond stood, completely naked as the others were, smiled and winked at Frank, then reached between the legs of the kneeling woman. Her knees moved apart to allow better access.

Frank could not restrain his excitement. While he leaned forward several times in a feeble attempt to control his arousal or at least hide it, he eventually gave up. He considered joining the three women with his own self-gratification, but chose to absorb the scene and endure the ache. The hurt of his excitement continued to distract Frank. All three women partially giggled and partly murmured as they acknowledged Frank's state.

"Would you like some help?" asked the brunette.

Frank remained frozen like a block of stone. The darker blonde took up the brunette's position with the lighter blonde between her legs. The brunette moved without the slightest restraint directly in front of Frank.

"Would you like some help?" she repeated.

Frank's chest heaved with excitement and uncertainty. What exactly did she have in mind? The lack of any inhibition meant anything could happen. He could only look into her deep green eyes.

She leaned forward to remove the towel across Frank's lap.

"My, my, what a specimen we have here girls," she said. The other two did not respond. "May I?" she asked, motioning with her eyes toward his groin. Frank moved for the first time, nodding his head ever so slightly.

The woman gently grasped him as if to feel its characteristics, and then slowly began to stroke it. Her touch seemed to amplify his ache, verging on pain. Frank knew the woman had done this before; she was better at it than he was. The sensations overwhelmed him. Here he was in a public sauna, where anyone, male or female, could walk in on them, and he was being manually satisfied by a female stranger while her friends worked on one another.

His climax came quickly with all the visual and manual stimulation. His attendant recognized the signs and began to murmur something. Frank convulsed with his eruption. The woman gently milked him. A different kind of pain replaced his ache as she worked on him licking up the residue that remained attached.

Frank tried to figure out what she was doing. The evidence of his conclusion adorned her back, face and hands. What else did this woman want from him? She continued to work on him gently with her lips, tongue and fingers until he felt his state of arousal returning to her touch, much to his surprise.

"He's drained and ready, girls. Anyone want some?"

"Oh, yes," said the darker blond. "Thank you, Jan. I'm ready, too." She walked over to them as if she was next in the hair stylists' chair, straddled Frank and lowered herself onto him. The brunette guided him into her. She settled onto him with a moan of satisfaction. Her breasts moved in front of his face as though he was not present.

Frank reached for one of the modest size mounds with it deep brownish red point swaying before him. The woman did not miss a stroke, nor did she acknowledge Frank's participation. She continued until her legs began to tire. The lighter blond took her turn on Frank with the same detached focus on herself. Frank tried to move several times thinking he could add some effort, but the women kept him in the position they wanted.

All three women took their turns on Frank. All three of the women were experienced and determined as though they were participants in an athletic contest. It was the third pass of the lighter haired blond that Frank felt the approaching peak. He tried to divert his path.

"Yeah, that's it," the woman said. "I've got it. I've got it. Come to momma," she said as her stroking assumed certain urgency. Frank could feel her muscle grip him tightly with each upward movement. "Give it to me. That's here. Oh, yes," said nearly shouted as she felt his convulsion begin. "Yes, yes," she shouted, as she moved hard against him. She kept moving on him until all of Frank's muscles went limp. She stopped, extricated herself, and then stood up with her friends in front of him. She moved her legs to regain her strength as she wobbled a few times. "I win," she said as the three women high-five'd each other.

They walked out of the sauna without a word or glance to Frank. He was just the instrument of some contest between the three women like a pole vault or broad jump. His legs were rather rubbery as he stood for the first time. He ladled some water out to clean himself as well as the residue of his pleasure. He wondered if he might be dreaming, but seemed content to accept the benefits of the bizarre moment in his life. No one would ever believe him, if he ever told the story. He smiled as he left the sauna devoid of the inner tension he brought to the gym that evening.

—

Emily

—

John's affair continued to leave me with confusion, anger, resentment, curiosity and dread. His repeated claims of innocence . . . he fell victim to his carnal curiosity . . . did not satisfy my concerns and worries. Something was missing between us. We generally had good sex, although maybe not as often as we both might like. Two young teenage children did have a profound effect on one's sex life. If there was one complaint both of us had, and yet neither of us seemed capable of transgressing, it was the routine of our relationship. Even the words boredom and monotony crept into our speech. John told me the affair was not important to him, he still loved me and wanted to stay together, and he wanted more from the physical side of our marriage.

In this instance, I shared his need. I wanted more as well. In this search, I sought the counsel of my best friend since childhood. Grace and I had been through everything together. At one point, Grace and I talked about her joining us in a *ménage à trois*. It was our concern for her husband that stopped us. After several conversations approaching ever closer to the edge, Grace introduced me to a good friend of hers from college.

Joan was a delicate woman. She was tall, nearly six feet, with medium blond, naturally curly hair. She had luscious full lips most women would die for, and she kept them painted bright red to accentuate them. Her light blue eyes always seemed balanced with the light make-up she wore. Her exquisite unblemished porcelain skin did not need make-up, but it did give her an even more feminine quality. Her light, wispy voice matched her features. Joan had the best legs I had ever seen on a woman. All of her extremities were long and slim, but shapely. The most impressive part of her character was her personality. She always had a smile, a subtle sense of humor, and an effervescent view of life. Nothing seemed out of place.

Everything Grace told me about Joan was so true. She was married without children. She had a rather kinky relationship, but they remained happy and devoted to one another. Since Joan could not become pregnant, they also enjoyed a rather open sexual relationship. She seemed to enjoy sex in all forms, was willing to experiment with what she did not know and displayed no inhibitions that I could sense.

While Joan did not have a large bust, she often wore provocative clothing – short skirts to show her legs, and blouses unbuttoned to show her cleavage. Joan accepted my request to help John and me on only one primary condition – I had to see her completely nude. If after that, my offer was still good, then she would participate. Joan and I had accomplished the task last weekend. Joan and Grace had been together several times before, so it was no big deal for her. Joan's appearance and body had such an impact on me, as it always did for Grace, the three of us enjoyed each other. I had never done anything like it before, but it did prove what Grace had said. I did not know how John would respond, but I knew it was worth a try.

Tonight was the night.

Joan arrived on time looking stunning as ever. The tight, bright red bodice of her dress accentuated her breasts and erect nipples from the cool evening air. A pullover skirt hid her legs. The introductions and dinner went quite well. John had no idea what lay ahead, or at least he was doing a great job of concealing his thoughts. With dinner complete, I moved us into the living room. Joan sat opposite John and me.

"John," I said wanting to move on to the next phase of the evening's experience, "there is another reason I invited Joan to join us tonight."

"Oh, yea?"

I looked toward Joan, who smiled patiently and demurely at me, and then to John. "We've talked about spicing things up in our lives, and Joan is the spice." I smiled a serious, warm smile.

"What exactly do you mean?"

"You've always been pleasant with me, but we've both know I was never really good with fellatio." John just stared at me waiting for the rest of the statement. "I talked to Grace and Joan. We think Joan is the best. So, she's here to do you."

"You're kidding? Right?"

I looked to Joan and nodded my head, and then returned to John's eyes. "No. We're not."

Joan moved smoothly and slowly to John, and knelt in front of him. John's eyes remained on her shifting from her eyes to her breasts plainly visible through the thin material of her dress. Joan slowly reached for his zipper, pulled even more slowly so that you could hear each tooth of his zipper release, and then reached into his trousers.

I moved closer to John to stroke his hair, to reassure him, and to watch Joan do what she said she was the best at doing. Her blond curls bobbed over his lap for several minutes. John managed a quick glance at me before he closed his eyes to enjoy the experience.

As she worked on him, Joan moved gracefully to remove John's trousers and underwear. I removed his shirt, the last of his clothing, as Joan spread his legs and moved between them for better access to items of her attention.

The exhibition of her skills was fascinating to watch. She used a combination of hand strokes precisely delivered over his glistening shaft along with licking, sucking and head motion carefully timed to accentuate and build the sensations for John. He groaned, stiffened, and then relaxed as she shifted from one activity to the next. She moved in rhythm; as he stiffened, her pace would quicken, only to slow as his muscles release their tension. There was a poetic aspect to her artistry. The scene produced the expected effect within me.

I could feel the wetness now soaking my panties, and an ache that needed fulfillment. The shiny features of his manhood as they flashed into view between her strokes had never looked so appealing, so magnetic, and so desirable. I wanted his hardness to fill the need deep within me.

The tempo of her motion and the more pronounced rigidity of his body broadcast the approaching climax. Joan brought nearly all her actions into play as she pushed him higher and higher. The tremors in his tense muscles preceded the very pronounced arching of his back almost as though he wanted to give her more of him.

An odd, animal growl, deep and heavy, came from the farthest reaches of his being as his body erupted into convulsions that shook the whole couch for what seemed like minutes. Joan moved in careful calculated actions to keep him convulsing. She swallowed most of his essence although several rivulets were clearly visible on her chin. She licked him until he nearly doubled over in what appeared to be pain.

Joan eventually released him. As his body continued to shake from the exertion, Joan unfastened the top of her dress exposing her bare torso. She cupped and rubbed her breasts several times, maybe in recognition of their liberation, or maybe just because she enjoyed their feel. She squeezed and rolled her nipples until they were erect, hard and quite prominent. Then, she leaned forward to drag her nipples across John's still erect penis. Every pass of one of her hardened nipples jolted him.

She stood, still fully exposed to her waist. Her modest but perfectly round breasts with almost no aureole around her large nipples attracted me for the strangest reason. I moved to her, reaching to lightly caress the sides of her breasts, and then feeling the hardness of her nipples between my fingers. They possessed what anyone might say was perfect shape and texture. Her breasts felt like what every woman thought they should feel like.

I looked into her waiting eyes. She remained motionless. An unreal attraction compelled me to kiss her. I stopped as a drip of John's release fell to her chest. I leaned forward extending my tongue to lick up the residue on her chin. She smiled, but did not move. Her light scent of lilacs could not overcome the musty, earthy aroma around her. The warmth of her mouth and the caress of her tongue made time disappear.

When I did grasp a moment of awareness beyond Joan, I looked at John. He sat spread-eagled on the couch with only a broad, most approving smile across his face and in his eyes. I liked what i saw. He returned to a partial reawakening that attracted Joan to return to her kneeling position. As she renewed her efforts, I kept John's eyes as I slowly undressed for him accentuating every move. I kept his eyes as long as I could with sensual and sexual gestures and motions. Joan's expertise eventually took his concentration.

I touched Joan's back, feeling the muscles move in a distinctive rhythm. I caressed her breasts, and then released them just enough to feel her nipples move across my palms. I watched John's fullness flow into and out of Joan's mouth. I waited for a segment of hand manipulation to pull her dress up, now gathered around her waist, and then slowly and lightly move my hand up the inside of her thigh. She looked over her shoulder with an asking expression. I smiled, nodded my head and gave her a wink. She returned my wink.

As a hermaphrodite, Joan was blessed with a functional vagina as well as a working penis with small testicles in place of her clitoris. Her parents had rejected corrective surgery as most doctors advised and raised her with a healthy attitude toward her anatomy. She had learned to enjoy the benefits of her body. Her only regret was not being able to experience the rock crushing orgasms some women enjoyed. She still enjoyed a 'male' orgasm, but it just did not seem to have the power of a 'female' orgasm. Joan responded to my strokes. While she was not large, she was hard. When her hips began to move to my rhythm, I stopped, and then moved over John. I felt her touch me, caress my lips, and then probe me as if to verify my readiness. She maintained her connection with me as I lowered myself to John. She guided him into me. He groaned in a different way.

I moved on him, feeling his rigid member fill me, for several dozen full strokes. The swelling forecast his pinnacle. I slowed, kept his eyes with mine, and then rolled to move him on top and keep him from noticing Joan. As he promptly picked up his deep stroking, intent on his climax, I looked around him to see Joan stroking herself still in an erect state. When John's eyes closed in concentration, I nodded to Joan. She smeared KY Jelly on herself. The contrast struck me for the first time.

Joan was a slim, toned, attractive woman in full glory, except for the odd appendage she had at the juncture of her legs. She twisted and stroked herself to ensure the lubricant was evenly spread. The residue that remained on her hand she applied to John, to ready him to accept her. John did not miss a beat. He had to assume he was going to get a finger or dildo. He did finally stop as she pressed gently into him. His muscles tightened, and then relaxed as he accepted her. I fought to contain my glee and laughter as the image of his recognition flashed before me.

I gripped him, and then thrust my hips to him urging him to continue.

John gradually worked his way back up the tempo scale. Joan's hands grasped his hips to feel his motion and match our rhythm. As he withdrew from me, she pressed into him. The collective motion between the three of us enhanced the incredible sexual energy building. The view of both John and Joan enjoying the sensations along with the rapidly swelling hardness of John thrusting between my legs set me over the edge.

The speed and height of my climax scared me. I had never felt anything so powerful. My noises or contractions, I have no idea what happened, had a similar effect on both John and Joan.

John was the first to go over the top. His thrusts were so deep and big I thought I could feel him in my throat. As he came down off his peak, he glanced over his shoulder to see Joan still pumping away into him. He fell forward onto my chest giving her full deep access to him. To my amazement, John relaxed on my chest and under my caress.

Several minutes passed before Joan reached her own climax marked only by the convulsive tempo of her hips and the heaving of her chest. I could feel her pinnacle through John. It was a fascinating sensation. As she finished, Joan fell forward onto John's back. We lay together for several minutes before we began to disassemble the mass of flesh we had become.

John waited for Joan to disengage, and then he rose up. Before he withdrew, he leaned forward and kissed me passionately.

"I love you," he whispered to me.

I nodded my head, smiled and winked at him.

Joan was standing with her hands on her hips about six feet from us when John turned to see her. Although I could not see his face or his expression, I could sense his eyes quickly moving from her eyes, her chest, then her groin.

"Jesus H. Christ! What the hell is this? I thought you used a dildo."

Joan smiled. "Well, in a manner of speaking, IT is. It's just a live dildo."

"What the hell does that mean?"

"John," I said as I placed a hand on his shoulder and felt him tense. "There is no reason to get excited."

"The hell there isn't. I've just been plugged by something that's a cross between a woman and a man. I was wondering why you kept going." He turned to face me with anger in his eyes. "I've got his . . . her . . . its jism in my ass, and you're trying to tell me not to get excited. Why did you do this to me? Why did you trick me like this?"

"Calm down, John."

"Calm down, hell! What the hell is this?" he asked, motioning over his shoulder with his thumb toward Joan.

She started to respond, but I held my hand up. "To be technically correct, she is a hermaphrodite...a person with both male and female sex organs. In some ways, I think she has been blessed. She gets to live in both worlds."

Joan remained motionless and silent, not ashamed of her displayed anatomy. Concern could be seen in her eyes. I tried to reassure her with my expression. She eventually nodded her head in recognition.

"John, I thought doing something different would add some spice to our sex lives. Maybe I was wrong, but I had good intentions."

"Well . . ."

"You've said several times, you wondered what it would be like to be a woman. Gracey introduced me to Joan," I said nodding toward her. "She is an incredible person who agreed to help me."

John turned to Joan. "I don't mean to offend, but are you a hooker?"

She laughed. "You know that is probably the most common question I am asked in situations like these."

"So, this is a regular thing?"

"John, I have always been proud of who I am. My parents were good to me despite my abnormality. While I may not be 'normal' in the usual way, I am thankful for who I am. No, I am not a hooker. I am a happily married woman. I also happen to thrive on sex. I love every aspect of it. My husband and I enjoy an alternative lifestyle...an arrangement, so to speak. No, it is not a regular thing, but it is also not the first time I have done this."

John looked at her as she stood before him unashamed of her anatomy. I wondered what John was thinking and what he might do, but his calmer, more purposeful actions indicated he was coming to grips with Joan's uniqueness.

"And, you're not a transsexual with some freaky surgical...what should I say...some surgical adjustments?"

Again, she laughed. "No. I am as I grew up."

I knew he had not disliked the experience. He has always felt good about me playing with his rosebud, but that was just a finger pressing against the muscles. It was a sure way of getting him off quickly when I wanted to, or making his climax more powerful. This was definitely a first for him, as far as I knew.

"If you put your macho-male crap aside, how did it feel being a woman?" I asked him. Joan laughed once more.

Even John smiled. "Well, other than my wounded male pride . . . and, I would never admit this to another guy . . . and, I'd call you a liar if you repeat it . . . I would have to be honest, it felt pretty good once I got used to it."

"My, my, I think you may have grown a little, John," I added since I could not resist the opportunity. Then, the thought came to me. There was more he could experience. "Let's go take a shower together."

"Won't that be a little crowded?" asked Joan.

"Nope. We are quite proud of our gang shower. John and I take showers together as often as we can. It was especially designed for us."

The mutual involvement in the shower was slow to start. With my initiative and within a few minutes of stiffness, the three of us washed, touched, explored, laughed and enjoyed each other. I was surprised, pleasantly so, how John warmed to Joan. The play produced two erections. I felt like the odd person out because I did not have a penis to play with, but both of them made sure I was not neglected. The expenditure of all the warm water in the house ended the shower play. My genitals throbbed with a need for more. I kept my desire to myself as we dried off and talked of sex. Joan's abilities commanded the center of attention as would be expected. John's curiosity had taken solid root.

As John led us out of the bathroom, I caught Joan's attention to make a gesture that we should coax John into taking the next step. She nodded her agreement. We both knew this would be more difficult, since we needed John to be active rather than passive, but I also knew if successful, it would go a long way to loosening him up.

Our bedroom was the natural destination. Fortunately, we had a super king size bed, so we had plenty of room. I moved first to raise John back to full attention. Joan and I switched on him as he sat on the edge of the bed. When he laid back to enjoy the final sensations, I reached to Joan indicating for her to stand. I stopped on John and shifted my attention to Joan. I took her in my mouth and quickly brought her to full stiffness.

I could see him out of the corner of my eye. He raised his torso onto his elbows with an expression of 'what about me.' I kept moving on Joan, and then reached up to fondle her breasts, and squeeze and pull her nipples. Soon, he began stroking himself without satisfaction. John then touched my arm to signal me, he wanted our attention. I waited until the third attempt, and then stopped with Joan.

"Why don't you do this?" I asked with a smile and a nod toward Joan's genitalia.

"Are you crazy?"

"Oh, come on now, John. Let's cut out all the macho crap. You know you've always wanted to try it."

"I have not," he protested.

"It's OK," added Joan. "I can take care of it." She started stroking herself.

"No, maybe this will help." I placed my hands on John's knees and moved my hips toward Joan. She did not need another hint. I felt her slide smoothly into me and begin beating with the rhythm of life. She was not large by male genitalia standards, but she made up with technique. There was more than the old in-out. She used herself to rub my magic button with the desired effect. As she worked on me, I tended to John. He was ready. I could feel him about to explode. He was certainly closer than Joan or me. I concentrated on him and took him over the top. There was not much from him, but enough for a decent taste. I touched Joan's hip to indicate a change. We separated.

"Now, this should help," I said, standing up beside Joan.

"What do you mean?"

"She will taste like me," I chuckled.

"I'm not sucking on her."

"That's it, John. Just think of it that way. Joan is just blessed with something else to play with. You know you want to."

He stared at me, and then looked into Joan's eyes. She was smiling and waiting patiently. He looked at her erect appendage for the longest time. He glanced at me to find my approving eyes, and then moved to her like the bear drawn to the honey.

At first, he reluctantly accepted her. Joan remained patient and calm. He moved on her at his own pace gradually picking up variations to enhance her sensations.

"That's it, John. Do what feels good to you, what you want us to do to you. That's it."

I moved behind him to rub my breasts across his shoulders and neck. I would fondle her breasts and squeeze her nipples hard, which seemed to multiply her sensations. We kissed and our tongues danced until I could sense her approaching peak. John must have felt the same as he picked up the pace until her shouts began from so deep and far away, and then blasted out to us in a sharp set of reports like cannons firing a broadside. Her body shook with convulsions of pleasure just before her knees buckled, and she collapsed to the floor.

Joan lay on the floor, her chest heaving for air. I pulled John back to kiss him deeply. I could taste and feel her all around his mouth. I licked up what residue I could find. I enjoyed his efforts.

In time and to my surprise, John was ready again. The urges within me became uncontrollable as I mounted him, grinding my hips forward against him. The itch was too great. I moved on him with a vigor I had not produced before and supplemented the filling sensations of him with my own touch to the correct spot. John could only lay back and remain motionless as I used him for my satisfaction. With the combination of contacts in the right places, my finale did not take long to achieve. It blasted through me like a rocket at full thrust. I could hear my own shouts off in the distance somewhere far beyond my body.

The clarity of events after my climax blurred substantially. All three of us must have dozed off for many minutes before movement in the room brought me back.

Joan was slowly dressing. I moved slowly as well to allow my aching joints and muscles to adjust. I helped her dress without words. We kissed several times to convey our mutual appreciation.

"I must be going," she said, finally as if to end the exchange.

"I know. Thank you, Joan. It was great . . . everything I dreamed it would be and more."

"Good. It was great for me as well."

"Thank you."

"No, thank you. We'll have to do it again sometime."

"Yes, we will."

She went to the bed, leaned over and kissed John. He responded but without passion . . . maybe he was just too spent. I put on a robe and walked her to the door. We kissed one more time before she left.

———

Karen

—

The long day took its toll and added more weight when I was the first to arrive home. Yet, family made the fatigue of work dissipate, but this was not to be the case this evening. Somehow, life always became easier when I walked into the house, to the smell of spaghetti sauce simmering, hamburgers frying with a hint of cheddar cheese, or the aroma of a freshly created Italian dressing on a green salad with some aromatic feta cheese.

Julie, our daughter and only child, usually beat us both home. At just 13-years-old, she accepted quite a bit of family responsibilities including, more often than not, starting dinner. We gave her considerable latitude as long as she adhered to the limits we all agreed to years earlier. She faithfully respected those limits. While it was not often I beat her home, it did happen for one reason or another.

I was not particularly enthusiastic about fixing dinner myself. The mail & unread newspaper were sufficiently attractive to allow me rationalization. Dinner could wait until we could all share its preparation. We could get some take-out, or as a last choice, go out to get something to eat. There was nothing interesting or even noteworthy in the mail or the newspaper.

The door to the garage opened. I fully expected to see Julie's smiling face. It was Mike's solid frame that entered the kitchen.

He looked withdrawn and haggard which meant it had not been a good day. Impulsively, I asked the question that needed no answer. "How was your day?"

"Don't ask," he grumbled.

"That bad?"

"Yeah, that bad. Between this damn traffic, the weather and these crazy subbies that don't give a damn about schedule, it's amazing we accomplish anything."

He needed a break. "Why don't you go have a seat? I'll turn on the news for you and bring a cold beer."

"I'm OK."

"I know, but go on now. Julie's not home, yet, so we have a little time, and it sounds like you need to relax."

Mike grumbled and grunted, but did as he was asked. With him settled into his chair and absorbed in the news of the day from our local TV station, I watched a little until Julie came in.

Rather than bother Mike, I joined Julie in the kitchen.

"Hi, Mom," she said with a cheery voice. "Sorry, I'm a little late. Ashley,

Molly and I got all wrapped up in boy stuff."

"Now, that sounds like a serious topic."

"We think it is."

I knew this could turn into a lengthy conversation. "Before we get too deep, what do you want for dinner?"

"Is Dad home?"

"Yep. He's in the living room, watching the news with a cold beer."

"Tough day."

"So he says."

"How about you?"

"Not so bad, just long."

"Then, how about let's order in some pizza?"

It was uncanny sometimes how she could read my mind. "My thoughts precisely." Before I could move to the phone, Julie dialed, ordered and returned to the kitchen table. The smile on my face undoubtedly broadcast my pride in her initiative and thoughtfulness. "So, what have you three decided about boys?"

"Nothing really. It's just that . . . well . . . we think they are a puzzle."

I laughed at the seeming contradiction. I want to tell her what I thought, but knew it was listening time. "In what way?"

"They seem so thin, or maybe shallow. There must be more to them. But, they all seem the same."

"Why is that a puzzle?"

Julie thought for a moment as she moved her right index finger around the table like a pencil beginning some abstract image. I let her take the time she needed to collect her thoughts. We also shared our thoughts, even some very personal ones, so I was not worried about her withholding something important from me.

She looked into my eyes. "There must be more to them, and we can't figure it out."

I chuckled, maybe inappropriately, but I could not restrain the urge. "Maybe there isn't."

"What do you mean?"

"Well, let me think." How did I want to say this? How much did I really want to get into with her? "What makes you think of boys as a puzzle, then?"

"There must be more hidden beneath the surface. That's the puzzle. All three of us agree. Girls are so much more interesting. We know what each other is thinking without saying the words sometimes. We know how the other is feeling without saying it."

"Is it emotions, then?"

"Yeah," she smiled. "Maybe that is it. They try so hard to never show any emotions, it makes them like a black and white photograph."

I laughed again. The doorbell rang. Julie started for the door. I reached into my purse and wallet. Before she reached the kitchen entrance, she returned to retrieve the $20 bill I held for her.

She placed the large pizza box on the table. Perhaps with intention or otherwise, she placed several pieces on a plate, grabbed a knife and fork as well as another cold beer, and took it to Mike. I had done the same for both of us except we would drink Diet Coke instead of beer.

"It sounds like you are beginning to see the differences our culture, our society, imparts upon our children," I said.

"Why?"

"I wish I knew. It is just the way it is. Maybe it is the hunter mentality that has been our heritage for millennia. Maybe it is just what society thinks it must be. Babies come out all the same as far as I can tell...well, other than anatomy. It is how we raise them, teach them, encourage them, that makes us what we are."

"What's wrong with emotions?"

"Nothing as far as I can tell, but I suppose emotions might not be good for the hunter."

"But, Dad hasn't hunted anything in his life, as far as I know, and neither have any of these boys, or at least most, I guess."

"Hunting is not just stalking wild game for food. It is competition, sport, and war for that matter. It is something much different in today's world."

"Is it really necessary? Can't they hunt and cry at the same time?"

It was my turn to contemplate the questions and possible answers. "I suppose that is a question that is beyond me. I don't know. Maybe, maybe not. There is part of me that rationalizes the results."

"What do you mean?"

"Well, we have survived and prospered because of those traits. Right or wrong, they have worked for many generations of human beings."

Julie drifted into her thoughts and abstract motions on the table. Mike snatched another couple of slices of pizza without words and returned to the TV. I ate a little as Julie considered some issue or another as she ate a few bites. She and her friends had been thinking about some rather large topics. Her expanding curiosity and inquisitive mind brought more warm waves of pride. I reveled in Julie's stretching her mental abilities as well as her physical characteristics. I truly enjoyed these discussions with her, even the ones that made me a little uncomfortable. Mike and I had agreed before we made a baby that we would not pass judgment on our children's questions. We would do our best to give her the best, most accurate information possible.

"Molly is afraid of sex," Julie blurted out almost matter of factly.

"A little bit of reservation or caution is a good thing at your age."

"No, Mom," she said looking directly into my eyes. "She is really afraid."

"Afraid of what?"

"Her mom told her, sex is pain. Pain of a dirty act. Pain of birth."

This was one of those topics that could pit one family against another -- a fundamental moral disagreement. The balance had to weigh on the side of Julie's attitude toward sex. We always wanted her to have a healthy knowledge and respect for the most intimate of human interaction.

"We've tried to tell you the facts, Julie. We've also told you, honestly, our feelings about sex. Does Molly's mom's view sound anything like what we've told you?"

"No."

"There are always differences of opinion about almost everything. Sex happens to be one of those really sensitive topics that seem to encourage such enormous extremes of opinion. In time, you will judge for yourself. I want to emphasize -- in time. Please do not rush into fulfilling your natural curiosity too fast."

"Oh, Mom. That's what you always say."

"Maybe, but I do worry that sometimes we've given you too much information too soon in your young life."

"Haven't I always done the right thing?"

"Yes, but I still worry."

"It's OK, Mom. I am very proud of your trust and honesty. It makes me feel stronger, more prepared in a way."

"Good."

Julie returned to the last few bites of her pizza. I could tell her mind was still grinding away on something. The best thing for me to do was let her work through her thoughts without any prodding from me.

"Mom, I know what you've told me about a man's penis and erections, but there are so many . . . strange . . . ideas about them. Is it one of those things I'll never know until I experience it for myself."

"I suppose."

"It does make me wonder what it will really be like."

"Don't wonder too much."

"Did your mom have these kinda talks with you? Did you feel you knew what to expect before you experienced it for the first time?"

I laughed at the thought of my mother trying to talk about sex. It was such an odd thought. "Actually, no, sweetie. In fact, it was probably the lack of information from my mother that pushed me to experiment far too early in my young life. I don't want that to happen to you. I want your knowledge, experience and curiosity to be gradually expanded, so you don't get into trouble with these natural forces."

"What does it feel like?"

This was beginning to make me a bit uncomfortable, but I could not back down, now. "Well, let me think . . . I suppose it feels like flesh that gets hard like a muscle when it tenses up."

"But, Ashley says it grows a lot. Muscles don't grow like that."

"She's right."

"She also says it gets so big it will tear you apart."

I chuckled again, partly from discomfort and partly from the image. "Has she seen an erect penis?"

"No."

"Well, then she doesn't really know, then does she?"

"Not really, but it is what she thinks, or at least says."

It was my turn to think about things. Mike and I had talked about this moment many times even before Julie was conceived. We knew it would come some day, and I thought we were prepared for it. Reality seemed too real, maybe even surreal. I decided it was time to press the limit.

"I suppose there is only one way to set your mind at ease. Let's get a real live penis in here. You've seen your dad's penis many times, but I don't think you've ever seen it erect, have you?"

"No."

"Then, let's see if we can do a little live anatomy lesson. Mike," I called in a much louder voice. He did not need to be called again. He entered the kitchen without words and a 'what do you want' expression. "The day we've talked about is here. It is time to put our money where our mouth is, for the sake of our daughter."

"What does that mean?"

I looked at Julie who returned my glance with an expression of curiosity and anticipation. Any doubt disappeared. "It's time for Sex Ed 101, and you're the exhibit."

"You're kidding?"

"No, I'm not. Now, take off your clothes."

Mike hesitated, and then did as he was requested. Fortunately, we were both comfortable with nudity and had brought Julie up to respect the body but not be afraid or ashamed of it. Mike was soon standing in front of us completely naked.

"A fine specimen of a man, even if he is your father," I said bringing laughter to all of us and relieving a little residual anxiety. "Before we begin, I want to make sure we separate the physical phenomena associated with the human body and sex. The difference in my mind is, sex is the physical, emotional and mental intimacy between a man and a woman; well actually, between any two people or even with yourself. Sex is certainly the body and all its attributes, but it is more significantly in your mind and heart. We will be walking a fine line here, so I want to make sure we are clear. In our society, sex between a parent and child is wrong, in fact, against the law. Let's make sure we keep these separate. Do you understand?"

"Yes."

I began by pointing out Mike's male anatomical features. "You notice his testicles have drawn up just from the short time he's been standing here. It's a normal response as his body tries to keep his testicles warm. When they are warm, they hang quite low with distinct balls. When they get a bit chilly, they draw up like this into a tight little ball to keep warm. His penis is also flaccid or limp, otherwise unexcited. It is also quite common among men whether circumcised or not for their penises to draw up as well. You can see your father's penis is quite small in the flaccid state. Some men don't shrink up like this. They remain very long when flaccid. There really is no difference, just like some women have large breasts and some small."

Julie remained intent and quite clinical which was amazing to me.

"I want you to see and feel what happens when a man gets an erection."

"Really?"

"Remember what I said earlier. This is an anatomy lesson. Anything beyond this is wrong."

"Sure."

"OK, now. I want you to touch him."

Julie slowly reached for Mike's penis, as she glanced back and forth between Mike and me to seek reassurance. Mike nodded once, then looked forward as though frozen as an animated statue. Julie touched him with one finger like she was testing a utensil to see if it was hot.

"Like this," I said as I grabbed Mike with two fingers.

Julie followed my lead.

"Feel how soft and flexible it is?" Julie nodded. "While every man is different, this is fairly typical for most men. I might add that younger men tend to get erections without any manipulation, but the older men get they need a little extra involvement."

"Oh, thanks," Mike protested.

"No offense, dear . . . just trying to teach our daughter the finer points." She almost naturally began to move her finger over him. "See how it's beginning to lengthen?" Julie nodded her head. "As it gets a little longer and fuller, you can use more fingers, then eventually your whole hand."

Julie continued to stroke him as he responded to her touch. She also moved to position her wrist better.

"Sometimes, especially if the man is having a little trouble, you can squeeze the base, as you stroke. It seems to help. Also, try not to ever draw the skin taut on either end of your strokes. That's it. Can you feel it beginning to stiffen?"

"Yes."

"Feel the texture change. Doesn't it feel like the shaft inside is separating from the skin? They felt nearly the same at the start. Now, they are becoming different. The shaft is hardening while the skin remains soft and flexible." Mike was not quite fully erect. He continued to remain frozen before us. "You should be able to hold him in your whole hand. That's it. Feel how the skin moves over the shaft." He looked like he was fully erect or nearly so. "Try not to rub the head directly. It's very sensitive. That's it." I let her continue for a few more minutes. "Here, let me feel."

I stroked Mike myself. He was quite rigid. I could feel my own response to his erection. I was concerned what I should do next. I needed to separate the anatomical lesson from the sexual one I was about to give. I released him completely.

"Now, this is what an erect penis looks like. You've also felt it grow in your hand, so you have seen and felt it from one extreme to the other." I looked at Mike, who could only return a 'what now' expression. "That's about as far as you should go. From here on out, I want to show you some things, but this is only for a man and a woman, definitely not for a father and daughter. Is that clear?"

"Sure."

With that, I stood, reached under my skirt and removed my panties. Sitting on the tabletop, I quickly removed my skirt as well as blouse and bra. It felts perfectly natural to be naked with Mike in my kitchen. "I've shown you the details of the female genitalia, so we don't need to go over that again. However, you haven't seen the female equivalent of the male erection." I spread my legs, so she could see. "Here you can see the clitoris is swollen and protruding from its hood. It's becoming erect much like the male penis.

Also, feel this," I added as I pointed to the folds. I could feel her fingers gently probe the petals. "Feel how slippery that feels." She nodded. "That is the normal lubricating response of a woman." I let her explore a little longer as I anxiously awaited the next stage.

"I think we'll take this to the natural point."

I reached for Mike and drew him toward me. Julie watched intently as though she was observing some critical biological demonstration in the classroom. I rubbed Mike's little head against my most sensitive spot, as well as among the moistened petals. I guided him to the entrance. He did not need further direction. He pushed slowly and gently into me until we were joined to the fullest extent.

"Ohhhh," I heard myself groan deeply. When I opened my eyes, I met Julie's beautiful green eyes riveted on me.

Mike began stroking into me. We moved together. It felt so good to be filled by his flesh and to feel the slippery sliding of our organs. He seemed somehow larger. Each stroke tickled my throat.

His pace quickened sooner than expected. I could feel his swelling even further within me. His pinnacle approached much faster than I wanted, but for the sake of Julie, it was probably a good thing. I selfishly did not want him to go over the top so soon, but it was best.

I could feel his body beginning to tense. His chest began to heave in an irregular beat. I pushed him back, to separate us, so Julie could see the product of his excitement. I reached for him.

Although the angle was quite odd, I managed enough contact to stroke the hot, slippery flesh covering his rock hard member. The conclusion was only a few strokes away. He made shallow pumps against my hands.

"Uuuuaaaooohh," he growled without opening his mouth.

His glorious white stream shot across my abdomen to my chest. I kept at him.

"Ummmp. Ummmp," he said for some reason as we produced two more, smaller streams from him. His deposit was more plentiful than usual. A fine example for his daughter.

"That, my dear, was an ejaculation." Julie nodded her head almost wide-eyed and speechless. "This is semen," I said pointing to the streaks of thick, white fluid across my torso. "Feel it," I added as I led her.

She ran her finger along one stripe, and then rubbed the substance between her fingers. "It's slippery and sticky at the same time."

I chuckled. "The nature of the beast, I'm afraid."

"It shot out like a big squirt gun."

"Again, as it should be. This is part of God's creation, the natural mechanisms, or processes, is to ensure the millions of little sperm contained in the semen go as deep as possible into the woman to enhance the chances of fertilization. Do you remember our discussion about the creation of life?"

"Sure."

"Well, now you've seen it all." I pointed to Mike's deflating organ. "While we're here, your father's response is typical and normal. This is usually what happens after a man ejaculates, although it is possible for him to remain hard depending on the circumstances and stimulation."

We began to clean up. I used a paper towel from the countertop. Mike grabbed his clothes and left the room. When I finished, I reached for my clothes.

"Do women squirt like that?"

I looked at her and smiled. "Certainly not like what you just saw, but sometimes when a woman has a particularly strong orgasm, a very slippery fluid does come out, so I guess I would say similar, but not the same."

"Will you show me?"

I concentrated on her eyes, as I considered her request. With all that excitement, I did need to get off. Her expression remained innocent and curious.

"Have you felt yourself after you've masturbated?"

"Yes, but I'm not sure. I would just like to watch you again to see what happens."

"I don't know."

"Please, Mom. I just want to know."

Julie remained focused and intent. I had masturbated for her before, when I showed her the fine points of female self-gratification.

"OK."

"Thanks, Mom."

I sat down with my buttocks on the edge of the cushioned kitchen chair and leaned back in the chair. I decided to separate myself from the situation to give her the best view possible without worrying about her being so close. Somewhat reluctantly but with anticipation I began stroking myself. Julie moved between my legs to get a close, clear view. I closed my eyes to eliminate her presence.

The sensations of my excited body did not take long to overcome the discomfort of having my daughter so close and attentive. The electric currents of my efforts quickly took me to a fantasy world of fingers, hands and other sensual body parts covering me with strokes. The images in my mind. The magic worked.

The rolling waves crashed over me sending electric shocks to every limb of my body. The delightfully warm shudders eventually gave way to the shaking fatigue of my enormous exertion. I went limp as I fought for air.

A few minutes later I opened my eyes to the beaming face of my daughter kneeling between my legs. I managed a feeble smile in return.

"I saw it, Mom," she said, with the excitement of an adolescent at Christmas time.

"Saw what?"

"I saw you squirt. It was a slightly cloudy liquid. It nearly hit me."

"Good."

"That was so impressive. Thanks, Mom," she said as she stood and hugged me.

"You are welcome, sweetie. Now, just remember to be responsible with what you've learned."

"I will, Mom. Trust me."

———

Jackie

"**W**hat do you think?"

"We may have chosen the wrong party," Jenny said while she continued to scan the upper crust crowd in the large art gallery.

"Maybe, but I haven't given up yet." This artist, whatever his name is, appeared to be quite popular as indicated by the crowd too large for the substantial gallery. Photography, painting, sculpture . . . this guy did it all. Some of his erotic work did not help my growing sense of frustration over the difficulty of finding an appropriate specimen for my purposes. Several excellent candidates from their appearance turned out to be quite the opposite. "Let's keep looking for a little while longer."

"OK, but this may be a waste of time."

"Maybe, but let's try."

"As you wish, my love," said Jenny, as she turned and disappeared into the crowd.

I took a deep breath to help me relax, took a sip of my wine and moved off in the opposite direction. Most of the people were dressed in black tie tuxedos or dark, elegant gowns. Some men wore conservative business suits, as if they did not have time to change clothes after work, or maybe came directly to the show from work. A couple of men chose to be different wearing denim jeans and their favorite sneakers. A few of the women stood out with bright colored dresses or substantial cleavage on display.

The various, multitude of conversations became a pronounced din, as most guests seemed to be content with conversation rather than the artist's work. There were plenty who paid the requisite attention to the art as though it was their duty.

As I moved among the crowd, I searched for eyes -- the eyes I needed, I wanted, I craved. With each passing, I used the soft cushion of my chest to touch an arm, elbow or back. The majority offered an apology. Many gave me a second, captured glance. A few had lusty eyes. Several women made the connection, but that was not my mood tonight, as Jenny knew quite well.

My third glass of wine seemed appropriate, but was not helping my predicament. I needed to concentrate. Time kept clicking away. Maybe Jenny was right.

I chose to lower my standards just a little. Doubling back, I found a couple of marginal candidates. They were attractive enough, but did not appear to be interested. As I had become quite skilled at doing, I maneuvered to pass directly in front of my target brushing my hand across their crotch.

Both men backed away, as if they had been the transgressor, and offered an apology. No connection.

Frustration mounted. The ache within me continued to grow. The first vestiges of resignation crept into my thoughts. Perhaps I would have to allow Jenny to have her way.

Her face appeared among the shoulders, backs and other upper body parts. As we made eye contact, she winked and nodded with her head for me to follow her -- a sign she may have found a viable candidate. I followed her from several bodies back through several other rooms.

Jenny stopped at the entrance. "There's one that looks like our type," she said nodding into the room of wall-mounted, framed, photographic images. I quickly scanned the room. From an appearance perspective, there were two men and at least one woman who would qualify as 'my type.' I tried to single out the target she had identified, but could not.

"Which one?"

"The one on the far side," she whispered, "with his back to us...light brown, curly hair...kinda big, and appears to be alone."

"I've got him," I answered, as I left her to focus on my prey.

I moved through the thinner crowd. Several images of beautiful women enabled me to feign interest as I timed my scans of the target. He had a modestly attractive face -- clean shaven, distinct facial lines with lusciously full lips and emerald green eyes. He was perhaps three or four inches taller than me with a sturdy build. He qualified.

Several well planned steps moving around other people to close on my mark. My right breast made contact with his right arm. He did not withdraw. He simply turned his head. Our eyes met.

At first, they were neutral eyes that quickly turned to interested eyes. He did not speak, and he would not break eye contact.

"I'm sorry to disturb you. I must have stumbled."

He winked. "Quite all right, I should think," he answered in the most delightfully, soft, English accent.

I nodded, smiled and began to move past him. A warm, strong hand grasped my right elbow gently.

"No need to rush off."

I stopped, but did not turn immediately, as if I was considering his proposition. I turned slowly. The connection shot across the space between us. The interest in his eyes transitioned to warmth with maybe a touch of lust. "Do you like his work?"

Without releasing my eyes for an instant, he smiled, and then responded, "Definitely."

"What do you find the most attractive?"

He smiled more broadly and still maintained our eye contact. "Difficult to say, actually."

The fact he did not take the bait made him all the more attractive to me. This one will do for my purposes tonight. I looked over my shoulder toward Jenny and allowed my hand to touch him. He did not move away. The bulge meant more than casual interest. Jenny smiled. I winked.

I turned back to him. "What if we try something different?"

"You lead. I'll follow."

Without an instant hesitation or further contact, I weaved my way through the crowd, passed Jenny and eventually outside the gallery. I needed a test, something wild, something satisfying. I looked both directions down the street -- nothing obvious. I quickly assessed the far side of the street -- again, nothing. There had to be something. I started to walk left from the gallery.

The adjacent alley appeared to be closed. A moderate, chain link, fence protected some portion of the area. I stopped at the entrance to the alley.

"Do you still want to follow?"

"Surely. Why not?"

I slowly walked into the alley quickly assessing the risk -- some and certainly enough. I turned to face him. The puzzled expression did not dampen his smile. Too much time had been wasted already. I reached for him. "I want this, now."

"Now?" he said with incredulity. "Here?"

"Yes."

I did not wait for further discussion. He also did not resist, as I removed the object of my desire from his trousers. He was not quite ready.

"What is she here for?" he asked nodding his head toward Jenny as if he objected to any witnesses.

"She's my friend. She'll stand guard and help me, if I need it."

The explanation satisfied him as he lowered his head and eyes to the point of our attachment.

I lowered myself to my knees. The few pebbles on the asphalt punished my knees, but somehow that did not matter. Only a few complete strokes were needed to bring him to the fullness and rigidity I needed.

Standing, my hands touched his shoulders and pushed him against the chain link fence. I grabbed the fence cap bar on either side of his shoulder, pulled my weight up, and then climbed the fence to place my toes in the fence on either side of his hips. My knee length, pleated skirt sans panties enabled me to settle on him. Feeling with my hypersensitive lips now slippery with the moisture of anticipation, I did not need to guide him to the point I sought.

He started to lunge with his hips overly anxious for the union.

"Not so fast. Don't move. You stay perfectly still and let me do this," I commanded softly.

He focused on my eyes. His inaction confirmed his agreement. I knew at that instant, this man was going to be a perfect specimen.

I teased the connection with only the slightest penetration then withdrew. A little bit more, then another pull back. I loved the sensations of the initial penetration. I could feel the tension in his body as he resisted the urge to a full and deep union. I wanted it too, but I wanted the thrill of the journey more than the conclusion. I continued to sit down on him allowing him deeper and deeper into me. He was a healthy size. The fullness nicely complemented the friction of the hot contact.

Once I reached a full and complete joining, I moved my hips to thoroughly appreciate his hardness.

Jenny moved closer standing beside us blocking the view from the street. I could feel her hand touching various spots on him and me. Knowing her, she would probably fondle his sack, as I tended to the rest.

Ever so slowly, I began to move my hips in the inexorable rhythm of life, as I moved on him suspended from the fence now supporting both of us. Jenny found her mark. I could feel her hand with each down stroke.

My most immediate objective approached faster than I guessed. His breathing quickened. His eyes closed to the world, as he ascended the peak. I could feel him swell even more. He felt like a hot steel rod occupying the most intimate space within me.

The fence began to rattle as I picked up the pace of my movements on him.

A deep, groaning, "Ohhhhhhh," preceded his convulsive climax. As he crossed the pinnacle, his knees buckled slightly nearly separating him from me. I quickly adjusted, although he regained his position as I moved to compensate. He grimaced as his hands grasped my hips pulling them tightly to him as if any movement caused acute pain although he made no sound.

His cue kept me motionless even though the ache in my arms and legs leapt to the forefront of my awareness. Several minutes passed. I waited until the rigidity connecting us began to dissipate before I began to extricate myself. The play became the task, as I squeezed my muscles as tightly as I could to hold him in me as long as possible. At the limit, he snapped away like a rubber band drawn too tight.

"My God, woman, you are good."

"Oh, thank you," I answered with coy humility. "You haven't seen nothin' yet."

"You don't say."

Jenny smiled. "She has many more surprises, but not for the faint at heart," she said.

"You don't say," he repeated looking back and forth between us with a broad smile on his face.

He was the one; there was no doubt. So, let's take this to the next stage, I told myself. "You got yours, are you up to giving me mine?"

"What on earth do you mean?"

"She wants it her way," said Jenny.

"Which is?"

"One step at a time. Are you game for an adventure in orgasmic delight?"

"Actually, I do believe I am."

"Then, let's get a cab."

We got him tucked back in and straightened up. I had simply to stand up. My skirt fell, as it should although the ache in my knees made the act of standing more difficult than usual.

The three of us took a cab across town to my loft apartment above a paper products warehouse. Another glass of wine along with peripheral chit-chat occupied the space until I decided to take the first step. I undressed as if I was alone. I stood stark naked holding my hands out as though to say, why are you still dressed?

The other two did not need a second invitation. In less than a minute, three naked people stood in my living room.

"I have a special room for our carnal enjoyment," I said with a wink to Jenny.

He nodded his agreement. I led them into an adjoining room.

"Dear God, woman, what is this?"

"This is my play room."

"This looks like a combination of hospital room and den of horrors."

Both Jenny and I laughed. "The floor is a continuous cast floor for easy clean-up."

"Clean-up of what?"

"Sometimes we have experienced unexpected excretions or emissions . . . the product of powerful orgasms . . . nothing cruel."

"Really?"

"Are you up for some great sex?"

He scanned both of us. "Let's do it."

"If you don't mind, since you've had your off at the gallery, would you mind tending to my pleasure first?"

"Certainly not," he answered looking around as if he wanted to find the bed he would need for that purpose. "What do you want me to do?"

With Jenny's assistance, I guided him through the process of securing the appropriate straps to my thighs, knees, ankles, shoulders and wrists. They hoisted me into the position I had come to enjoy the most. Using a system of pulleys in the high ceiling, I was soon suspended in an upright position with my arms free to move above my shoulders but prevented from attaining the lower reaches. My legs were spread not quite laterally and nearly horizontal making my genitalia feel completely exposed and open for anyone to examine. As best Jenny could determine, my crotch was at the height of a seated man's head. I felt as though my groin was hanging there . . . the focus of the room . . . the universe. The anticipation made me feel as though I was already dripping from excitement.

"Now what?"

"I want you to do exactly as I tell you."

"OK," he responded with some hesitation and reluctance in his tone.

"Work my nipples until they are fully erect. If you want to finger me, you can."

He immediately set out to suckle at my breasts. He spread his attention to them well. At first, he fondled the round, fleshy mounds near his mouth. Then, I felt a finger lightly touch me at the juncture of my legs.

"My God, you are wet."

"It's the anticipation of the pleasures to come."

"Indeed," he said, as he returned to my breasts and began to explore.

He found everything in due course . . . my readiness, the swelling organ above the folding, wet lips as well as the looseness of my rosebud.

"That should do." He stopped to look into my eyes. "Now, get those nipple clips over there and attached them at the base of each nipple." Fortunately, it did not take him long to find the tool, nor did he question my command. He gently placed them precisely where I wanted them. The firm squeeze of the clips sent jolts of electricity through my body shaking all my restrained and suspended limbs as well as evoking an audible groan of pleasure. This was going to be a good one I just knew it. The anticipation and nipple stimulation were nearly enough to take me to the peak, but I resisted the temptation...going now, would not be as powerful as later.

"Connect the electrical lead Jenny is holding to the chain between my nipples."

He hesitated with an expression of incredulity as well as inquiry as if he wanted to ask if I was sure.

"It's all right. It is low current...just enough for stimulation, not injury." He did as he was asked. "The button is for you to push at the correct moment. You must push it just as you feel my climax begin."

"But, I've never felt your orgasm."

I chuckled. "Isn't that the fun of it? The question in your mind as you feel my body responding . . . is this it or not? All I can say is, I think you'll know the time. Give me a brief push to make sure it's working." He did it. The electric shock leapt through me and went instantly to my groin. I struggled in the straps to prevent the orgasm that nearly took me. "It's working," I said, once I regained control.

"Are you sure you want me to do this?"

"Absolutely. Now, get to work."

He started by caressing the inside of my upper thighs . . . a nice touch. Moving slowly, he began playing with the folds and soft flesh.

"It is so sexy when they're shaved and smooth like this."

"Don't talk."

He continued until he had touched each little spot and appreciated the subtlety. He recognized the need for a chair. I smiled in recognition. Yes, this was going to be a good one. Most others tried to figure out how to get their own satisfaction while tending to mine in this suspended position. This guy got it.

Before he began his task in earnest, I wanted to add one more dimension. "Here's the challenge." He looked up at me without a word. "Jenny is going to tend to you as you are doing me. You must not climax before me. OK?"

"Sure."

"Are you up to the challenge?"

"I should think so," he answered with a smile.

I nodded my head for the games to begin. He reached for the button, as if he though he would be successful in short order. I liked his attitude. I saw Jenny move beneath me and between his legs before I closed my eyes to concentrate on the touching and the hot waves of pleasure soon to be cascading over me.

He used an exceptional combination of sucking, licking, squeezing and probing. It was the simultaneous flicks of his tongue, while he sucked rhythmically, that had the most profound effect. He began to add some pressure on my rosebud as he prepared to probe my interior that convinced me to take the final preparatory step.

"Wait." He stopped instantly as if he thought he hurt me. "One more thing." Again, he waited for his instructions. "I want you to insert a butt plug. Jenny will get it for you."

She pulled the proper device from a drawer. After applying some KY Jelly, she handed it to him. He bent over to have a proper view of his target. I was already relaxed and ready for the device, but I appreciated his slow considerate manner. My muscles accepted the bulbous object, and then contracted on its neck to hold it in place. As he straightened up, Jenny plugged it into the wall outlet. The swirling motion inside me added even more stimulation that could have taken me over the top if I let it, but I fought the seductive urge.

I waited for Jenny to return to her position. "This definitely won't take long now. Are you ready for this?" I asked, as if it was his orgasm that was approaching. He nodded his head, retrieved the button and returned to his expert task.

He squirmed a little, as he began to work on me. Jenny performed her task perfectly. I could tell he was struggling against his own stimulation. His excitement added quickly to my pleasure. His finger danced within me in complement to the gyrating plug separated only by thin layers of sensitive flesh. He kept touching all the right spots. His efforts brought a rapid rise toward the pinnacle. I sucked in a deep breath and held it, as the small tremors in my limbs shook me.

The jolt of electricity from my nipples to my hanging and exposed groin to every fiber in my body shook me in violent convulsions. Hot, burning waves pulsated through me like some huge pipe at a nuclear plant. I could hear screams beyond my consciousness. I could not recognize the source, and I really did not care. The consuming fires of my climax lasted longer than anything I could remember, but not forever, as I would have liked.

The transition of ecstasy to pain came as the pleasure eventually began to subside. "Stop, stop," I screamed, as the pain became more pronounced.

Everyone did as they were commanded. Jenny unplugged the electrical connections, and then without needing further instruction, she first removed the nipple clips that now felt like they were going to rip off the hypersensitive points of flesh. Jenny massaged my breasts for a few moments to take my awareness away from the raw spots. When I nodded my head, she knelt down and ever so slowly removed the last object within me. I could feel her delicate, soft, pointed tongue licking the inflamed petals just in front of the spasmodically constricting muscles. She carefully avoided the one organ that was the most sensitive in my entire body. Her touch, sensitivity and knowledge of my needs never ceased to amaze me; it always brought us closer together. I found his eyes riveted on me with an expression of amazement and wonderment.

"She likes the taste of my passion after a great orgasm," I said to him, as Jenny continued her efforts.

He could only nod his head with the most bizarre smile across his face. His eyes spoke volumes about his curiosity and appreciation. He obviously enjoyed the view.

"OK, it's time to get me down from here."

They lowered my legs and un-strapped my legs before they lowered my entire body to the floor. It took several minutes to work out the pain in my joints and muscles. The exertion of such a powerful climax had taken its toll on my body, but there was no question it had been worth the pain.

Once I had walked around for a few more minutes, I returned to the two who stood patiently. "Who's next?" I asked.

He looked at Jenny. Jenny looked at me, and I winked.

"I want mine last," she said.

"I've already had mine. It is your turn after all," he said, as quite the naked gentleman.

"I nearly had you off before Jackie went, and you're still hard as a rock. I think you need it sooner than I do."

He considered the situation, then as any man with a hard erection would do, he agreed to the relief of his passion pain. "I don't need the straps."

"Sure you do. This will be an orgasm you'll never forget."

"The last one was rather memorable, if I do say so."

"This one will be better."

"I can't wait," he said, as he positioned himself in the same starting position I had.

Jenny and I made quick work of preparing him, and then hoisting him into position. Between the two of us, we made certain his focus organ received sufficient stimulation. We shared his conventional oral stimulation until the first signs broadcast the approaching conclusion.

"OK, Jenny, let's harvest this stud."

"Harvest?" he asked.

As Jenny retrieved the appropriate apparatus, I explained. "Have you ever heard of milking?"

"Like a cow?"

"More or less," I answered with a smile.

"You must be kidding."

"Actually, no. Guys love it once they get used to it."

"I think not."

We ignored his lack of consent.

As we had done many times before, we suspended the equipment so that he felt very little if any weight. Suction was checked. He squirmed in the straps and protested as most first-timers did. We continued undeterred. Lubricating him and the mouth of the receptacle, we position the flexible tube over him and turned it on. As the rhythmic suction took effect, his protestation disappeared. We moved over his entire body touching him, fondling him and applying pressure in the right spots. The end came predictably and quickly. His back arched against the straps, and his body shook as every muscle convulsed. He groaned with the pleasure of his relief.

We waited for his muscles to relax and the groans of pleasure to transform into pain. We stopped the machine and let the last few drops descend along the transparent, slippery tube to the collection receptacle.

"Not bad," I said to Jenny. "What do we have?" I held the graduated tube up for inspection. "Twelve cc's . . . not the biggest load we've seen, but certainly not the smallest either." I emptied the collector into a proper storage container to be preserved for future use.

"I think he has more in there for us," Jenny added.

"I think you're right, my dear."

"Wait just a moment. All righty then, that was fun. I've had enough, now get me down from here."

"*Au contraire, mon ami.* Our experience has shown that with a deposit of greater than 10 cc's, especially on the second pass, you've... what would you say Jenny... maybe three or four in him."

"Dear God, no. You'll kill me."

"Oh, now, doth thy protest too much," I said mocking his heritage.

He struggled against the straps until he convinced himself they would not give way. As he relaxed, we removed the apparatus and cleaned it. We also used a warm, moist, silk cloth to clean him. While everything else was ready for the next episode except him, we naturally set about pleasing each other. We could have fun together virtually any time and any place. We knew each other's body, desires, sweet spots and levels. I knelt before her. She opened to me. Her body responded to my touch as my gentle sucking did the rest. Her first climax of the evening came almost instantly with all the stimulation of the night without relief. Her knees buckled, and she fell on me.

We embraced on the cool floor and laughed at the product of our efforts. There was always something magical about bringing pleasure to a lover.

"Thank you, Jackie," she whispered.

"You're welcome, my love," I responded.

We kissed a few more times before Jenny asked, "How's our friend?"

We both looked up to find his smiling face beyond his nearly ready organ. "I think he's ready."

Without skipping a beat, Jenny took him in her mouth, as I prepared the equipment for the second harvesting. She had him ready in short order. This time he did not protest in the slightest. The objective took only a few minutes to achieve and required no additional assistance other than our normal touching and expertly applied pressure.

The cycle was repeated two more times. The collected semen diminished in quantity, and he was beginning to feel pain from the repeated attention. There was probably only one more in him, and he would need some additional stimulation to get it out of him.

I watched as Jenny carefully worked on him to reach a sufficient state of arousal for the equipment to operate properly. He groaned quietly with a mixture of pain and pleasure. We knew this would probably be his last event. His eyes closed as he entered his own oblivion.

As Jenny applied the collection device, I sterilized the plug used on me earlier. We would have to stimulate his internal organ the plug was specifically designed to do for males, if we hoped to get a reasonable amount of product.

I waited for the machine to move him along the way before I smeared the KY Jelly to prepare him to accept the plug.

"What the hell are you doing?" he shouted.

"Just giving you a little help."

"I don't need any help."

"I suspect we have more experience at this than you do, and you need the help. Now, just relax and enjoy it. You'll be amazed at what this does for you."

His meager struggle and protestation ended as the tip of the plug began to open his tight muscle. Jenny moved to the wall plug, ready to turn it on once inserted. I pressed up slowly allowing him to adjust to the intrusion. Surprisingly, he accepted the aid readily and without further complaint. Jenny plugged it into the wall outlet. It had a noticeable and desired effect as it inflated further.

As the collection machine began its calculated rhythmic action, Jenny and I concentrated on stimulating the rest of him. We rotated between face, lips, chest and sack trying to tantalize every spot of sensitive and sensual flesh.

We patiently and gently worked on him. The signs of the approaching limits of his stimulation coaxed us to suspend Jenny in a companion harness, so she faced him. I moved the various chords moving her much like a puppet, allowing him to suckle at her breast, and then I moved her so that he could taste her excitement. Access to Jenny's intimate organs did the trick. I secured her in place and quickly descended beneath him to take his sack in my mouth. I licked and sucked at the same time. I could feel the pulsating of the extraction device as well as the rotation of the plug.

"Jesus Chri . . . ahhhh . . . my go . . . ohhhhh," he screamed as the substantial stimulation catapulted him over the top. His groans of pleasure and pain rapidly transitioned to the latter. "No, no . . . stop, no, stop. Stop the damn thing!" he commanded.

I quickly jumped up to switch off the collection machine, and then unplugged the support device. He seemed to go limp in his straps. His head fell forward burying his nose in Jenny's still suspended and presented genitalia. He remained motionless for the longest time. Jenny kept still, to let him recover some strength.

After several minutes, he raised his head. "Do you have enough from me, now? Will you let me down from here?"

I lowered Jenny to the floor and unbuckled her without answering him. We checked the collection receptacle. There was perhaps only a few cc's of fluid. We had milked him of all the semen he could give us. It would probably take him several days to recover to full quantity levels.

"Yes, I think we have," I answered, as I removed the last remnants of his bodily fluid from the machine. We stored it in a new vial and placed it along side the others collected earlier. We slowly began to lower him; first his legs which did not quite touch the floor, and then we lowered him completely. He allowed us to unstrapped him and did not put up a fight as some previous specimens has done. As always, we were prepared for anything.

He remained partially hunched over. "Well, you said at the outset this would be an experience I would never forget. I do believe you have achieved that distinction. I feel like you two have turned me inside out."

"That's normal. It will pass in a day or so."

"Why did you do this to me?"

Jenny and I looked at each other, then back at him. "We collect worthy specimens to artificially inseminate women who don't want conventional impregnation, or they want our specific certifications."

"Certifications?"

"Yes, we note fundamental physical attributes as well as other characteristics that are of particular interest to our clientele."

"Like what?"

"I'm afraid that's a trade secret."

"Oh really, well, maybe, to put in typically American terms, I should sue you for a violation of my personal rights."

"You could. Others have tried. You are most welcome to do as you see fit. The most I will say is, we do take precautions to protect ourselves. Now, with all the negatives hopefully out of the way, let's look at the positive. For the price of your semen without restrictions, you received some of the best sex you've ever had."

"With a damn machine?"

"Now, now, let's not get prejudicial. Ignore the facts. Think about the sensations."

"I don't know if it's that good."

"Maybe for you it isn't. So, if that's the case, we'll make you a deal. Jenny and I will make ourselves available to you for your sexual pleasure in partial compensation for this session as long as you agree to another collection session."

"Both you?"

"Yes."

"At the same time?"

"If that's what you would like."

"OK, I guess. It was rather fun and exciting, for the most part. I will do it."

"Thank you for being such a good sport about this."

"Quite. Can I go now?"

"Certainly, and thank you again."

As he dressed, Jenny and I played with each other. It was approaching dawn, and it had been a long night. However, I knew Jenny needed her release, and I needed to feel her, to taste her, to smell her.

We stopped for just a moment, but remained in our embrace as he made his way to the door. "Wait," I said. "What's your name?"

He turned to give us a feeble smile. "Jeremy. Jeremy Lawrence. I was wondering if you even cared."

"Sure we do, Jeremy. See you next time," I said, and then immediately interlocked tongues in a passionate kiss with Jenny. We heard him shut the door behind him as we moved to the bedroom and the comfort of the large, cool bed. Jenny would soon give me an explosion, and I could barely contain my anticipation.

———

THE END
of
Volume I

J. Laux Perren
Author

—

     J. Laux was born in Toulouse, France. She immigrated with her parents to the United States before her school years and still resides in New York City – a metropolitan city she truly enjoys. J. Laux spent all of her school years in the city and proudly graduated from Columbia University with a Bachelor of Arts degree in Sociology. She is fascinated by the human condition and experience.

—